What Others Are Saying About Dawn Crandall and *The Hesitant Heiress*...

The Hesitant Heiress features a rich cast of characters set in a fast-paced world of intrigue, faith, and drama. Dawn Crandall is a new author to watch!

—*Elizabeth Camden*
Author, *Into the Whirlwind* and *Against the Tide*

Like the petals of a lovely flower, the secrets in Crandall's debut novel slowly unfold as the romance blossoms. If you enjoy reading inspirational romance, you'll love *The Hesitant Heiress*!

—*Melanie Dobson*
Award-winning author, *Chateau of Secrets* and *Love Finds You in Mackinac Island, Michigan*

A love story to savor, *The Hesitant Heiress* is a gentle Gilded Age courtship that delightfully teases, taunts, and takes the heroine—and the reader—by surprise with a tale of mystery and true love revealed.

—*Julie Lessman*
Award-winning author of three series: The Daughters of Boston, Winds of Change, and Heart of San Francisco

Dawn Crandall's debut novel is a heart-stopping work of art. The first chapter was all it took to captivate this eager reader. Watch this up-and-coming author. I truly believe she's about to take us on some pretty exciting adventures, so let's buckle our seat belts!

—*Sharlene MacLaren*
Award-winning author of four series (Little Hickman Creek, The Daughters of Jacob Kane, River of Hope, and Tennessee Dreams) and two stand-alone titles (*Long Journey Home* and *Tender Vow*)

What Others Are Saying About The Everstone Chronicles Series

Romantic! Engaging and absorbing! Dawn Crandall brings America's Gilded Age to life on the page with vintage amour and emotional depth.

—Kristy Cambron, author of The Butterfly and the Violin

Visit a bygone era filled with romance, intrigue, and characters who will stay with you long after you close the book. Dramatic and engaging, The Everstone Chronicles is one series you won't want to miss.

—Michelle Griep, author of Brentwood's Ward

Readers of Laura Frantz' dramatic historicals and Julie Lessman's twist-filled sagas will love The Everstone Chronicles.

—Rachelle Rea, author of The Sound of Diamonds

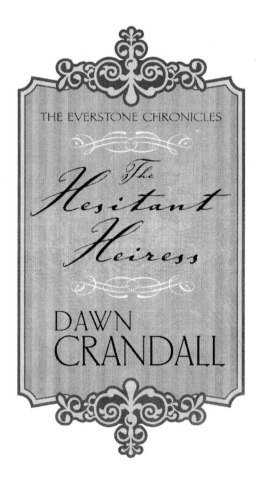

THE EVERSTONE CHRONICLES

The
Hesitant
Heiress

DAWN
CRANDALL

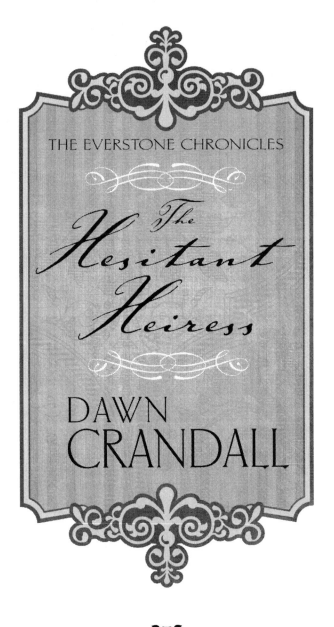

THE EVERSTONE CHRONICLES

The

Hesitant

Heiress

DAWN
CRANDALL

WHITAKER
HOUSE

The Hesitant Heiress
The Everstone Chronicles ~ Book One

dawncrandallwritesfirst@gmail.com
www.facebook.com/dawncrandallwritesfirst
www.twitter.com/dawnwritesfirst/@dawnwritesfirst
www.pinterest.com/dawnwritesfirst

ISBN: 978-1-62911-658-7
eBook ISBN: 978-1-62911-229-9
Printed in the United States of America
© 2014 by Dawn Crandall

Whitaker House
1030 Hunt Valley Circle
New Kensington, PA 15068
www.whitakerhouse.com

Dedication

This is for my husband, Jonathan,
who never failed to believe in me from the moment he found out
about my secret dream of writing a book…even if he might have
felt a little sorry when what ensued for years was my talking his
ear off at every given moment about my characters and plotline.

Acknowledgments

This book is for and because of so many people—which seems strange to me now, since I started writing it solely for my own enjoyment while my husband was busy working full-time and earning his MBA. But now that it's gone this far, I have so many wonderful people to thank—so many who have helped me in the last four years as I learned my way through writing and self-editing a book. Much to my chagrin, my husband began bragging about me to my friends from church—"Dawn's writing a book, and I'm sure it will be good enough to be published." I didn't dare believe him, but it was certainly good to hear. After those friends began to read what I had written, they jumped on the bandwagon of encouragement, as well. Not that I believed them, either. They were my friends—they were obligated to tell me they loved it. Well, Narissa, Beth, Lisa, Amy, Susie, and Lindsey...here it is. I suppose you must have been telling the truth, after all.

On top of encouraging friends, it also took my joining the American Christian Fiction Writers and their Scribes e-mail crit-group to really start getting my story/writing up to par. Within months of joining, I signed with my ever-encouraging agent, Joyce Hart, but still didn't have a critique partner. I prayed and searched for "the one" and finally found her when she e-mailed me and admitted to having followed my story on Scribes for all those months, even though she'd been too busy to submit anything. I don't know what I would have done thus far without Susan Tuttle, a writer who, despite writing the opposite of me in almost every way, is my perfect match.

There are so many others to thank—too many to name—who have spurred me on through the different stages of waiting these last few years. Most of all, I want to thank God for creating this desire in my heart back in high school, before I was even His.

ONE

Claudine Abernathy's Boston

"Beauty is not only a terrible thing, it is a mysterious thing.
There God and the Devil strive for mastery,
and the battleground is the heart of man."
—Fyodor Dostoyevsky, *The Brothers Karamazov*

February 16, 1890 · Boston, Massachusetts

M iss Brigham, may I have a word with you?" Professor
Silvious strolled down the aisle toward the stage of
The Boston Conservatory of Music's auditorium.

I'd just finished playing Chopin's *Raindrop*, a favorite of mine.
I'd long been in the habit of taking every chance I could get to play
the grand piano at the center of the stage in the auditorium, but I
never could rid myself of the nerves that doing so created in the pit
of my stomach.

"Yes, sir."

Professor Silvious always had a frown on his face, ever since
the moment I'd met him over three years before, so it didn't surprise me to see it there now.

He stopped short, evidently deciding that the central aisle of
the empty auditorium was as good a place as any to tell me what
was on his mind.

"Miss Brigham, I received a letter today concerning you." The tone of his voice was sharp, as if I'd somehow offended him by forcing him to receive said letter. He stood stoically, both hands behind his back, as I walked the remainder of the way to stand before him.

"Was it from my Aunt Claudine?" I could not imagine who else would have bothered. She was the only one who wrote me anymore, the only person who seemed to care I even existed. My cousin Lawry had been a faithful correspondent for a few years, but after his graduation from Dartmouth, his letters had stopped.

"No, it was not from your Aunt Claudine. If you indeed have an Aunt Claudine, that is."

"Claudine Aberna—"

"Yes, I know who Claudine Abernathy is, Miss Brigham— it's her connection to you I highly doubt. And the letters you say you've received from her while she's been conveniently out of the country these last three years."

"I have every one of them, if you'd like to see them." I'd saved them all, rolled up and tied together with a black ribbon, hidden in my hollowed-out version of *Great Expectations*.

"This letter is the only one I need to see, Miss Brigham. And from what it tells me, you are not the kind of young woman we at The Boston Conservatory wish to be affiliated with…no matter your talent."

I swallowed hard. "Whoever sent the letter is obviously lying." It was unheard of to speak back to a professor in such a manner, but who else would defend me if I did not defend myself? There was no one.

"There's no contest when it comes to my judging the truth of this letter. You are a young woman with an unknown past, no relatives, and now a very trustworthy account from Bram Everstone against you."

It took only a moment to understand what was happening. The professor would, because of some slanderous letter, believe the worst of me.

Me—Amaryllis Brigham, whose most fervent desire was to be good.

"I am the epitome of self-control and perseverance, Professor Silvious. There can be no truth—"

"So says you. But we know absolutely nothing of your life before the age of fourteen. You seem to have appeared out of the woodwork, which is where you will return. We cannot have someone of your ilk contaminating the good standing of our institution."

"You mean—"

"I mean, Miss Brigham, from this moment on, consider yourself expelled from The Boston Conservatory without references."

"But I—"

"It matters very little what you think or what you say. The decision is final."

⌒

March 14, 1890 • Back Bay, Boston, Massachusetts

My stomach churned with anxiety as I stood just inside the formidable leaded-glass doors of one of the largest mansions in Back Bay—Hilldreth Manor—waiting.

Within the hour I would meet the closest relative I had—a great-aunt.

Claudine Abernathy.

Her letters from Europe over the last three years had made mention of my coming to live with her once I finished my extensive schooling. Little did either of us know back then that it would turn out to be the other way around.

I watched as a couple walked slowly down the Pedestrian Mall at the center of Commonwealth Avenue.

Commonwealth.

Such a strange name, but it was fitting for the street where I'd been sequestered for weeks on end. I'd never been one to notice all of the intricate architectural designs upon the buildings in Boston before, not until I'd found myself tucked away and hidden in the virtual castle built by my Landreth grandparents. All I'd been able to think about for years was my dream and how I would accomplish it.

With the piano.

In all the years since leaving Washington, it was all that had mattered.

And what had it all come to?

A month of solitude piled directly atop a mountain of questions.

In that last month, not once had I been outside to walk down the street. Not once had I even taken my horse, Truelove, out for a ride. And not once had I ventured past the front door since seeking the comfort of having it close behind me, shutting out the world.

Until now.

I emerged onto the front portico, knowing my time had come. With Claudine back from Europe, there was little hope of being able to stay hidden for long. I would be stuck with her and her life of social affairs and Boston Brahmins as much as she was stuck with me.

When a smart black carriage drove up and parked in front of the house, I hid in the corner of the porch, peeking around the edge of the massive brick wall. A fashionably dressed elderly woman climbed out and strode up the cobblestone walkway. Right away, I noticed the tautness of her face, much like the way my mother had always looked...so solemn. But then, when Aunt Claudine saw me, she charged straight toward me, exclaiming indistinct words disguised in high squeals.

I came out from my hiding place but halted before descending the steps. Was this gregarious old woman indeed my somber mother's aunt Claudine?

"Amaryllis!" Her light brown eyes took me in, and at once, all my fears of being hated and rejected vanished.

I nodded, and the woman raced up the steps, reaching her arms out to me and taking me in a surprisingly strong embrace. I wasn't used to hugging anyone, especially virtual strangers, so I hardly knew what to do but stand there and awkwardly endure it.

"Amaryllis! Amaryllis! Oh, that's the coat I sent you from Paris, isn't it?"

There was no doubt she was happy I'd decided to stay.

And suddenly, so was I.

"It is." I smiled. "And thank you. You really didn't need to do such a thing."

I'd never had a coat like it—brown velvet with strands of black braided silk loops down the front to fasten the buttons. I still couldn't believe she'd bought it for me without having first met me. It must have cost a fortune.

"Buying you a coat was only the beginning, Amaryllis!" She took hold of my jaw and turned my face toward hers for inspection. "You do have the Abernathy nose, just like your cousin Lawry... and your dear mother, of course."

My smile faded a bit, despite the fact I'd grown into my nose over the years.

"And your father's bluish-green eyes...."

I was about to ask how she knew what my father's eyes looked like when I recalled the many times I'd been told as a young child that Aunt Claudine had been the one to escort Mother on her Grand Tour, where they'd met my father and his family.

"How has Higgins been treating you? I don't call him the Keeper of Hilldreth for nothing, you know." Claudine pulled me through the front door into the house, all the way to the back parlor, disregarding that we were still in our coats.

She took a seat on the settee and motioned for me to sit beside her.

"Have you heard anything from your father's lawyer?"

"No."

Claudine responded with a wide-eyed stare. Obviously she, too, thought this odd. And it was. My father had been dead for three weeks, burned in his home during a fire that had ultimately taken out his entire horse farm in Maine only a week after I'd arrived at Hilldreth.

A loud thud announced the arrival of Aunt Claudine's trunks being unloaded into the house through the back door.

"Well, regardless of what happens with your father's land, I have news of another matter that I'm certain will lift your spirits. You see, Mr. Harden has been rather strict concerning everything, dear, and I wasn't allowed to mention a single word until now. Are you ready?"

"Of course." I liked the way she spoke with such honesty. Not a common attribute in most women I'd met, no matter their age.

"Amaryllis, I wanted to tell you years ago, but your grand-mother's will strictly stipulated I wait until you were finished with your schooling. And what young lady, besides you, would rather attend college twice than be presented to society?"

"I didn't dare pass up the scholarship to attend The Boston Conservatory, Aunt Clau—"

"Simply call me Claudine, Amaryllis. We're both adults, are we not? And, dear, none of that matters now." She kneaded her hands together in her lap. "What I mean to say is that you've been cited as the sole inheritor of the Landreth fortune."

Shock tingled from the back of my neck all the way to my toes.

"Was I not disowned along with Mother?" I asked. "I never even knew them. How—"

"Your grandparents were good people, Amaryllis. Your great-grandfather, Jasper Landreth the Third, was a shipping merchant and an early investor in Back Bay land. He purchased large areas of the undeveloped tidal flats prior to the district's being filled and developed. He built this house during the Civil War—a mansion among town houses." She took my hand in hers. "Your inheritance is a great sum of money and includes both Hilldreth Manor and Truesdale Cottage on Mount Desert Island. You'll be set for life."

I sat back against the plush cushions and stared evenly at her. "You must be jesting."

"No, I'm not." She stared at me blankly and seemed genuinely confused by my reaction.

"Do you know what this means?"

It meant it didn't matter that I'd been expelled from The Boston Conservatory with no references. And it meant absolutely nothing stood between me and my desire to return to Washington. I would have the freedom to found my own academy of music.

For with that much money, anything was possible, wasn't it?

"I know it means you'll be provided with a sizable dowry."

That awful word hung in the air between us as I comprehended just what all those two syllables entailed. "A dowry?"

"Yes, a dowry, Amaryllis." She gave me a sideways smile. "Your grandmother made the will very specific, dear. In order to claim the inheritance, you must be married within the year of finishing your schooling. Which means you'll have until February sixteenth of next year to find a suitable husband."

"Husband?" I practically stumbled over the distasteful word. "Is that the only way?"

"It will hardly be difficult, Amaryllis. You're even more beautiful than your mother, and that's saying something. You do have a photograph of her, don't you?"

"No, I don't."

She rummaged through the reticule still in her hand and passed me a close-up photograph of two women. They stood on a rocky beach, barefoot.

"That's her with her friend Grace. Those two were almost like sisters once...."

I really did look just like my mother. We shared the slight bump at the bridge of our nose, thick black hair, and small stature. Was that the reason Father had abandoned me after her funeral? Had it simply been too much for him to look at me?

On the back of the photograph was scribbled, "Elinorah and Grace, Bar Harbor."

"Lawry will be here soon and will be of some help, dear. I'm so happy you've decided to quit The Boston Conservatory. I wrote to him as soon as your plans were confirmed."

"Is he using his law degree alongside Uncle Edward in Bar Harbor?"

"He does work for his father—only here in Boston. But he also travels for his father, in the name of research. He's on his way back from an extensive trip, primarily to Washington State."

I forgot all about the photograph in my hand as the deep longing to return to the West Coast burned in my chest.

"How long has he been gone?"

"Oh, let me see...I suppose it's been nearly two years. He's always insisted that he'd eventually return home. Never mind that it took having you and me in Boston at the same time to make him follow through with it. You see, Lawry never forgot how much you loved the West Coast, Amaryllis. He told me all about your letters full of plans to go back someday to build a music school, if I remember correctly." By the tone in her voice, I could tell she thought such an idea to be silly and perhaps even childish.

Though the short and often funny letters Lawry and I had exchanged throughout the years had begun to dwindle about seven years earlier, I could not blame him. He was four years older than I and surely had better things to do than write letters to me. It seemed odd, though, that he'd never informed me he planned to someday head west. Surely he knew I would have been thrilled for him. Perhaps he thought I would have given up my opportunity at The Boston Conservatory to join him.

If only I had.

"Nathan Everstone has been traveling with him, of course."

Everything about that particular gentleman's father rushed to mind—the vindictive letter, his hatred for me and my mother, and the nightmares I'd had since the day I'd met him almost eleven years earlier.

"And a gentleman named Mr. Crawford, whom I don't think I've had the privilege of meeting. He was recently acquired by the Boston Inland Mission Society and is in search of a wife to take back to Washington with him."

"Is that what Lawry and Mr. Everstone were doing in Washington? Mission work?"

"Heavens, no! Lawry's interested enough in attending church, but I daresay he has little interest in becoming a missionary. And Nathan? Absolutely not. He would be a very sad candidate, indeed. Lawry likely had to persuade him to let Mr. Crawford aboard his private railcar. Can you imagine a poor missionary being escorted across the continent in such style, and in the company of an Everstone?"

"Are the Everstones so entirely wealthy?" I tried to seem as uninterested as possible. For all I knew, Claudine might expect me to be friends with him.

"My dear, Nathan Everstone's father owns a massive chain of resorts and hotels that extends from Maine to Florida, as well as the Greaghan Lumber Company. They're one of the wealthiest families in the region."

"Oh." A shudder ran down my spine.

"Now, Amaryllis, about Nathan—he'll likely still want to spend much of his time with Lawry. He visits us quite often, you know."

"How often is 'quite often'?" I dreaded the answer.

"Almost on a daily basis. It is surprising, is it not? One of New England's most eligible bachelors choosing to spend his evenings at Hilldreth instead of at the endless supply of parties and dinners to which I'm certain he's always invited."

The more I learned, the less happy I became. With every additional word, I realized I'd placed myself in the very heart of the Marriage Market of Boston's most elite society.

Was all this part of God's will for my life? Did He care about my inheriting the Landreth fortune? My thoughts again dwelt upon the horse farm on Whidbey Island where I'd spent the first fourteen years of my life. Wanting to begin again after my mother had died, I'd long supposed that Father had sold it, permanently robbing me of the only home I'd ever known.

It was my stubborn belief that God would make a way for me to return to Washington, even if I wouldn't be able to have my Brigham Shires of Bruckerdale on Whidbey Island again. God knew my heart better than anyone and knew that my being trapped in the gilded cage of Claudine Abernathy's world was not what I wanted...or needed. Especially in light of how closely she seemed to be associated with Bram Everstone and his family.

"It is best you know from the outset, Amaryllis, that Nathan's as charming as God ever made a man, even when he's being disagreeable. I'm certain he could have any young woman he wanted, and at times, he acts as if he has no qualms about flirting with all of them. You'll have to take care with that one. He—"

"Oh, have no fear, Aunt Clau—Claudine. Inconsistent men hold no appeal for me whatsoever." The mere fact that he was Bram Everstone's son was more than enough reason for me to steer clear of him.

"Such a smart girl, but don't think for one minute I say these things because you couldn't snag such a man's attention. You could, without a doubt. Just look at you. However, Nathan claims, much as Lawry does, that he's hard-pressed to find any young female truly worth being serious about. Both of them insist that most of the young ladies they know are merely done-up packages of ribbon and silk, full of nothing more than fluff and manners."

"I cannot blame them," I muttered under my breath. Most of them were indeed.

"And the man barely gives a girl the chance to prove herself otherwise. Though, I must say, it did seem that before he left in such a hurry all those years ago, he was on the verge of forming an engagement with Nicholette Fairbanks. But everyone knows it was his father who desired the match."

I unbuttoned my coat. I was getting rather warm.

"You see, Amaryllis, Nathan stands to inherit his share of the Everstone's twenty-million-dollar inheritance upon his thirtieth birthday next February. And rumor has it that Bram threatened to withhold it from him until he marries her."

"Twenty million dollars!" I tried my best not to get involved in the love triangles Claudine was obsessed with, but it proved to be far too engrossing.

"And if you ask me, Nathan can hardly tolerate the girl."

"Would his father do such a thing? Would he leave his own flesh and blood penniless, for the sake of—"

"There's no telling what Bram will do, Amaryllis, though I doubt there's any danger of Nathan ever being left penniless, no matter what the outcome of this forced engagement is." She shook her head. "Fortunately for Nathan, his father is still in Europe and will not be back for some time."

That tidbit of information was the best news I'd heard from her yet.

I sat up with a start, still shaken, my knees bent and my face in my hands. The nightmare always played out the same, no matter how long it had been since the last time I'd dreamt it.

All of the excitement and, yes, even the joy from meeting Claudine was gone.

My eyes adjusted to the dim moonlight, and I took in my surroundings—my mother's bedchamber at the end of the hall on the second floor at Hilldreth. As soon as my feet hit the thick, carpeted floor, I was again reminded of the drastic turn my life had taken in the last month. Anyone else in my predicament probably would have considered such a turn of events to be a blessing.

I stood and walked around the massive cherry four-poster bed and across the room to the oversized bay window overlooking the corner of Commonwealth Avenue and Berkeley Street. I sat upon the burgundy velvet sofa and ran my fingers over the intricate detail of the lace covering the windows as the moon shone through.

Turning my attention back toward the chamber, I again marveled at the size of the room and wondered what my grandmother could have been thinking to will everything to me after treating me as if I didn't exist the one and only time I'd ever seen her—at my mother's funeral. Had I been her last, delusional hope of restoring what was left of her family to Boston's most prestigious aristocratic circles? Or had she truly regretted disowning my mother all those years ago?

Whatever the reason, I already knew it wouldn't work. I was certain my inheritance would only attract the most desperate of opportunists. Who was I compared to the elegant young debutantes who'd circulated through the balls and banquets of Boston already this year?

But no matter how much I could use the inheritance, I could not use a husband. Unless perhaps the missionary was interested....

I put a stop to that illogical thought immediately.

What did I know of men? They were controlling. Insensitive. Undependable. Inconsistent. And liars. Just like my father—and just like Bram Everstone.

But surely a missionary wouldn't have such irredeemable qualities—would he?

With those two little words, I realized I'd actually allowed myself to consider something I had never imagined I would.

Marriage.

But even that unpleasant subject wasn't enough to fully take my mind off the nightmare. I stared for a long time at the moon's reflection upon the now-familiar flourishing crimson swirls of the silken wallpaper, trying to forget the pain the nightmare had trudged up.

For eleven long, lonely years, I'd taught myself to fight against the unwanted feelings it produced, but my efforts always proved pointless. In the midst of the dreams, I always remembered my mother.

And the reason she was gone.

TWO

The Train Station

"All generalizations are dangerous, even this one."
—Alexandre Dumas

Claudine rushed into my room early the next morning to inform me that Lawry and his friends were scheduled to arrive back from their extended vacation that very day. She'd wanted it to be a surprise and undeniably got her wish.

My fingers clutched the leather seat in Claudine's carriage on our way to the train station. I couldn't help but wonder if I'd be able to tell which of the gentlemen was Nathan Everstone before we were introduced. I'd already decided he would most likely have the same dark brown hair and brooding eyes as his father, along with an arrogant attitude evident upon first sight.

Claudine and I arrived at the train station early and waited in the warmth of the carriage for Lawry and his two friends. Having spent hardly a day settling into life with Claudine, I'd not had time to think of all the implications of Lawry arriving home so soon.

When the train drudgingly arrived through the snow and ice, a loud screech rent the air. With endless billows of steam surrounding us, Claudine and I exited the carriage. We found the Everstones' long black private railcar attached to the end of the train. Red velvet curtains in the windows closed off the interior from my prying eyes.

Claudine caught my arm and guided me toward the balcony at the end of the railcar, where I saw a door with a coat of arms painted upon it—the very same coat of arms that had been emblazoned on the coach that had carried me off to boarding school eleven years earlier. Bile crept up my throat. How far had Bram Everstone's hand reached into and tampered with my life already before the sixteenth of February?

Suddenly a familiar face peeped through the curtains of a nearby window. Lawry smiled, waved, and then quickly emerged through the door. Two impeccably dressed gentlemen came out behind him. The one with brown curly hair and brown eyes—the same dark features as his ominous father—leveled a cocksure grin my way as soon as he spotted me.

Avoiding eye contact, I focused my attention on the gentleman with straw-blond hair standing beside him. He had an astonishing face with deep-set brows, which I had a chance to examine closely as he took off his hat and bent over the railing to scour the crowd. What I liked best about his face was his nose. It was aristocratic and remarkably straight, quite the opposite of my own. Was this perfect-looking man the Washington-bound missionary?

When he turned and caught me staring, I noticed the dark green color of his eyes. I was unable to turn away, even as I realized he was glaring down at me with a vexed expression. Before I could gather my erratic thoughts, Lawry clanked down the metal stairs and headed directly for me. His friends followed behind him as he caught me by the waist and gave me a quick embrace. "Why, Amaryllis, you've not changed one bit."

"I sincerely hope that isn't the truth." I forced myself to pull my gaze from his friend. "Despite your lies, it is so good to see you again."

Once he let go of me, Claudine slowly walked to the dark-haired gentleman and asked rather oddly, with no lack of surprise to her aged features, "Mr. Crawford?"

I looked back to the light-haired gentleman. He still stared at me, as if transfixed.

This was Nathan Everstone? Surely not!

"Nathan!" exclaimed a young woman as she broke from the busy crowd surrounding us, her maid in tow.

"Sis!" He finally turned his troubled eyes from me and wrapped his arms about the young lady, twirling her about.

The young woman seemed to cling to his shadow once he put her down. She spoke to him so intently, it felt as if those of us standing around them were eavesdropping. "Nicholette was quite upset when you left, Nathan. I don't know how you'll ever be able to repair things with her, not to mention with Father."

"They'll both be happy I'm back, won't they? Ready and willing to do everything that's asked of me. Within reason, that is."

"Oh, do be serious."

Nathan, who had again become conscious of my blatant regard, took his arm from about his sister's shoulders, turned to me, and bowed. He took my hand in his and met my gaze directly. "You must be Lawry's cousin Amaryllis Brigham. It's an honor to finally meet you." No matter how smoothly he could speak, he didn't fool me. It was as if he had taken his forced smile and put it into words.

"Amaryllis, meet Nathan, Natalia's twin brother. You remember Natalia from the summer you came to Bar Harbor, don't you?" Lawry asked, coming between us. "And I told you all about Nathan in my letters, remember?"

"Yes, I remember, Lawry."

"I meant for you to meet the last time you came," Lawry said, as if it had been only last year. "Oh, and this is his other sister, Miss Estella Everstone."

Once I had a good, long look at Estella, I realized what an extraordinary resemblance she, at least, bore to their father.

"I'm pleased to meet you, Mr. Everstone, Miss Everstone."

"Likewise." Estella looked at me as if I weren't interesting enough to deserve her full attention.

Her brother said nothing but only continued to stare at me. My cheeks burned under his scrutiny. What had I been thinking to ogle him so?

"And this is Jay Crawford, another old friend of mine." Lawry motioned to the dark-haired gentleman who quietly stared at Estella. "Amaryllis was born in Washington, just north of Seattle. It was all she spoke of the summer she visited Bar Harbor eleven years ago."

"A pleasure, Miss Brigham." Jay turned his attention to me and took my hand in a firm grip, as if I were a man. "I can understand why you loved Washington so. It's a beautiful part of the country."

However, as he said the words, I couldn't help but notice that his eyes drifted toward Estella for what seemed like the hundredth time since she'd made herself known.

⌇

As the horses moved Claudine's carriage down the road, I couldn't help but watch Nathan step into a red landau that also flaunted the ostentatious Everstone crest in gold gilt.

"Where exactly do the Everstones reside?" The words left my mouth before I thought better of asking.

Lawry turned from the window to face me. He'd been staring at something outside and, in all honesty, looked as if he were about to bolt. "Estella lives with her aunt Miriam—"

"Miriam Bancroft is one of the imperious Boston Blues, Amaryllis," Claudine cut in. "No doubt Estella's been waiting for Nathan to return home so that she can move back into Everwood. Their father has been in Europe all winter, and Everwood has been closed up since he left. As for Nathan, he usually lives on the top floor of his father's Grand Everstone Hotel."

Of course. Nathan Everstone likely wouldn't know what to do with himself without the backing of his father's name and money.

"Nathan knows about the fire, doesn't he, Lawry?" Claudine stopped a moment, then continued after Lawry nodded his head. "The hotel burnt down weeks ago, Amaryllis, and with his father traveling abroad. I'm sure he'll have his hands full, since Bram isn't hurrying home anytime soon—"

"Is that the reason Mr. Everstone has returned home? To rebuild the hotel?" I inwardly kicked myself for even being interested.

"I don't know what his plan is." Lawry still gazed out the window.

Surely Nathan had told his friend something of his plans. They'd just traveled together for weeks on end.

"I know he could just as well move to Everwood," Claudine continued. "But I thought I'd invite him to stay with us at Hilldreth for the next few weeks. What do you think, Lawry?"

"I think that's a splendid idea. He'll be at Hilldreth most of the time, anyway." Lawry turned to smile at me, watching for my reaction. "Amaryllis, I'm sure you'll like him. Everyone does."

"Surely he'd rather stay in the comfort of his own family's home," I added halfheartedly.

Claudine looked at Lawry and then at me. "Oh, Amaryllis, we'll be the talk of the town. You're not afraid of him, are you?"

I opened my mouth to answer but was at a loss for words.

"Amaryllis, dear, I had no idea you would take such an aversion to Nathan from what little I said yesterday." Claudine gave me an impish grin. "He's quite harmless."

"Is he?" Lawry asked with a wry smile. And Lawry would know.

"I know you've never had much of a chance to fraternize with gentlemen over the years, Amaryllis, but I think having Nathan stay with us will have just the effect we're looking for."

"And what effect is that, exactly?" I asked.

"Why, with Nathan at Hilldreth, it will drive more men to take notice of you. There's nothing like a little competition to incite jealousy among men. And if Nathan likes you, everyone will."

And what if he didn't like me? What if he hated me, even? Had Claudine missed the look on Nathan's face when he'd first noticed me? It was obvious he already knew of his father's distasteful opinion of me.

The feelings of anxiety I'd experienced earlier that morning were back and swirling out of control, churning my breakfast. What could Claudine be thinking to invite him to stay with us, coercing him to pay attention to me to enhance my popularity?

It sounded like torture.

⌒

As soon as we entered Hilldreth, Lawry's melancholy dissolved, and he began to exude the same brotherly devotion I remembered from the summer my mother and I had spent at Truesdale Cottage in Bar Harbor. I wondered, for the first time, how it was that Lawry's family seemed to have always lived in my grandparents' summer cottage. They seemed to have enough money to purchase it if they wanted it for their very own.

Lawry and I stole away to the large wood-paneled study that took up two stories on the west side of the house, in an effort to stay out of the way of the busy preparations for the evening's events. Claudine had a "surprise" dinner party planned in honor of Lawry's homecoming. There would be a much more elaborate party later, I was certain, but for that night, it would be just a small gathering of friends.

From the moment we sat down on the deep leather sofa, Lawry handed me photograph after photograph, telling me where each one had been taken. His agreeable manner immediately put me at ease. And seeing that he didn't have the same self-consciousness about his Abernathy nose as I still did made me think that perhaps it wasn't such a travesty to have such a feature.

It just wasn't straight. Like Nathan Everstone's.

"This one is of Niagara Falls. Have you ever heard of it? It's near the Thousand Islands and is the widest waterfall you could ever imagine." He handed me a pile of photographs. "From there we went down to Chicago to visit a friend from college."

"Dartmouth, correct?"

"Yes. Nathan, Crawford, and I graduated together back in eighty-three."

"You'd rather live here with Aunt Claudine than in Bar Harbor? I thought you and your parents were close."

"We were, but I've found there's more to living than what that secluded tourist town can offer." He handed me another pile of photographs, even though I'd hardly made my way through the ones already in my hand. Pointing out the Everstones' railcar stopped at an unmarked train station, he added, "From Chicago, we took the Northern Pacific Railroad to Washington and ended up staying. I suppose you expected us to show up in Boston looking like cowboys, didn't you?"

"I did imagine that you'd all look a bit rougher than you do, being out west for so many years." It was so good to be with Lawry Hampton again. Having spent just one summer with my distant cousin, and that over a decade ago, I was thrilled that we still got along so well.

"We cleaned up just for you, Amaryllis. No young lady wants to witness what three bachelors look like after two years of...well, you know what it's like out there. Sure, there's civilization in the big cities, but we weren't out there looking for civilization."

"What were you looking for?"

"Oh, you know. Adventure. Escape. Freedom."

He was purposefully not giving details about anything. I decided to ignore my curiosity. After all, I would have wanted him to do the same. As I continued to sift through the photographs, I noticed there were hardly any featuring him or either one of his friends. That is, until I came across a photograph of Nathan Everstone dressed in hiking apparel, standing in front of what looked to be Deception Pass, the northernmost point of Whidbey Island. His hat was on the ground beside him, and his shirt was stretched tautly across his chest, his collar wide open, his sleeves rolled high.

And I'd thought merely his face was perfect.

What had Lawry and Nathan been doing on *my* Whidbey Island?

Despite the multitude of questions the photograph brought up, the fact that it was an image of Whidbey Island wasn't the reason I couldn't drag my eyes away. Even as I shifted it to the bottom of the pile, Nathan's smile was burned into my mind. My stomach contracted, and I didn't have the heart to look at any more photos.

I put the stack of photographs on the desk and stood to leave. Lawry followed me to the door. Resting his shoulder against the doorjamb, he handed me one last photograph.

"There aren't many pictures of me, but I wanted you to have one. Nathan and I were hiking on your beloved Whi—in your beloved Washington."

I knew very well that he'd almost said "Whidbey Island." Did he really think I wouldn't recognize the one place on earth my heart felt was home?

I took the photograph from him and studied it for a moment. It was similar to the one I'd hidden at the bottom of the pile, only this one included Lawry, as well.

"It's beautiful." For more reasons than one. "Thank you, Lawry."

The familiar vistas vividly reminded me how much I missed living on the ranch where I'd grown up, surrounded by those mountains. I would go back someday, even if attaining what had once been my father's first horse farm was impossible.

I held the photograph at my side, as if it didn't interest me in the least. I certainly didn't need the image to remind me of Nathan's smile, those green eyes, or the rest of his remarkably sculpted physique. "Is Mr. Crawford staying somewhere near Back Bay?"

"He's staying at a boardinghouse downtown. He plans to stay in Boston for only a few months."

"Oh, yes. He's in search of a wife."

"Do your own plans still involve heading back to Washington, Amaryllis?" I felt Lawry's unyielding gaze measuring me. Was he guessing that I might settle for marrying Jay in order to gain my inheritance—which I was certain he knew about—and move back west in one strategic move? What would he say if he knew it was the truth?

"Perhaps someday." I allowed a small laugh to escape.

"Would you really go back?" Lawry watched me, practically guarding the doorway.

"Yes, of course." I paused for a moment gathering my courage. "Lawry, do you happen to know anything about my grandmother's will?"

"Claudine mentioned it in a letter a while back. It won't be long until all of Boston knows about it, though. Harden hardly has a reputation for keeping anything to himself."

"I had a feeling that was how things would be."

"Are you not interested in inheriting the Landreth fortune, Amaryllis? After I did my part and brought you the two best men in the world to choose from?"

"I don't especially want a husband." The words, now out, refused to be unsaid.

"Wouldn't you want to marry if you fell in love?" He pushed himself from the wall and walked back to the desk.

"That sounds so trite."

"But not impossible." His smile held the same brotherly countenance I remembered.

"Do you know who will inherit the fortune if I don't?"

"I wouldn't worry about that. As Claudine mentioned, having Nathan stay at Hilldreth will help accomplish that particular goal. I'm sure there will be someone you end up liking well enough." Lawry sat down at the desk with an air of persuasiveness.

"I don't think you understand. I don't want—"

"And if all else fails, I'm sure Claudine will simply convince Nathan to marry you."

I snorted. As unladylike as it was, I couldn't help it. "From what I've heard, that route doesn't work so well on him. He was told to marry Nicholette Fairbanks." My cheeks flamed.

"He sure was."

"Not that I'd ever consider such a thing."

"No woman would refuse a marriage proposal from Nathan. Not even you, Amaryllis." He smiled as he gathered up his photographs.

Taking my chance while he was distracted, I quietly left the room, no matter that it seemed I was running away from where the conversation was headed.

As I climbed the small stairwell to the second floor, I realized Lawry had never answered my question regarding who else was in line to inherit the Landreth fortune. I knew of no other relatives besides him and his two younger sisters. They weren't related to Jasper Landreth III but to his wife, Marielle Abernathy-Landreth, the woman who'd disowned my mother before I was born.

When I reached my bedchamber, I placed the photograph of Lawry and Nathan between the pages of my Bible, alongside the one of my mother and her friend Grace.

I hoped to have the strength to never dwell upon it again. But no sooner had I decided that I wouldn't than I found myself sitting on the edge of my bed studying every square inch of it.

The mountains. The trees. Nathan Everstone.

I put it back again, lay down on my bed, and stared at the ceiling. I dreaded his paying any kind of coerced attention to me. Would he truly do it as a favor to Claudine? I sincerely hoped not.

I flipped to my stomach and opened my Bible again, looking at the photograph once more. I told myself I wanted to see the background, for I could still picture in my mind those mountains I'd loved so much. But of course, Lawry and Nathan were there, too, both grinning with unmistakable mischievousness that told of the special bond between them.

They really did look like the best of friends. And Nathan Everstone, as much as I wanted to hate him, did look quite stunning when he smiled.

THREE

The Dinner Party

*"Through the ingenuousness of her age beamed an ardent mind,
a mind not of the women, but of the poet;
she did not please, she intoxicated."*
—Alexandre Dumas, *The Three Musketeers*

L ater that night, I sat at the vanity in my bedchamber, already
dressed for the evening. Agnes, the young maid who'd been
appointed to me when I first arrived, was busy taming my dark,
unmanageable hair into some sort of braided knot at the crown of
my head.

"You look stunning, Miss 'Marillys! Just like perfection."

"Thank you." I stole a wary look at my reflection in the mirror.
Agnes really was a master at getting my hair to do as she wished.

"Well, you don't seem very happy about it." Her jovial response
didn't surprise me, for we'd developed quite a comfortable relationship with one another in the month I'd spent at Hilldreth on
my own. "Do you not like the way I've twisted it up into the back
here?"

As an answer, I simply lifted a finger to the bump at the bridge
of my nose.

"But there's absolutely nothing wrong with your nose. It's the
very same famous Abernathy nose that Master Lawry has. You're
not insinuating that he's ugly, are you?"

"No, Lawry is the farthest thing from ugly."

"Miss Brigham, I promise you, no one else sees your nose as you do. Everybody has one, and they're all different. I daresay, the shape of yours adds character to your face. Without it, you might even look plain."

Hmm. "Plain" instead of "unsightly" didn't sound so bad.

"You're not listening to a word I'm saying, are you? You look marvelous, from the top of your head to the tip of your toes. Please believe me."

There was a loud knock upon the closed door of my bedchamber.

"Amaryllis, may I enter?"

I knew the moment Claudine saw my dress, she would make me change. I was surprised Agnes hadn't mentioned it already.

"Yes, come in."

Before Claudine spoke a word, she immediately began to unhook the back of my dress. "Dear, you'll need to show yourself off at your best advantage tonight. If you wear this, every woman invited will outshine you the minute she enters the house. What were you thinking letting her put this on, Agnes?"

"I'd prefer it if they did outshine me," I mused. "I'm really not cut out to make men notice me."

"You're being a silly goose," Claudine said as Agnes helped her pull the dress over my head. "Of course you want men to pay attention to you. You just don't know what it's like. All you have to do is be a little mysterious and, of course, make use of your fan." Claudine handed me the fan she'd presented to me the day before, part of the entire wardrobe she'd bought for me in Paris. "It really is the best tool there is for flirting."

My thoughts switched from the subject of flirting to Nathan Everstone. I didn't want him to think I was trying to entice his attention. What I did want was to let him quietly ignore me—as I was sure he wanted to do.

"Please believe me, dear. No one wants to marry a young lady who doesn't carry herself with confidence." All her talk of marriage frayed at my nerves. It really was all she thought about. I was surprised she'd never married. She seemed a great advocate for the institution.

Claudine rummaged through my wardrobe and held out a simple lacy cream-colored evening gown. I recalled, from having tried it on the day before, that it showed off my shoulders and hugged my body quite closely.

"This one, I remember, shows off your figure very well." She gathered the bottom, heaved it over my head, and situated its fabric about me. Never in my life had I been so primped and primed for one measly dinner.

My eyes met Claudine's eyes in the mirror. "I don't want men to like me for my figure." Not that I was certain I wanted any of them to like me for any reason.

Claudine left the room with an exasperated huff, taking Agnes with her.

To tell the truth, I was just as exasperated with myself. I exhaled, my chin in my hands, staring into the mirror.

Was that stunning young woman looking back truly me?

⌒

As the guests trickled in through the front door, I stood next to Lawry in the foyer of Hilldreth, in case Claudine's attorney, Wyatt Harden, tried to capture my attention. I was already weary of that particular gentleman, as he had come around the day before to meet me. Answering his tiresome questions with the utmost politeness had tried my patience.

He'd already annoyed me with his habit of pinning me with a stare whenever I glanced about the room. I couldn't tell if it was my inheritance that intrigued him so much, or if he was genuinely attracted to me as a person. Either way, the thirty-something-year-old bachelor made me feel uncomfortable to the point that I could barely stand the sight of him. Given the choice, I would have rather had to deal with an encounter with Nathan than Wyatt any day.

"Nicholette Fairbanks, meet my cousin, Miss Amaryllis Brigham." The buzz of voices filled the room, and I was barely able to hear Lawry's voice. "Amaryllis, meet Miss Nicholette Fairbanks."

I smiled, as Claudine had instructed me to, but the look that registered on Nicholette's face was one of irritation. That withstanding, I couldn't help but notice how stunningly beautiful she was. With her glowing youth, perfectly upswept golden tresses, and deep hazel eyes, she looked flawless. I was surprised Nathan hadn't wanted to marry her two years earlier.

As she turned her eyes back to Lawry, I expected her expression to change, at least a little. But it remained the same. Did she really look at everyone so indifferently? How exhausting.

After a few minutes of listening to Lawry describe his trip to Washington for Nicholette, I heard Higgins announce Nathan and his sister Estella. Unfortunately, my notions of facing him in place of Wyatt became a reality.

Nicholette took my arm and led me straight to them, looping her other arm through Estella's. Before I knew it, all three of us were positioned before Nathan in a way that felt ridiculously worshipful. It was likely the first time Nicholette had seen him in two years. Perhaps she felt the need to prove something to him.

And yet Nathan practically ignored her presence, directing his gaze to me.

"It's so good to see you again, Miss Brigham." He couldn't have shocked me more with such unexpected civility.

"Good evening, Mr. Everstone."

"Have you had a chance to see Lawry's photographs yet?" As he tried to charm me with his gorgeous smile, the only photograph I could recall was the one I wanted to forget.

"Yes." I could think of nothing more to say as he stared down at me with his intense green gaze. The skin around his eyes crinkled when he smiled. I forced myself to look away.

"And what did you think?" Why was he suddenly so courteous to me? Had Claudine already spoken to him? Had he truly meant to ignore Nicholette so completely?

"They were stunning." I felt terribly warm.

"Which ones did you like best?"

"Deception Pass." My eyes met his again. Everything I wanted to say was entirely unsuitable, so I turned instead to Nicholette for a moment. She seemed more than perturbed by the fact that he'd spoken so exclusively to me.

His eyes drew my attention once again. He was still focused solely upon me. "Lawry read your letters aloud to us on the train back."

"Did he?" Betrayal was one emotion I'd never imagined I would feel toward my cousin, but there it was. I willed myself to forgive him, though. For what were those letters but a lonely adolescent girl's means to escape reality while confined at Miss Pelletier's School for Young Ladies for years on end?

"They've been quite helpful in my efforts to understand a good many things concerning you."

"Why should anything concerning me matter to you?"

"That's a very good question, Miss Brigham. And one I'm glad you've had the forethought to ask."

"And the answer?" I hated how easily he'd entrapped me, but I couldn't help it. He was so enigmatic. He'd hardly had to try, and there I was, eating out of his hand.

"We'll get to that eventually, I promise, Miss Brigham." He smiled again. "Now, back to Lawry. Honestly, I was shocked he was willing to come back when he received word that you would be staying with Claudine. I thought he'd end up staying in Washington indefinitely."

"Were you not also tempted?"

He lifted a corner of his mouth. "I wouldn't say that. I just wasn't tempted enough to give up the opportunity to meet you." He slanted a brow, and I glanced away. It was proving to be quite difficult to keep my eyes off him.

"You took the train all the way from Washington to Massachusetts to meet me?"

"Don't be ridiculous," Nicholette said, standing rigidly beside me. By her defensiveness, she clearly thought he was serious in his attentions toward me, but I saw right through what he was doing. He was most likely launching Claudine's nonsensical charade, intent on using the stunt to also play with Nicholette's emotions.

And if that wasn't it, he was surely the most talented flirt I'd ever met.

Nicholette let go of my arm and led Estella over to Lawry. I was surprised she was willing to leave me alone with Nathan.

Watching the two young women cross the room, I wondered if perhaps Nicholette and Nathan didn't deserve each other.

"You smile." He drew my attention back to his face—too easily.

"Do forgive me. It was quite unintentional."

"Are you not enjoying my company, Miss Brigham?" I could not believe the gall the man had. "Or do you simply loathe this masquerade called high society as much as I do?"

Fortunately, I was saved from having to answer his absurd question by the call to dinner.

⌒

Claudine had transformed the long dining room into what looked like a garden of pink and white roses. She'd gone a little to the extreme in adorning the table with vase after vase of long-stemmed roses and pussy-willow branches. Claudine and Lawry were seated at either end of the table, while I sat at the center between Jay Crawford and Mr. Fairbanks. My seat directly faced

Nathan's, which thankfully meant I wouldn't have to speak with him. How could I, with such a wall of flowers and twigs erected between us?

During dinner, I found that Jay had a good deal to say—to Estella, who sat to his left.

Out of sheer boredom, I peeked across the table through the roses and pussy-willow branches. Nicholette must have forgiven Nathan for his earlier misconduct toward her, for she spoke quite endlessly to him about something I could tell didn't interest him in the least.

When he turned quickly and caught my eye, he smiled.

Averting my gaze, I witnessed Wyatt steal a glimpse my way, his ice-blue eyes half hidden under his long, effeminate black eyelashes. Thoroughly frustrated, I looked down just as the next course was set before me. I was happy to see dessert finally arrive. I'd picked at every unidentifiable course up till then, certain I would never get used to the French cuisine Claudine's cook was accustomed to preparing for every meal, even while Claudine had been in Europe.

Intent on eating the strawberry sponge cake, I had to stop short when I heard Jay ask, "How do you like Boston, Miss Brigham?"

The question captured not only my attention but also that of Nathan, whose deep green eyes were again watching me from across the table.

"I'm not new to Boston, Mr. Crawford. I've lived here for years."

"How is that?" Finally, he seemed interested in something about me. Not that it would have been my first choice of subjects to speak to him about.

"I used to attend The Boston Conservatory. But I didn't get out much back then."

"Did Miss Abernathy not—"

"My aunt has been in Europe for the last few years. She's only just returned."

"What did you like to do when you did venture out?" He seemed to measure his words.

"Sometimes I went to the library. But that was all. We were encouraged to stay close and to practice much."

"What instruments do you play?"

"Only the piano."

His smile lit up his warm brown eyes. "If you attended The Boston Conservatory, then I'm sure you play the piano quite proficiently. Will we have the pleasure of hearing you perform for us this evening?"

"It's quite likely, if my aunt has anything to say about it." I looked down the table and realized dinner was almost finished, and I had yet to take a bite of dessert. "May I be rude by changing the subject, Mr. Crawford? I would much rather hear about your work in Washington than speak about my time in Boston. Where exactly is your mission?"

"I'm being sent to a town called Aberdeen, near the coast. Have you heard of it?"

"I have not."

"It isn't a pleasant place, but it's in much need of a church, as well as a hospital. Where in Washington were you born?"

"Whidbey Island, just north of Seattle in Puget Sound. I'm from a very small town called Greenbank."

"I've heard of it."

"You have?"

"Sure I have. It's where Nate—" He seemed tense for a moment, then abandoned his comment completely. Obviously, Lawry, Nathan, and Jay all wanted to keep quiet about my Whidbey Island.

"Are you interested in moving back to Washington one day, Miss Brigham?"

"It's my dearest wish, Mr. Crawford."

I could tell he was indeed interested in furthering our conversation along that specific line, but some of the gentlemen were already helping the ladies from their seats. I still hadn't taken a bite of my dessert.

As we left the table, it seemed that everyone was speaking to someone else. All except Nathan, that is. He was staring at me again, only now with a look of concern knitting his brows.

⟁

"I noticed Nathan watching you throughout dinner, Miss Brigham." Nicholette took my arm and led me to a far corner of the drawing room, while the gentlemen congregated in the study near the back of the house. "He's becoming about as shameless as his younger brother Vance. I wanted to be sure to make a point and warn you about him."

"Oh, I know all I need to about Nathan Everstone, Miss Fairbanks. And he's the last person I'd ever want to encourage." I could see straight through her cautionary advice. She desired him for herself and didn't want anyone to get in her way.

"Amaryllis, would you be a dear and play the piece I chose for tonight?" Claudine asked, and then returned her attention to her guests. "She's amazingly talented at the piano. Just wait until you hear her play."

Thankful for an escape from the small crowd of women, I left Nicholette's side in search of the sheets of music I didn't need and remembered I'd taken them to my room.

On my way back downstairs, I heard the gentlemen file out of the study and into the hall. I decided to head down by way of the servants' stairs to avoid meeting them in the foyer.

As I dashed through the hall past the study, Nathan Everstone walked out in front of me, and I collided directly into his hard wall of a chest.

"Oh, I'm so dreadfully sorry!" I glimpsed up in time to see a crooked smile spread across his face. "I really must try to be more watchful of where I'm going."

"Apparently." His hands cradled my elbows, holding me up, although I was quite certain I could have stood perfectly well on my own. "Where are you going in such a hurry?"

"Through the back parlor to the drawing room." I feebly pointed the way.

When I tore my gaze from his, I discovered the sheet music strewn all over the floor.

His eyes followed mine. "You're going to play?"

"I am. You're welcome to come listen…if you would so graciously let go of me."

His eyes searched mine for a moment, and then he let go of me with a jerk. Without another word, he walked away in the direction I'd indicated through the parlor.

Kneeling, I gathered my music and followed not thirty seconds behind him.

Within minutes, I was seated at the old-fashioned box grand piano in the drawing room. As I played Beethoven's *Moonlight Sonata*, Nathan stood by my side, flipping each page of music for me.

Nicholette watched us from her seat with a hard look in her eyes. I was sure she hated me. Nathan had done an excellent job of making me seem exceptionally untrustworthy, as if everything I'd said to her was a complete lie. I hadn't meant to run into him, and I certainly hadn't wanted him to turn pages for me. I closed my eyes and focused on playing the notes, doing my best to ignore everyone else in the room.

As soon as Estella took my place at the piano, I realized I had the option of sitting either in the chair situated next to Nicholette or upon an empty settee, where Nathan was sure to join me.

I chose the safer of the two options.

"Unbelievable." I smiled down at Nicholette before I took the seat next to her. "What an insufferable man. You can tell what he's doing, can't you, Miss Fairbanks?"

It was unnerving to act a part that had been forced upon me, and I prayed she wouldn't see right through my little play. I'd never done anything like it in my life, but I didn't want to be caught in some sort of love-hate triangle between Nicholette and Nathan, or anyone else for that matter.

"I'm relieved to find you with such an opinion, Miss Brigham. It is difficult to resist his charm when he decides to use it."

I quickly concluded that Nicholette seemed as fickle a woman as they came.

"As wealthy as he is, and as handsome, I have no doubt Mr. Everstone is accustomed to having women fall at his feet. But I certainly won't be one of them. I have to maintain some degree of self-respect, after all."

From his seat nearby, I found Nathan's irritatingly steady gaze still on me. It seemed he'd heard the general meaning of my words, for he smiled to himself, as if amused.

⁓

"Miss Brigham." Wyatt greeted me in the hall as I was about to enter the empty parlor near the back of the house.

My only reason for going there was to stay out of Nathan's fiery line of vision. I was bewildered by him, to say the least. What made his green eyes watch my every move like a cat on the prowl? Surely Claudine hadn't asked him to do *that*.

"You play so very superbly, Miss Brigham. Mozart's *Moonlight Sonata* is one of my favorites." He followed me into the parlor.

"Thank you, Mr. Harden, but the composer was actually Beethoven."

I wanted with all my heart to tell him to leave me alone and never speak to me again. But, as he was Claudine's attorney and friend, I felt I should try to be as pleasant as possible.

I sat down upon a settee, and he seated himself beside me. "Is it one of your favorites, also?"

"It's tolerable, I suppose. I've always considered it to be rather listless."

"By Jove, I stand corrected. Now that you mention it, I've never heard a more listless tune in my life."

Nathan Everstone chose that moment to walk into the room. He lowered himself onto a cream-colored French Baroque Louis XV chair in the corner about five feet away, then picked up Claudine's small Bible, of all things, and pretended to read.

"But you did play it to perfection," Wyatt added, seeking to regain my attention.

"Thank you again, Mr. Harden." I moved farther from him and smoothed out my skirts.

The fact that Nathan seemed so intent on spying on our little discussion annoyed me. And what could possibly be of interest to him in the Bible that he felt the need to read it in the middle of a dinner party?

"You seem pensive, Miss Brigham. May I ask what's on your mind?" Wyatt asked.

"Oh, why...the Holy Bible—"

Nathan chuckled under his breath.

"Do you read the Bible, Mr. Harden? It seems Mr. Everstone is immensely amused by it. What on earth do you suppose he's found to laugh at?" It wasn't so much Wyatt Harden's general appearance that sent shivers up the back of my neck whenever he looked my way. He really wasn't an unattractive man, for his age. It was only that he seemed to exude some strange, purpose-driven ambition in getting to know me better. I still wasn't certain whose attention I disliked more, Mr. Harden's or Mr. Everstone's.

"Probably the general absurdity of the book as a whole, I would guess." Wyatt glared at Nathan, his mouth pulled down at the corners.

"Wyatt, are you ready to go?" One of Lawry's nameless friends had bounded into the room. "Let's give the University Club a try. I need a real dri—" The young man stopped in mid-sentence when he saw me.

The prospect seemed rather difficult for Wyatt to pass up. He excused himself from our company and left the room.

Nathan quickly took advantage of the empty seat beside me. I couldn't deny I half expected it of him.

"I see you've made quite a devoted friend out of Harden."

"It was done with absolutely no difficulty, I assure you."

"I imagine not."

All night I'd been thinking of what I'd tell him, and I had it down to two sentences that would make my stance very clear. "Mr. Everstone, you need not pretend we're friends. We both know very well your father will not approve of your associating with me."

He flashed his amazingly perfect smile my way with a perceptive glance. "I do appreciate your concern, Miss Brigham, in regard to sacrificing our friendship for the sake of what others might think. However, the fact is, I've been looking forward to making your acquaintance for over eleven years. Have I waited all this time in vain?"

He delivered each line flawlessly and without emotion. I hardly knew how to answer him. "Your father won't like it."

"He need not know anything about it."

"Why is it so important you do this?" I asked, referring to Claudine's plan to make me popular.

He looked puzzled for a moment, which surprised me. He'd seemed to guard himself so well up to that point. "I imagine you already know the answer to that question, Miss Brigham."

"Really, there's no need to interfere, Mr. Everstone. I can handle whatever my future holds."

"I might as well do what I can while your aunt has invited me to stay at Hilldreth for the next few weeks. It's quite the perfect opportunity, if I may say so."

"You accepted?" I had no idea why I was so candid with him.

"How could I refuse such an offer?" He flashed me a clever smile. "Not only will I be under the same roof as my oldest friend, but his mesmerizing cousin, as well. I could hardly resist."

FOUR

The Library

"*The soul, fortunately, has an interpreter—often an unconscious, but still a truthful interpreter—in the eye.*"
—Charlotte Brontë, *Jane Eyre*

W ith my nose buried in the midst of the advertisement section of a day-old newspaper, I heard the chair beside me creak as someone sat down. I looked up cheerfully, expecting to find Lawry, who'd been the one to escort me to the library in the first place.

But it wasn't my cousin at all. It was Nathan Everstone.

I took back my cheerful smile and returned my attention to the paper.

"What a joy, finding you here, Miss Brigham." Although the words sounded as if he meant them from the bottom of his heart, I knew better.

"So, it's officially begun, has it?" I asked, implying the game Claudine had asked him to play for the benefit of my finding a husband.

"If that's the way you want to view it, then yes, it has." He spoke entirely too loudly.

"You must speak quietly in the reading room."

He bent nearer, lowering his voice. "I must, as you say, Miss Brigham." I'd not expected him to sound so very amorous. He must have seen my stunned expression, for he awkwardly grabbed *Jane Eyre* from the top of my pile of library books and opened it to a random page. "You still don't like me?"

"If your last name is Everstone, then no." I'd hoped that would make him leave, but he didn't move an inch. "I'm surprised you aren't frequenting the athenaeum instead."

"Why would I want to pay dues to go there, when you are here?"

"I'm sure you didn't come in here looking for me. Or for *Jane Eyre*." I reached over, grabbed the book from him, and placed it back atop the pile I'd collected. "What is your true purpose in coming here?" I couldn't think of one thing in the entire building that would interest him.

"I've already found what I was looking for. Let's leave it at that, for now."

I folded the newspaper and laid it on the table. There was no point in pretending I was reading it any longer. It was quite impossible with him sitting beside me, saying such things.

His eyes were fixed on my face, and I decided it was probably best to start a new topic of conversation. "Do you read much, Mr. Everstone?"

"Quite often."

"The newspaper, I suppose?"

"Yes, but I also read novels. And sometimes even the Bible."

"Yes, I noticed that yesterday."

"'*Without ceasing I make mention of you always in my prayers,*' my dearest Miss Brigham, '*...for I long to see you.*'"

When I failed to respond to his ridiculous misuse of Scripture—which he obviously did not revere as I did—he continued further, "I'm honestly surprised you're not at Hilldreth playing the piano. It must take much practice to play with as much passion as—"

"Thank you, but I hardly need to."

"You don't need to practice?"

"I play by mem—" I'd not meant to mention it to anyone. How did he, of all people, seem to make me want to say everything that was on my mind?

"You play strictly by memory and don't need to practice at all?"

"If you must know, Mr. Everstone, I play quite faultlessly without having to read music." I picked up *Jane Eyre* again and began flipping through the pages.

"But I remember your sheet music, Miss Brigham. First, spread all over the floor of the back hall after you ran into me, and, second...don't you remember? I turned the pages while you played Beethoven's *Moonlight Sonata.*"

I put down the book to face him.

"I also remember Nicholette—who, I might add, believes she's still terribly in love with me—glaring at us with absolute hatred blazing in her eyes." He whispered at a decent level, but I would have much rather he'd stopped speaking to me altogether. The sound of his deep voice so close sent thrills down my spine, especially when his gaze fixed onto mine so persistently.

"Yes, I noticed that also." I blocked my view of him with *Jane Eyre.* I didn't care what chapter I'd turned to. Any chapter would have been an acceptable escape from what those green eyes were doing to my insides.

"That she was watching us so intently, or that she is—"

"Both." I refused to look at him. "Are you so sure she's not?"

"Not what?"

"In love with you." My eyes darted to him, just in time to catch his gaze again.

"She hardly knows the first thing about me. And it's my goal to keep it that way. Even if her mother is able to claim a link to the Everstone family, I, for one, care nothing about the keeping of such pedigrees." He sat back in his chair for a moment before leaning closer again with a playful grin. "Will you tell me why you were using the sheet music if you don't need it? You wouldn't be lying to everyone about your remarkable talent on purpose, would you?"

"I try not to make a huge deal of it." It had never seemed to work to my advantage. I wondered that I continued to bother.

"You shock me."

"I hardly want more attention, Mr. Everstone."

"I know just how that is, Miss Brigham."

"Yes, I suppose you do."

"You honestly have no sense of disguise, do you?"

"I hardly care what anyone thinks of me, least of all, you."

"Ah, but you do. Using the unneeded sheet music is a prime example." He leaned even closer. "But you have nothing to fear from me. I'll tell no one your secrets." I tried to ignore him, to focus on my book, but every venture was hopeless. "Miss Brigham, have you known anything of the affiliation between your father and Bram Everstone over the last ten or so years?"

"They both knew my mother." I knew there had to be more to it than that. I also knew that I'd have my work cut out for me trying to get Nathan to tell me exactly what he knew.

"You must know more than that. Is it not the reason you're so set against having anything to do with me?" When I refused to answer, he leaned back in his chair. "Is it not the reason you're so terrified of what my father might think of us being seen together?"

"If there's more reason to avoid you than the fact that you're Bram Everstone's son, I do not know it." Turning away from him, I asked, "Have you seen Lawry wandering about? He's been missing for the longest time."

"The Greaghan Lumber Company was your father's largest customer while he bred his famous black-and-white Shire horses in the mountains of Maine. Do you not think it somewhat interesting that they chose to do so much business together? You act as if my father was your greatest enemy in the world, when I can assure you he's not."

Immediately Lawry walked up to the table with a smirk of inquisitiveness on his face. How long had he been watching us?

I swiftly adjusted myself in my chair when I realized how closely I'd been crouched toward Nathan.

When Nathan glanced at Lawry and noticed his expression, he straightened in his seat, as well. Then, without another word, he stood and abruptly took his leave.

I did not see Nathan Everstone at all in the four days following our strange conversation at the library. Not one single glimpse of him, despite the fact he'd taken up residence at Hilldreth the evening after the dinner party. Lawry told me he was kept busy at the Everstone Square Offices downtown while his father was still away in Europe.

But I knew better.

I was certain I was the reason he hardly made an appearance at Hilldreth—why he never came to dinner or spent any time with Lawry.

It was quite obvious that he'd accepted Claudine's generous offer out of politeness, and that he would've preferred to make his home at his father's newly remodeled mansion, Everwood. I didn't know where in Back Bay that mansion was located, but I knew that Nathan's staying there was much preferable to him residing in the east wing of Hilldreth.

Nathan Everstone did, however, dine with us the evening of the fourth day, in the company of Claudine's attorney, Wyatt Harden.

Having both of them seated across the table, clearly watching me, made me feel anything but comfortable. I focused on my soup, disregarding everyone's comments as best I could.

"The last I heard, Vance and Father were together and visiting the spas of Baden-Baden in Germany." Hearing Nathan mention his father so casually blackened my mood considerably.

"Ah, yes. Vance met with him somewhere along the way, didn't he?" Claudine asked.

"They met in Paris."

"Do you happen to know when they'll return?" Lawry's glance passed over me as he asked the question.

"Father wants to be back soon after Will graduates from Harvard, most likely by June."

I jumped in my seat, and Nathan gave me a sideways glance.

"Young Will is already through with his studies? How time does fly." Claudine shook her head, saying the words almost to herself. "I suppose he's the one Bram's pinning all his hopes upon."

"Nathan, do you recall my telling you how Amaryllis so fearlessly responded to your father when she visited us on Mount Desert Island that summer?" Lawry practically interrupted Claudine, but she didn't seem to take much notice.

"I do." Nathan stared at me from across the table, spooning his soup slowly to his lips.

I turned from him to see bewilderment spread across Claudine's face. "Amaryllis, you've met Bram?"

"Only for a few minutes. He found Lawry and me at The Cleft Stone the summer—" I was physically unable to utter the words *"my mother died."*

"I remember that day well," Wyatt added. I was shocked to suddenly recognize him as the young man who'd been trailing behind Bram Everstone that day. Had Wyatt Harden worked for Bram Everstone at one time?

I felt as if I was going to be sick.

"Amaryllis, you never told me." Claudine reached her hand down the table toward me.

"It was a long time ago." I swallowed the lump in my throat.

Nathan's speculative green eyes met mine again, preventing me from saying anything more. My mind was still mulling over the implications of Wyatt Harden having been witness to most of what had been said that day. Would he tell Claudine everything now that he knew she was so interested? And what exactly was his connection to Nathan's father now?

"He wanted to know how Lawry and I were related. That is all," I reluctantly admitted.

Wyatt didn't venture to add to my story, although, by the look in his eyes, I suspected he remembered every detail that I'd purposefully omitted.

Fortunately, Wyatt departed right after dinner, and the rest of the evening passed uneventfully, except for the fact that I caught Nathan looking at me far too often. He was usually making polite conversation at the time, but I could tell there was something more to it than good manners allowed. Surely it wasn't the same way he looked at Claudine when he spoke with her.

Or perhaps it was. She did turn into a sopping pile of mush whenever he was around. I thought of her first mention of him and how differently I'd expected her to treat him. One thing was for certain—I hadn't pictured the doting host she'd turned out to be.

FIVE

The Piano

"You are very amiable, no doubt,
but you would be charming if you would only depart."
—Alexandre Dumas, *The Three Musketeers*

The following morning, while Claudine was attending a meeting concerning the upcoming Musicale Benefit for the Boston Inland Mission Society, I busied myself playing the French opera *Samson and Delilah*. Of everything inside Hilldreth, there was nothing of greater value—nothing that gave me more joy— than the beautiful old box grand piano in the drawing room.

When I was finished with the piece, I rested my hands lightly on the keys. The distinct sound of a page turning had me peeking over my shoulder.

Nathan Everstone had entered the room and now sat on a chair reading my book *Of the Imitation of Christ*, which I'd left on the end table. I'd been so engrossed in the music, I hadn't even noticed.

It didn't seem to matter to him that I'd stopped playing, so I took full advantage of the rare moment and stole a long, satisfying glance his way.

He really was entirely too attractive, in every way possible, with his straight nose, his disheveled, golden hair, and his long, athletic legs, crossed at the ankle and resting on the ottoman in front of him. I couldn't see his eyes, but I knew exactly what they looked like. They were that beautiful shade of dark forest green, and I could hardly keep my own eyes from drifting to them whenever the chance arose.

I turned back to the piano perfectly disgusted with myself and heard him lift his feet from the ottoman. I certainly didn't want to speak with him, but I couldn't find the will to stand and leave.

"I heard you from the hall. I hope you don't mind. I do enjoy listening to you play."

I turned on my stool to face him, fully aware that, had I known he was in the house, let alone in the room, I wouldn't have been playing quite so passionately.

"You must admit, Miss Brigham, although you entertained us quite well the other night, you did not perform then with as much passion as you could have. Why the difference?"

"I thought I was alone."

"Is there any such thing as being alone with a piano? Anyone who hears you playing like that would come searching for the source of such—"

"At The Boston Conservatory, there was such a thing." A cold sweat broke out on my back beneath my chemise. Did he know that his father had had everything to do with my expulsion? And if he did, would he tell me anything more than what I already knew?

"This is a very different side of Boston from the one you've been used to, isn't it?" He motioned with his hand, referring to the overall atmosphere of the room.

"I hardly mattered to anyone before I was considered an heiress." I opted for cowardice instead of summoning the courage to ask him anything.

"You mattered. More than you think." He paused awkwardly and flipped through my book. "Is this yours, perchance?"

"Yes."

"While you were playing, I read something that has particularly held my interest, and I wanted to share it with you. It actually holds much truth this morning." He looked at me for a long moment before sharing. "'Whensoever a man desireth anything inordinately, he becomes restless in himself.'"

"How moving." I had no idea what the obscure sentence meant, and I was certain that Nathan had no real interest in imitating Christ in his daily life—he was merely using the book to torment me.

"How about I try another?" He flipped back a few chapters, as if he knew right where to go. "'All men naturally desire to know: but what does knowledge avail without the fear of God?'"

"And what is it, in your opinion, that a man desires to know?" I asked, overlooking his odd behavior.

"You, Miss Brigham...if you were indeed asking me specifically. The fact that you're in the midst of reading this particular book has, in fact, only multiplied my determination to know you." He spoke so evenly, I hardly believed a word he said.

"You care so much about imitating Jesus Christ in the way you live your life?"

"Very much indeed." He stood and walked around the perimeter of the room. "You see, I've come to realize there's more to life than the never-ending cycle of making and spending money that everyone seems to like so much. The impressiveness that comes from having such a large amount of it is quite overrated. Were you aware that all anyone really cares to know of me is the fact that I am born into the Everstone family, and that I am therefore wealthy beyond reason?"

I stood to take my leave. He was only saying what he thought I wanted to hear. I needed to be careful before I found myself believing him.

"You know, I remember the day you met my father," he said next. "It was July fourth, eighteen seventy-nine."

"You weren't there that day. How do you know?"

"And you're not at all what I expected." He seemed to be incredibly proficient at bringing an intimate air to any conversation. It almost seemed as if we had some sort of shared past, but that was far from the case. We were two people on two different sides of a circumstance. "Are you not at all interested in what I mean?"

"I hardly care what you mean by most of the things you say, Mr. Everstone."

"That was the first day I remember ever hearing your name, Amaryllis Brigham, reverberating off the paneled halls of Rockwood. And then later, Natalia told me all about your visit to The Cleft Stone that day. And Lawry never stopped singing your praises, at least from what he knew of you as a fourteen-year-old. I suppose I could simply blame him for the fact that I've always looked forward to meeting you, but it's more than that. You know it is."

My curiosity was piqued. I couldn't leave now. I sat upon the sofa, where he soon joined me. He set the book between us.

"First, Madame Pelletier's School for Young Ladies in Concord, then Mount Holyoke Female Seminary, and then The Boston Conservatory? You must admit, that's quite a list of institutions. Most young women aren't keen on continuing their education to such an extent. Do you like that caged-in feeling so entirely, Miss Brigham?"

"It's none of your business why I was—" *Caged-in* was such a good term for it.

I took up *Of the Imitation of Christ*.

"But it is my business, since my father's the one who funded your way through all three schools."

A new fire burned in my chest, fueled by an anger running so deeply through my veins, I wanted to scream. "And why would he have been the one to do that?"

"You truly didn't know?" He seemed genuinely astounded.

"No. But, to tell you the truth, it shouldn't surprise me." Just as I was about to turn from him and leave the room, I decided that it might be best that I stay and play his little game. Perhaps he would tell me more.

He searched my face for a moment. "You're telling me the truth."

"Of course I am. All I know of Bram Everstone is that he hated my mother and me. That he was the one who took me from my father, and that my father essentially let him. And that he—" I didn't finish that sentence. *He wrote the malicious letter that essentially ruined my life.*

"Are you so certain Bram hates you, and not—"

"I'm really not certain of anything, Mr. Everstone. I've been living under a veil of riddles for the last eleven years, and I've become numb to the point of hardly caring anymore."

"Amaryllis, I don't think you understand."

I was unable to keep from looking up at him. He seemed so sincere.

"And I'm quite certain you don't!" I stood and marched to the closed pocket doors that led to the hall. But no sooner had I thought my escape successful than Nathan stood firmly before me, one hand on the wall behind me, the other grasping the crook of my arm, holding me in place. The contact was so sudden. I could feel the heat creep up the back of my neck.

He contemplated something as his eyes sought mine.

"I'm on your side. No matter what you think of my father—or of anything he's ever done." His face was so incredibly close.

As I looked away, his hand quickly slid down my arm, catching my fingers in his.

Like a magnet, my eyes were drawn back to his, and I stood paralyzed. The undistinguishable look I saw on his face startled me. But I was determined. I would not allow myself to be deceived by him.

Not Bram Everstone's son.

"Am I supposed to trust you?" I tried to pull my hand away, but he held it fast.

"Yes." He paused. "You are."

"Mr. Everstone—"

"And I wish you'd stop addressing me by that infernal name. I'd much prefer you call me Nathan."

"No." My breath caught in my throat. His hand held on to mine, and as I looked down, I realized my treacherous fingers had relaxed and were entwined with his. Without another thought, I tore my hand from his, pulled the pocket door open, and bolted from the room.

Even as I left him standing there, I wished I'd been courageous enough to stay. What would he have done if I'd allowed myself to stand there one moment longer?

And, more important, what would I have done in return?

As I walked toward the stairs, my heart raced with the ridiculous hope he might follow. All the while, I repeated over and over under my breath, "Keep thy heart—keep thy heart with all diligence...."

Surely my greatest desire was to be alone in my room. Safe from him. Yet remembering the touch of his fingers sent shivers through me.

Oh, he flustered me so! What were his reasons, with no one else around?

Whatever the truth was, the last thing I needed to do was fall for his superfluous charms and become infatuated with him—or do something equally ridiculous.

An hour later, Claudine and I were waiting in the front foyer as Nathan headed down the front staircase carrying a small trunk.

"I'm taking my railcar up to Maine this afternoon with Estella," he told us. "I'm sorry, but I won't be able to escort you to Summerton." He seemed so stiff, almost as if he were trying not to look at me.

"Will you return soon?" Claudine was evidently hurt by his lack of concern for her schedule. After all, everyone already knew he had accepted her invitation to stay at Hilldreth for at least a month. What would they think if, after only a week of our company, he preferred to travel to cold and blustery Maine?

Even I understood her distress.

"It's uncertain how long we'll be." His eyes grazed past me. It was the first time he'd looked my way during the exchange, and I wondered if I'd offended him somehow. But then realized it was just what I should have meant to do.

Without even a "Good-bye" or an "It was nice to meet you," he went out the front door and hauled his trunk into his flashy red landau. I was surprised he traveled with so little, and that he hadn't thought to take Lawry with him. It had, after all, also been two years since Lawry had seen his own family in Bar Harbor.

"I was so looking forward to Nathan staying with us...longer than a week," Claudine announced when Lawry arrived a little later. "Did we do something to offend him, Lawry?"

"He's irritated about something, but I'm positive his departure had nothing to do with either of you," Lawry reassured us.

"Well, if you say so. But I don't know what he was thinking, leaving when Amaryllis needs him so."

"I don't need him." I flushed.

"Lawry, are you able to come to Summerton in his stead?" Claudine asked him. "Meredyth Summercourt and her family have just returned from visiting her mother's people in New York, and you haven't seen her at all."

"I have too much to do." Lawry's gaze shifted to the floor, and I could tell he was very politely making up excuses. I wondered why he wasn't excited to see such an old family friend. "I'll see her here tonight at dinner." He rushed past us to the front door, although he'd only just returned to Hilldreth not five minutes before. "I have too much to do before then."

Lawry's odd behavior concerning Meredyth was interesting, but it didn't do much to distract me from my last encounter with Nathan. I wanted to be happy he was gone. It was the correct thing to feel. He frustrated me to no end, to be sure. Everything he'd said to me in the past week blurred together into a mass of conflicting words. But it wasn't so much *what* he'd said that made me certain of his dislike of me. It was the many times I had caught him glancing at me with those brooding green eyes that bothered me the most.

SIX

Meredyth Summercourt

> *"Warmth and tenderness of heart, with affectionate, open manner,*
> *will beat all cleverness of head in the world, for attraction:*
> *I am sure it will."*
> —Jane Austen, *Emma*

Annabelle Summercourt's daughter, Meredyth, is about your age, Amaryllis, and we've already decided the two of you are to be the closest of friends," Claudine said as she practically pulled me down the sidewalk a little while later. "She really is a dear girl, only she's never gotten on very well with the young ladies in our set. Having only older brothers, I don't think she quite knows how to relate to young women. Or perhaps she simply doesn't like them. I don't know."

"How old is she?" I wondered if any such "friendship" had even a chance of forming, no matter how many mamas and aunts were involved.

"Three-and-twenty, I believe."

"Is that not rather old for not having married yet?"

"Yes, as is five-and-twenty, dear." She gave me a sideways glance. "But it isn't for Meredyth's lack of beaus that she isn't married. She's much like Lawry and Nathan in some regards, for she seems extremely particular. That, too, probably has much to do with her having so many brothers. She always preferred to spend her free time cavorting with the boys, even after they grew up and became young men."

"I would think that would help her chances."

"If she would stop being their friend and start flirting with them, yes, it would." Claudine pulled at my arm. "It's been good that Nathan and Lawry have been away, and that both of Nathan's younger brothers have been away either at university or traveling in Europe. For the last few years, Mere has had to branch out more, finding herself left with only her older brother Garrett and his friends to occupy her time and attention. And let me tell you, they are much more interested in flirting with her than becoming kindred spirits." She turned to me and winked, her wrinkly brown eyes sparkling with a slight smile. "It's a pity Nathan left so suddenly. I really wanted him to join us. Nicholette should be there soon."

By then, we had almost arrived at Boston Common, so I knew we had to be near our destination. Almost upon the moment we reached the steps of a great limestone town house, the door opened, and a young woman stood in the doorway, as if waiting for us to ascend. With her ginger hair and bright blue eyes, she was a stark contrast to almost everything about me.

And she was smiling. She was exceptionally pretty, but in a very different way than the utter perfection of Nicholette Fairbanks's rigid manners and glances of disdain. Meredyth Summercourt's beauty was more natural, as if she didn't even need to try.

"Good afternoon, Aunt Claudine." I thought it odd that Meredyth Summercourt called Claudine "aunt," while I, her own grand-niece, had been instructed to call her simply "Claudine."

"Is this Amaryllis Brigham?"

"You know very well it is, Meredyth." Claudine almost giggled.

So much for fretting over proper introductions.

Once we were in the foyer, Meredyth turned to a woman who I presumed was her mother, and said, "Isn't she just lovely?"

I had a difficult time believing her. No one with a nose like mine, I was convinced, could be considered as such. It was impossible, no matter what anyone ever said.

"What a beautiful dress. The color matches your eyes to perfection," Meredyth said as she linked her arm through mine.

"Thank you." Before I could decide whether to refer to her as "Meredyth" or "Miss Summercourt," she turned to Claudine. "Did you pick out this dress for her in Paris?"

Claudine beamed. "I bought her an entire wardrobe while I was there. That is, after sending for her measurements and her overall opinion on a few fashion plates."

I looked down at the ruffled sea-green creation they were referring to, lifted the train off the floor, and shifted it around me. I was still somewhat in awe of the thing, even though I felt a bit uncomfortable in so many layers of fabric. For twenty-five years, I'd worn only simple day dresses, and just one per day.

"Do you like the color?" Claudine asked her. "I ordered many of the dresses in this shade, knowing from what everyone had told me that Amaryllis has her father's eyes."

I wondered if it was common for Claudine to speak about someone as if she were not standing directly next to her.

"I daresay"—Mrs. Summercourt was looking at me but not quite speaking to me—"if it weren't for those light eyes from her father providing such a beautiful contrast to her dark hair, she would be the very image of Elinorah, God rest her soul."

When Mrs. Summercourt guided us into her drawing room, Meredyth held me back. "Would you mind terribly if I took Amaryllis up to see my roses before joining you, Mother?"

"Of course not, dear. But remember, it's almost ten o'clock."

"Yes, I know. We'll be back presently."

I obediently followed Meredyth up the stairs.

Over the years, I'd been used to the feeling of having absolutely no control over my life. Not that I liked it; it just didn't shock me anymore.

Not much compared to the devastation of being forced into an empty black carriage directly following my mother's funeral and then, just hours later, being delivered to Madame Pelletier's School with only the clothes on my back.

Well, except perhaps that last day at The Boston Conservatory.

"—a conservatory?" Meredyth's words caught my attention for the first time since leaving the ground floor.

"Pardon me?" I stood paralyzed on a step halfway to the third level.

She was looking at me from over the railing of the next flight of stairs. "Have you ever been in a conservatory?"

"Of music?" I was still unable to move. Did they already know?

"No, of plants." She smiled. "It's on the roof."

Meredyth guided me up the remaining flights of stairs to a space at the top of their house—a room literally filled with a jungle. As I followed her inside, I was struck not only with the strange misty atmosphere of the warm, glass room, but also with how tall Meredyth was. "The real reason I brought you up here is that Nicholette Fairbanks is expected at any minute. Our mothers insist upon it, every Wednesday at ten o'clock, without fail, though we really cannot stand each other."

I hoped, even though I'd known Meredyth only all of fifteen minutes, that she would not come to see her time spent with me as such. I had never had a close female friend—or really any close friend at all. Unless I counted Lawry.

"I've met her." I focused my attention on a strange orange-and-purple spiked flower, hoping Meredyth wouldn't detect my nervousness.

"At the dinner party in honor of Lawry's return? I wished I could have come. How did Nicholette behave?"

"She warned me about Nathan Everstone."

"Then you already know she cares about only one thing on earth, and that's marrying him—and his fifth of the twenty-million-dollar inheritance. I advise you to stay away from her as much as you are able. Be polite if you must interact, but don't let her get under your skin." Meredyth crinkled her nose. "She will try."

The glass door of the spacious conservatory opened, and, to my surprise, Mr. Crawford walked in.

"Meredyth, I cannot believe you took to hiding her away the moment she walked into the house, and you didn't come find me." He was smiling as he teased Meredyth. Were they such good friends? What was he doing there, wandering the halls as if he owned the place?

"Amaryllis." Meredyth motioned a hand in my direction. "You've obviously met Jay Crawford."

"It's a pleasure yet again, Miss Brigham." He took my hand and bowed. "But may I please have the honor of using your Christian name? I've been used to hearing it all these years. It's not a name one is likely to forget." He refused to let go of my hand.

"Of course."

"And you may call me Jay or even Crawford, if you prefer."

"What are you doing here, Jay?" I asked, hardly certain what was proper; but, as he was such a friend to both the Summercourts and Lawry, I felt that it was all right to use his Christian name. Truth be told, I was rather tired of being referred to solely as Miss Brigham, as I had been all the way through school.

"I came to see Mere's brother Garrett." Jay finally released my hand. "I'm amazed by the fact that you've known Meredyth all of— what, twenty minutes?—and she's already brought you up here to exchange secrets." Jay nudged me with his elbow. "Meredyth doesn't like most girls, you know. You must have quickly impressed her. It's very strange."

"Crawford, you are impossible." Meredyth's eyes filled with ire. "It's really not that strange, Amaryllis. Before he left for Washington, Lawry told us all about you. I feel as if I've known you for years."

For a moment, I felt almost elated. Lawry, too, had mentioned his friends in his letters over the years...Meredyth and Nathan, mostly. But never in a million years had I thought any of them would ever care to meet me or look forward to becoming my friend. What on earth had Lawry told them about me? And how long would it be until they were all terribly disappointed?

"So, what did you come up here to speak about? Nathan, and how all the unmarried ladies of Boston are anxiously awaiting his return from Bar Harbor?" He sounded about as disgusted with the prospect as I felt. It was my first clue that perhaps Meredyth had taken me up to the conservatory solely for the purpose of staging a reunion between Jay and me.

"It must be past ten o'clock now," Meredyth remarked. "Nicholette's probably already here and furious at me for making her wait." She pulled at my elbow. Leaving Jay behind, we exited through the glass door and hurried down the stairs.

Our conversation about Nicholette was still vivid in my mind as I passed back through the halls of Summerton to the cozy parlor at the front of the second floor. The Summercourts' town house was nothing like Hilldreth, which was much larger and one of the only detached houses along the street. I liked Summerton more. Hilldreth had a starched feel to it, despite its four stories of dark wood-paneled excellence.

We made it down to the second floor just in time to meet Nicholette following the Summercourts' butler into the room.

"Amaryllis, Nicholette, I believe, you've met."

"Miss Brigham." Nicholette nodded. And that was all.

"A pleasure to see you yet again, Miss Fairbanks." I tried to copy Jay's comment to me.

I sat on a sofa, Claudine to one side and Nicholette on the other; Jay, Meredyth, her mother, and her mother's pug dog were seated on another sofa facing us. Garrett Summercourt had been summoned to join us, but we were soon told he had left the house, unbeknownst to his mother.

The tea had been rung for and set out, and we were all silently sipping, when Claudine said, "Oh, did you know Nathan is staying with us at Hilldreth?"

"Yes, I heard," Meredyth answered. "I'm sure Lawry is as happy as a clam."

"Yes. Well, he was. Nathan and Estella just left for Maine to visit Natalia. But he will be back soon enough."

I was more interested in what Nicholette thought of the news than anything else we had discussed before the tea had been served. I glanced her way and noticed that absolutely nothing changed in her silent, steady poise.

"I'm so glad you're back where you belong." Meredyth was suddenly speaking to Jay.

"It's good to be back...at least for a little while." He took a tea biscuit from his plate and fed it to the pug dog, which was now sitting at his feet.

"Will you be able to join us for dinner tonight, Mr. Crawford?" Claudine asked. "The Summercourts will be dining with us."

"I'm afraid I can't. I have an important meeting at the mission society tonight."

"That's too bad. You'll have to come to dinner soon."

I thought it odd that my aunt was so interested in entertaining Mr. Crawford. I'd assumed Jay Crawford was the last eligible bachelor in Boston she'd ever want me to form an attachment with, since he was supposedly leaving Boston so soon.

"Did Lawry bring back hundreds of photographs like he promised to?" Meredyth asked her. "I do wish we'd been back in time to attend the welcome-home dinner. Was he not able to come with you today? I was certain he would join you."

"No, he was busy, dear. You know, getting himself reacclimated with the firm and all," Claudine answered.

Actually, it had seemed that Lawry had purposefully not come when we'd given him the chance. Was he avoiding Meredyth?

"Of course he has hundreds of photographs—it was the whole reason for his trip." Jay beamed at me, and I turned to Nicholette. She still had yet to say a word or move an inch.

From what Claudine had disclosed to me, Jay's comment about Nathan's reasons for leaving was only partly true. What had Nicholette thought when Nathan had run off instead of obeying his father by entering into an engagement with her? Surely she'd been humiliated. Did she truly still want to marry him after that?

"Do you think Lawry's photographs do the West Coast justice?" Jay looked at me.

"Nothing compares to really being there, as you well know."

"Is it not fortunate Nathan has made it back before his father is due to arrive home from Europe?" Meredyth's unexpected words in regard to Bram Everstone sent a tremor down my spine.

Nicholette, with just the slightest hint of disdain, turned to Meredyth and spoke for the first time. "I hardly think it matters when his father is destined to return. We all know what the end result will be."

SEVEN

Answers and Questions

*"I've dreamt in my life dreams that have stayed with me ever after,
and changed my ideas; they've gone through and through me,
like wine through water, and altered the colour of my mind."*
—Emily Brontë, *Wuthering Heights*

When the Summercourt family came to dine at Hilldreth that evening, Mr. Summercourt was still shocked at the news of Nathan's departure. It was all he spoke of during dinner. Afterward, Meredyth and I secluded ourselves on the far side of the drawing room while Claudine and Mr. and Mrs. Summercourt played cards, and Lawry holed himself up in the study.

"Do you know anything about the Boston Inland Mission Society, Meredyth?" I'd been thinking of the organization quite often since Claudine's first mention of it. My hope was that I could gain some experience doing something while in Boston, so that when I saw an advertisement in the newspaper that interested me, I would have at least some sort of reference.

"Do you mean, Crawford's Boston Inland Mission Society?" she asked with a sideways glance.

I leaned in closer. "Do you know Jay well?"

"I knew him quite well in the past. Nathan brought his sisters and him to Bar Harbor for the summer a few times when they were attending Dartmouth. Do you mean to marry him and run off to Washington? It would be exciting, would it not?"

I could tell she was only teasing me, but the validity of her words cut deep and made me realize how terrible the whole idea seemed.

"I'm truly not interested in selling myself in such a way for any price," I said urgently. "Not even for my inheritance, I promise."

"Settle your feathers! I was only giving you a hard time."

Across the room, Claudine looked up from her card game. I prayed she'd not heard my last, telling sentence. I much preferred her thinking I felt as she did about my inheritance—that it was an amazing opportunity for me to join her world. In reality, all I could dream of was escaping Boston's elite society as quickly as possible.

I turned to focus on Meredyth before Claudine could catch my eye.

"I believe you, but there's nothing I can do about what others think. Rumors about Elinorah Landreth's doppelgänger of a daughter who's been mysteriously held away all these years will abound no matter what you do."

As closely as I resembled her, I was nothing like my regal mother, and I wished everyone in Boston would simply recognize the facts. Elinorah Landreth had been born into this societal world, had been raised in it, and likely had fit into it quite well.

Meanwhile, I'd been born and raised on a horse farm on the other, wilder side of the country. How Claudine ever imagined I'd fit in here or find a husband was beyond me.

"Are you at all interested in marrying?" Meredyth prodded.

"I would, if a particular gentleman asked."

"Have you been waiting for Lawry to—"

"Marry Lawry? Of course not." She looked almost as disgusted at the thought as I felt. "Lawry's like an older brother, whom I love more than my three true brothers combined. That is all." "Were you surprised by Nathan's sudden departure?" she hurried on.

"Personally, I'm never surprised by anything he does. He's never cared a great deal for the conventions of society, you know. He probably realized he'd not seen Natalia in two years and decided to amend the situation posthaste."

"He should've thought of that before spending one day in Boston. It wasn't very considerate of him to say he would stay and then leave so quickly. Lawry said he seemed irritated about something since they'd arrived."

"Nathan's always irritated about something, Amaryllis. It's simply the Everstone way."

"Is it?" I wanted to ask about Nathan's father, but the topic seemed rather out of place.

Meredyth looked at me for a moment. "I'm sure Nathan's departure has more to do with the pressure of being constantly sought after by society than anything else. He's one of the heirs of the Everstone empire. You do know that his father is one of the wealthiest men in the country, don't you? Nathan will be welcomed back with open arms, no matter how long he's gone or how gravely he seems to slight anyone—even Claudine. Just wait—you'll see. He's done it enough in the past to prove it time and again." Her gaze darted to the other end of the room, where Lawry was sitting with his father. "It's the only way I can think of that Nathan and Vance are anything alike."

"Vance is his brother?"

"He's the middle brother." She straightened her posture and glanced back at me. I had the impression she thought the subject a distasteful one. "I've always thought it odd how Nathan and Natalia were born with such Nordic features, while the rest of them are all so dark. If I recall correctly, their parents both had rather dark features, also."

"Where is their mother?"

"She died when Estella was quite young."

At learning this, I felt a new sort of commiseration toward Estella. Perhaps losing her mother so young had been a traumatic experience for her, the same way it had been for me. Perhaps that was the reason she was so quietly detached from everyone.

"Nathan rarely attends social functions, you know. It doesn't surprise me at all that he left town. He often feels as if everyone wants a piece of him. If you haven't noticed already, he snubs most of them as often as possible."

"Why would—" I stopped short, remembering his reference to society that first night as a masquerade...and how he could tell I thought the same thing. At the time, I'd thought he was just telling me what he thought I wanted to hear. But now, I wasn't so sure.

"It's his way of avoiding future invitations and having to deal with debutantes...and their mamas. However, it never works. Everyone keeps inviting him, trying to entice him into their social circles. Vance, on the other hand, goes out quite willingly. He's been gallivanting throughout Europe while Nathan has been hiding away in Washington."

"And there's another brother just finishing Harvard?"

Meredyth nodded. "I've heard that Will's the only business-minded heir Bram Everstone has, with Nathan being so unsociable and Vance being utterly out of control. He'll graduate just in time to be apprenticed under his father."

I was beginning to realize how little I knew of Nathan and his family, and how much Meredyth did know.

"Did you really not like having him around?" she asked. "Lawry told me earlier tonight, once I cornered him, that Nathan can't seem to keep his eyes off of you."

"Lawry said that?" I was shocked he would tell Meredyth such a thing. "Claudine already warned me that he's never been serious about any young lady, and I think that's why she decided to ask him to pay special attention to me."

"She asked Nathan to flirt with you?"

"She did."

"And he was more than willing to go along with it?"

"It would seem so."

"Well really, Amaryllis, that hardly sounds terrible. And I wouldn't be so certain it's all pretend. I can tell Nathan has changed quite a bit during his time away."

"How so?" I wanted every detail Meredyth could pass along.

"I can see it in his eyes."

"What do you see?"

"A sense of peace and determination that I know wasn't there before."

⌒

I awoke with tears streaming down my face.

Like always.

And with vivid images racing through my mind of a shipwreck off a rocky coast, it was difficult to stop them. The moment I awoke was always the same. Instead of Mother on the ship, it was I, sleeping in a cabin slowly filling with water, flowing over me, covering me like a blanket, until it reached my face…and I knew what she felt in those last, terrifying moments of her life.

There was the overwhelming guilt, knowing that it was my fault she'd been on the ship in the first place. And then, there was always Bram Everstone's vengeful anger toward me for stealing her away from him forever…and the awful feeling that he was still out to get me, to make me pay for my part in her death.

When I tried to fall back asleep, I could do nothing but toss and turn. I was terrified of what he would do when he came home to Boston and found that I'd been associating with his eldest son.

After what seemed like hours of tormented thoughts, all at once, I remembered Bram Everstone's angry words to my mother the very day she'd died.

"You had no right to come here and taunt me with your presence."

The words had been a mystery to me as a naive fourteen-year-old, but as an adult, I had an idea of their significance.

I dreaded asking Claudine what she knew. As wonderful and accepting as she was of me, I could tell she didn't like to discuss serious matters.

After lighting a tiny lamp and slipping into my dressing gown, I tiptoed along the hall and down the narrow back stairway with hardly a creak. A light shined from the crack beneath the study door.

As I turned to head back up the stairs, the door opened. Lawry stood with the glow of a lamp burning behind him.

"What are you doing awake at this hour?"

I could have asked him the same thing. He was still dressed in his dinner clothes, as if the thought of changing into something more comfortable by then hadn't even occurred to him.

"I keep having nightmares." I pulled the ruffled collar of my dressing gown to my chin and held it there.

"The same one over and over?"

"Yes." I'd never told anyone about the nightmare, and thought best not to tell Lawry exactly what all it entailed. "What are you still doing awake?"

"I couldn't sleep."

"Have you even tried?"

"Truthfully, no, I haven't." He turned his back to me and walked to the other end of the room. Obviously, he didn't want to talk about it.

"Lawry, do you remember my mother's funeral?" I held my breath, wondering if he'd be able to shed any light on what had happened that day.

He turned sharply, looking at me intently. "Of course I do."

"Do you recall if Bram Everstone was present?"

He squinted as his gaze roamed up the wall of books behind me. "I believe so."

I didn't remember his being there, but from what I did remember, my focus had been on anything but the reality of the situation.

Lawry studied me. "You left in his carriage, didn't you?"

"Yes, I know...but without him. I never knew, until recently. Did you not think it was odd?"

"If I remember correctly, he and your father had some sort of agreement, as unusual as that may seem."

"Why do you say that? Do you know much about my mother and father?"

"I know of a letter I once found concerning them. I read it, but I was just a child at the time. I didn't know what it was about. I bet I could find it again, knowing Claudine." He put a finger to his lips for a moment, then walked out of the study toward the drawing room. We were cloaked by shadows, save for the dim glow from my tiny lamp as I followed close behind. He headed straight to the overstuffed chair in which Claudine often sat.

"She always buries all sorts of things into the cushions. I can't tell you how many times I've had to find her spectacles for her." He reached into the cushions and produced a small leather-bound journal. Flipping to the back cover, he pulled out an old tin daguerreotype and a discolored, tightly folded letter from a secret pocket.

I reached for the image first, for it was only the second photograph I'd seen of my mother since her death. I didn't know what had happened to any of the belongings she'd brought east, or what had happened to our belongings at Bruckerdale after I was sent away to school and my father remained in Maine.

I was always struck by how beautiful and self-composed she'd always seemed, in life as well as in photographs. She and Claudine were posed together for a professional photographer, whose studio's name and address in London were printed on the bottom corner of the tin. I turned it over. A small, neat script covered the back.

Dearest Aunt Claudine,

Thank you for taking me on my Grand Tour of Europe, May 7, 1859–March 5, 1860.

With love,
Elinorah

Lawry slowly eased into the chair from which he'd pulled the journal. He'd unfolded the letter, and his eyes roved over the words I desperately yearned to see.

"May I read it?" My voice trembled.

He stood and let me take his place next to the lamp. Sitting in Claudine's comfy chair, I read:

August 21, 1860

Dearest Aunt,

Peter will come, I know he will. Though he loathes me, he will endeavor to save me, because he's that good of a man. No matter how wicked I was to make him my husband, he feels I am his responsibility. Therefore, I will go with him to the ends of the earth, even if it's the Washington Territory. What other option is there, Claudine? I must go.

It will be far from Bram, and that is all that matters.

With Bram's word against me, I shan't want to stay. Yes, he loves me still, I know, dear aunt, but I've hurt him so dreadfully, through lies and weakness. I blame only myself for this outcome. Please, please don't blame Bram, dearest Claudine, no matter what happens in the duration of our lives. Please don't hold this over his head. I know I've already caused him enough pain to last the rest of his life—he doesn't need more.

I have only one more favor to ask of you, Aunt. Grace needs a husband. I cannot divulge the details, but I've already spoken to her and have advised her to tell you everything in

*hopes that you can convince Bram to marry her. She needs a
husband, Claudine, and since I cannot have Bram myself—
oh, pray that God will make me strong enough to endure this!
If any good comes from all of this, it will be that Grace is able
to marry Bram.*

Your loving niece,
Elinorah

My fingers gripped the yellowed paper. "My mother was once
in love with Bram Everstone?" I felt as if a great fog was lifting
from around me.

"I've heard rumors throughout the years that your mother and
Nathan's father had once planned to wed that summer after her
Grand Tour." Lawry stood and rested his right elbow upon the
mantel of the fireplace, the fingers of his left hand rubbing the
bottom of his chin. "Her parents disowned her for marrying your
father instead of Bram. She lost her place in society. With her life
in shambles, she ran off with your father as soon as he was able to
make the trip from England. I remember that being a major part
of the scandal."

I took the small leather book from Lawry's hand and flipped to
the back in search of more. I found nothing but the indecipherable
scribbles of Claudine's handwriting. However, one of the pages
stuck out along the edge, so I tugged at it.

It was a loose piece, already torn out, with a small hand-drawn
family tree upon it.

Peter J. Brigham,
Born November 21, 1831, Cartmel, Cumbria, United Kingdom
Died February 21, 1890, Millinocket, Maine
Joined in Marriage on December 27, 1859, Cartmel, Cumbria,
United Kingdom, to
Elinorah S. Landreth,
Born January 3, 1840, Boston, Massachusetts

Died July 4, 1879, off the coast of Nahant Island, Massachusetts
A daughter, Amaryllis Lily Brigham
Born December 3, 1864, Whidbey Island, Washington Territory

I leaned against the door. "They were married in England... while she was engaged to Bram Everstone?" My thoughts swirled with these new, vague details.

Lawry was quiet for a long time, his even eyebrows scrunched together. "It's nearly three in the morning, Amaryllis. I think it's probably best you get to your room before we wake Claudine and then really have some questions to answer."

"Not that I'll be able to sleep now." I placed the ragged piece of paper into the old leather journal and stuffed it back into Claudine's chair. "Thanks for helping me."

"Of course." Lawry's voice was gentle as his resolute blue eyes continued to search mine. "That's what friends are for."

"I suppose you're right." Only, I'd never really had many friends before to know it. "Good night, Lawry."

I left Lawry in the study and headed up the back stairs. With every step, I was more and more convinced that in solving one mystery, I'd only discovered a hundred more.

EIGHT

The Trinity School for Girls

"It's never too late to be who you might have been."
—George Eliot

Lawry rushed up the stairs of Hilldreth a few days later, his intent, quite apparently, to find me and ask this most unexpected of questions: "Do you want to come with me? I'm going to Trinity Church to give them the funds for the school they've recently begun for less fortunate girls."

"You aren't serious." I really didn't think anyone from Claudine's level of society cared that much about orphans, especially not Lawry Hampton.

"I'm very serious. Do you want to come?"

"Of course." I dashed down the stairs behind him and gathered my shawl, all the while wondering what had prompted such a driving desire in Lawry to suddenly want to help orphans. I also wondered if this opportunity to go with him might be in direct correlation to my prayers about gaining some kind of reference in order to attain a job someday.

Once we reached Trinity Church, Lawry found the secretary and told her why we were there. She led us both to a door labeled "Dr. Grig Wellesley."

Lawry went in while I waited on a bench outside the office.

When Lawry walked out only a few minutes later, his face was drained of color. I had no idea how the tired-looking elderly man I'd caught a glimpse of inside the office could have terrified him so much.

"Your turn," he sighed. "I told him you might be interested in helping, and he said he has a few minutes to spare for a short interview."

"How did you know I'd—"

"Are you interested in volunteering at the school?"

"Yes, but…are you?"

"No, I'm just part of the funding. I don't need another reason to stay in Boston."

"You're not staying? Are you going back to Washington?"

"I'm not sure what I'll be doing in the future, but let's not get into that just yet. You have someone who can help you right now waiting to see you." I barely comprehended his words as he grasped my elbow and ushered me into the office.

"So, Miss Brigham, of twenty-five Commonwealth Avenue," Dr. Wellesley began as I took my seat in the wood-paneled office. His wrinkly, spotted hands were clutched together on the desk before him as he stared evenly at me.

"Yes, sir?"

"What is your desire?"

What a strange way of wording the question. Did he think I was just another spoiled young lady of Boston's elite society, full of nothing but fluff and manners, like the ones Lawry and Nathan reportedly loathed?

"I'm not here to offer you money, sir, despite how it appears." I looked down at the exquisite grass-green silk dress Claudine had insisted I wear that day. "I haven't any."

"Miss Amaryllis Brigham hasn't any money? That isn't quite the story the papers tell, miss."

"If you've read anything about me, sir, you will know the money is tied up quite tightly with the contingencies of my grandmother's will. And since I never plan to marry, certainly not by next February, I will not inherit as much as a dime."

"Interesting. Go on."

"I grew up on the West Coast, sir, where my father bred Shire draft horses for the nearby lumber companies. My family moved east eleven years ago, and I've attended boarding school, graduated from Mount Holyoke Female Seminary, and also attended The Boston Conservatory."

"Ah, yes, The Boston Conservatory. I've heard something about that. Things did not go well for you there, it seems."

"Sir, my dearest desire in life is to get back to Washington and to someday found a music academy of my very own. First, however, I need a reference, so that I may at least work at one." I prayed desperately that Dr. Wellesley wouldn't hold against me whatever he might have heard. I clasped my hands tightly in my lap.

"These dreams concerning a music academy, are they strictly personal? Or do you strive to live them out for the sake of fulfilling God's will for your life?"

"I believe my using the talent He's given me is His will for my life. Why else would He have bothered giving it to me?"

Dr. Wellesley smiled for the first time. "Mr. Hampton, you may join us now," he called toward the open door.

Lawry's eyes met mine briefly as he sat in the chair beside mine. We waited silently as Dr. Wellesley shuffled through some papers and began writing something. He finally looked up and asked, "Miss Brigham, would you mind playing something for me?" He pointed to the upright piano in the corner of the room.

I stood, crossed the room, sat at the bench, and played a flamboyant bit from Chopin's *Fantaisie-Impromtu*. Then I returned to my seat.

"Isn't she amazing?" Lawry asked with a laugh.

Dr. Wellesley was not laughing—or even smiling, for that matter. He didn't seem angry, per se, only incredibly serious. "I was thinking, Miss Brigham—would you consider teaching the girls music one afternoon a week? How does Tuesday at two o'clock work for you?"

I hardly believed my ears. "Very well," I said, trying desperately to hold back my smile. Excitement bubbled from deep within, and tingles surged all the way up my spine.

"Are you perhaps able to be back here today at two o'clock this afternoon?"

"Yes, of course, Dr. Wellesley."

"From there we'll discuss the specifics regarding where we'll have you teach. Mr. Hampton, you're more than welcome to join her, if you wish." He stood behind his desk and awkwardly stuck out his hand into the space between us.

I quickly stood and shook his hand, as did Lawry.

"And, Miss Brigham, would you mind staying an additional hour every Tuesday, beginning today, from three to four o'clock? Next Tuesday will be the first day our current pianist will be unable to play for the weekly prayer meeting."

"Of course. I would be honored."

He sat back down at his small, scarred desk and took up his papers again. "Well then, that will be all."

I had no idea what I was in for. Upon my return to Trinity Church that afternoon, the same woman who'd shown Lawry and me to Dr. Wellesley's office earlier led me through a narrow hallway to the back of the church where a very old carriage waited. Dr. Wellesley was inside waiting, ready to go. *Where to?* was the question resounding in my mind. Would there be no discussion whatsoever as to what was going on?

Memories from the day I'd been forced into the Everstones' carriage directly following my mother's funeral accosted my mind, as did an image from the last time I'd ever seen my father, standing at my mother's grave, staring at me solemnly.

Had Bram Everstone taken me by force, or had my father willingly let him have me?

"We're running a tight schedule, Miss Brigham. Do get in." Dr. Wellesley sat up from the worn leather cushions.

My feet refused to move, and I knew I was being unreasonable. Even the fact that the young secretary joined Dr. Wellesley inside the carriage did little to quell the sudden bombardment of emotions that had surfaced.

"You remember Miss Wilder, I suppose? She'll be accompanying us to the mission. You will be perfectly fine."

I forced myself into the carriage and perched on the edge of the seat. We were headed to the vocational school for orphans to help, not to be held prisoner. But no matter how many times I repeated this silently to myself on our way to the school, the feelings of terrified helplessness from being shipped off to boarding school at the age of fourteen without a parting word from my father permeated every inch of my shaking body.

We didn't drive far—only four blocks, in fact. I could hardly contain my relief when I realized we were stopping in front of the Boston Inland Mission Society's building.

"The Trinity School for Girls is situated in a newly built section at the back of this building," Dr. Wellesley explained before he hobbled from the carriage. "However, you will be using the small practice rooms on the second floor, which are still furnished with pianos from the days when the building was used as a neighborhood music conservatory. I've already spoken with the mission board, and they're more than willing to allow you to use them weekly for the sake of instilling some culture into these girls. I suppose we'll begin by offering lessons to each and every girl enrolled at the school, as a means of measuring their musical abilities."

He stopped only for a quick breath as we made our way into the building through two large, heavy doors. "There aren't many students yet. Perhaps two dozen. But that will soon change."

"And just how are the girls enrolled?" I asked.

"Every one of them is a charity case. Someone has taken it upon himself to fund the girls' education, strictly out of the goodness of his heart."

"Or some rake has been made to pay his dues for that which he's accidentally produced," Miss Wilder whispered in my ear.

"Miss Wilder, do you have something to add?" Dr. Wellesley demanded.

"It's so generous of them…to be paying those dues for others," she hastened to say.

"Yes, some give of their money—like your cousin, Miss Brigham—while others give of their time. The school would never have come to fruition if not for enterprising young women like you." Dr. Wellesley guided us to a large auditorium. "This is where the prayer meetings will take place every Tuesday from three to four o'clock."

At center stage stood a rosewood grand piano with intricately carved legs. I looked to the back of the room, noting the scrollwork framing each of the boxes along the upper balcony. It still looked very much like it should have been used as a concert hall instead of a prayer meeting room, and I wished I'd not agreed so quickly to Dr. Wellesley's request to play. Not if it meant playing that particular piano at the center stage in front of such a large room of people.

"The mission takes pride in having such a superb piano," Dr. Wellesley said. "It was given recently as a gift from Bram Everstone, in honor of his beloved wife's memory."

The implications sent chills down the skin of my arms. Trying to hide my discomfort, I asked, "May I see the music rooms we'll be using?" My mind raced with possible reasons I could back out of my promise to play for the prayer meetings. There had to be something.

"We've known for months now that we'd soon be without a pianist, and in all that time, I've not been able to find someone suitable," Dr. Wellesley supplied as he limped up the stairs. "Sure, there are plenty of young men and women who can play, but are they willing? I have not met any as willing and able as you, my dear girl."

I knew he meant it as a compliment, which was saying something, coming from Dr. Wellesley. But if I could have changed his thinking to conclude I was not so talented, I would have donated the entire amount of the allowance Claudine had given me to do so.

Upstairs, a row of small practice rooms lined the left side of the hall. Doorknobs were missing from many of the doors, and even the ones that were there did not work properly. There were ten rooms in all, each with an exterior window directly opposite the door. And each practice room, just as Dr. Wellesley had mentioned, still contained a piano. Most were outdated box grand pianos, like the one in the drawing room at Hilldreth, but a few rooms at the end of the hall had some newer uprights. One box grand in particular caught my eye, and I knew with certainty it was where I'd be spending much of my time in preparation for teaching my lessons.

I gravitated into the room. "Are the pianos tuned?" I smoothed my hands over the unique, almost striped wood grain.

"Tuned well enough for the girls, I suppose."

"May I ask, Dr. Wellesley, to have at least one finely tuned instrument?"

"You could take the girls down to the auditorium and play the Everstones' grand."

I sat on the burgundy-velvet-cushioned stool and placed my fingers on a few of the keys. The noise the beautiful instrument produced was absolutely atrocious.

"Perhaps I can convince someone to at least have this one piano tuned. Would that be an acceptable compromise?"

"Yes, sir. Very much so."

The more Dr. Wellesley spoke, the more I became convinced that he actually liked me. He was just a little rough around the edges.

Dr. Wellesley guided me down the stairs to a large empty classroom. There was no piano and no chairs in the room, but there was a lined chalkboard. Far from ideal, to be sure; but then, I would be working for free for a school that had only just begun enrolling students.

"Well, how do you like it? Do you think you'll manage, Miss Brigham?"

"These rooms, and everything else, will be perfect, Dr. Wellesley."

NINE

Plans

> *"The more I know of the world,*
> *the more I am convinced that I shall never see a man whom*
> *I can really love."*
> —Jane Austen, *Sense and Sensibility*

M iss Amaryllis." Higgins, who knew just where to find me when I had any spare time to myself, walked into the drawing room just as I was about to begin playing the piano. "You have a caller."

I stood as he presented me with a silver tray containing a single card that read "Felix Redding, Attorney-at-Law."

My father's attorney.

Standing, I asked, "Is Claudine still upstairs?"

"I believe so, miss. Would you like me to—"

"Oh no, leave her be. Please." I hid the card between my hand and the bodice of my dress, as if doing so would prevent Higgins from knowing what he already knew.

"As you wish, Miss." He left the room to retrieve my visitor.

I'd never met Mr. Felix Redding, but I'd known his name for precisely five weeks. It had been through a letter from Mr. Redding that I'd learned of the unfortunate fate of my father and his horse farm in northern Maine.

When Higgins returned with Mr. Redding, I was surprised by his youthful age.

"Mr. Felix Redding, miss."

"Miss Brigham, what an honor to finally meet you," he said as he took my hand. By his accent, I could tell he was British, like my father. However, he had fiery red hair, which gave me the impression that his ancestry contained more Scot than Brit. "Your father spoke of you often. He missed you terribly, I understand."

I immediately sat on the piano stool, as his words had taken me by surprise. I realized I'd completely disregarded the proper etiquette for the situation—etiquette Claudine had been endeavoring to teach me over the previous weeks.

I stood and motioned to the sofa. "Forgive me. Please, do sit. Do you have news of my father's will?"

"That I do, Miss Brigham," he said with a grin as we both took a seat. "It seems you've a bit of a thing for wills and inheritances lately."

I suddenly had the feeling Mr. Redding knew all about the rumors circulating about my grandmother's will, as well as my father's.

"Was there anything left besides the land?"

By the stunned look in his dark blue eyes, Mr. Redding had been unprepared for my directness. Yet I saw no need for niceties when my very future could be so entirely altered by what he might have to say. Perhaps the land in Maine was mine; if so, I would be able to sell it and, in so doing, forget all about Boston, Claudine Abernathy, Hilldreth Manor...and The Cleft Stone. Perhaps, if things worked out just right, I would soon be able to leave for Washington on my own, never having to look back.

"Ah, the land. You mean his horse farm in Washington, perhaps?"

"Did he still have possession of Bruckerdale when he died?" I asked, hoping desperately that I'd been terribly wrong all those years, and that my father hadn't sold it after all.

"Actually, no. He didn't. I'm sorry to say, Miss Brigham, but he sold the property on Whidbey Island mere months ago, right before his passing."

"Are you certain?" The thought that I could have gone back to Whidbey Island at any time during the last eleven years brought burning tears to my eyes. All I would have had to do, all that time, was to buy a train ticket?

A wave of nausea swept over me. If only I'd taken the initiative and written to my father years ago. If only I hadn't been so determined to resent him and his willful abandonment all those years ago. How differently my life could have turned out.

"Yes, I'm quite certain. I took care of the details myself."

I quickly realized Mr. Redding hadn't brought anything into the room with him. No papers and no will.

"Who bought it? Do you think they would reconsider?"

"I'm actually not at liberty to say who purchased the land in Washington, Miss Brigham. But no, the likelihood that they would reconsider is doubtful. The new owner is a young gentleman who is quite eager to relocate from New England. There would be little you could do to convince him to sell it back, even if you had the funds upon your marrying within the year."

"Did my father have no funds when he died, Mr. Redding? The money from the sale couldn't have vanished in such a short time—"

"Ah, but it did. Peter gave it all to Bram Everstone, who happened to own the land in Maine that his most recent horse farm was situated upon…though I haven't a clue how Peter could have come to owe him such a substantial amount of money."

I could hear Claudine making her way down the front staircase, then happily giving orders to Higgins about something or other as they walked through the hall to the back of the house.

Obviously, he'd refrained from telling her about my visitor.

"There's nothing left?" I whispered. "Why, then, are you here?"

"Forgive me, Miss Brigham, for having to be the one to tell you this, but Peter had nothing whatsoever to leave you. I'd written a will up years ago, before the sale of the land in Washington. Up until months ago, Bruckerdale would have been all yours. We meant to update the will after the sale, you see. And then there was the fire. As you well know, Miss Brigham, there was absolutely nothing left of the barns, the house…or the horses. Everything was lost."

Lost. Just like me.

⌒

A cool gust of wind fluttered the pages of my book, losing my place. I put it down, gathered my shawl closer around my shoulders, and fell back against the black leather seat of Claudine's carriage, the top of which was now open to accommodate the wonderful, almost springlike weather.

It had been over a week since Nathan had left for Maine, and this wasn't the first time I'd tried my best to forget him—and failed. Even from hundreds of miles away, Nathan Everstone perturbed me.

I hoped he wouldn't come back to Boston for a very long time. But, all the same, I'd resolved to finish *Of the Imitation of Christ* as quickly as possible, and have it well hidden, in case he did return to Hilldreth. I picked up the book once more and turned to a random page, my eyes grazing over a familiar string of words.

"Whensoever a man desireth anything inordinately, he becomes restless in himself."

I realized I still didn't know exactly what the word *inordinately* meant. I took a pencil from my reticule and circled the term, resolved to find it in the dictionary once we returned to Hilldreth.

"Mr. Crawford!" Claudine shouted. The carriage immediately came to a halt. "Amaryllis, do look up. It's Mr. Crawford." I glanced up from putting my pencil away to find he'd approached my side of the carriage.

"Good afternoon, Miss Abernathy, Miss Brigham."

He took my hand, and Claudine practically shoved me out of the carriage, causing my book to fall to the ground, my beloved pages crumpling facedown on the curb. I was beginning to cease being surprised by Claudine's random and often thoughtless ways. She was a quirky old woman, that was for sure.

Jay bent to retrieve the book and handed it to me.

"Mr. Crawford." I tipped my head politely once I stood next to him.

"We were having a wonderful time enjoying this impeccable weather, Mr. Crawford," Claudine said from her carriage seat. "Would you like to take Amaryllis for a walk through the park? She's always trying to escape from the hectic world of society into which I've thrust her. She actually brought a book to read at the Common! Can you imagine?"

"I'd be delighted, Miss Abernathy."

As Jay's dark brown eyes were directed to Claudine, I noticed the quality of his suit. It was almost as fine as Nathan's, which surprised me. How was it possible that he had such money? Weren't all missionaries quite poor?

"I'll be going back to Hilldreth presently," Claudine added. "If you would be so kind, Mr. Crawford, could you return Amaryllis home when your walk is through? And you can stay for dinner."

After Claudine rolled away in her carriage, Jay walked beside me in silence. He seemed so serious. What a difference there was between him and Nathan Everstone. Jay seemed so sensible, while Nathan exuded an arrogance that made me feel I was from an entirely different world.

In all actuality, I was.

I didn't know much about Jay's background, but I did like his smiling brown eyes. The more I saw of them, the more I liked the rest of him, too.

As he faced forward, walking beside me with my arm linked through his, I took the chance to study him, knowing full well that Claudine was probably watching my every move.

Jay wasn't nearly as handsome as Nathan, but not many men were. However, Jay had proven himself to be a man with noble priorities and unselfish goals. That counted for something, didn't it?

What were Nathan's goals? Gather more wealth and make everyone jealous by flaunting it whenever possible? He'd denied he cared for such things, but one never knew. In twenty years, would he be just like his father?

It was a rather depressing thought, for even I had to admit that, at times, he really didn't seem that bad.

Jay reached out his hand for my book. "*Of the Imitation of Christ?* Did Nathan recommend this book?"

"No." I was taken aback. "Would he?"

"He was reading it on our way back from Washington." Jay must have seen something related to curiosity on my face, for he said, "It surprised me, too. He's a different person, on all accounts, from the man I met a decade ago at Dartmouth."

"Is that so?"

"Believe me, Amaryllis." He tried out the sound of my name with a smile. "Let's leave it at that. Have you read the book before?"

"I haven't. I generally read novels."

"Novels are quite pointless compared to works like this."

Striving to avoid a lecture about how the novels I loved were polluting my mind, I was about to steer the conversation in another direction when he asked, "Do you still have family in Washington?"

"No. My father has lived in Maine for the last eleven years. But he's gone now."

"Oh, I'm sorry for your loss. Has it been long?"

"There was a fire a while back."

I really didn't want to speak about it. The more attention I brought to the fact that he'd died recently, the more people would question why I was not in mourning. But how was one expected to mourn the loss of someone one had never known?

"Is that also where you've been hiding all these years? Maine?"

"No. I attended boarding school in Concord—"

"Miss Pelletier's School for Young Ladies?"

"How did you—"

"My sister, Magda, attended there also. You see, I'm originally from Concord—" His words stopped on his lips.

Had I paid any attention to the other students during the years I'd attended, I might have had the chance to know her; but, being as I'd been lost in my own world, which involved a small room filled with little more than a relatively new grand piano, I doubted it. "I don't recall any students by the name of Crawford."

This bit of information seemed to ease some of his tension. "And then what did you do?"

"I attended Mount Holyoke." Bram Everstone's interference concerning the degree I'd always been so proud of attaining came to mind, and my stomach lurched. "And then, of course, I was awarded a scholarship to attend The Boston Conservatory." Again, the thought of Bram Everstone being involved made me pause. Had he provided that scholarship? And if so, why? So that he could bring me so close to the culmination of my dreams, only to then rip them away?

"You do play quite well. I remember that much from the night of your aunt's dinner party." He became strangely quiet for some minutes as we walked down the path, seemingly lost in his thoughts.

"Will you tell me more about your mission in Aberdeen?" I hoped this time we'd actually have a chance to discuss what it was like there. He'd asked me question after question, and now it was my turn. "Who's taking care of it while you're gone?"

"It's actually not mine yet. I was only there visiting, exploring my options."

"They really won't let you serve without a wife?"

"No, they won't." He handed the book back to me and placed his hand on mine where it rested at the crook of his elbow.

"Are there no suitable young women in Aberdeen to choose from? Or are they all the sort one wouldn't want to marry?"

His face turned beet red. "There are a considerable number of those, yes. Not many at all like you, Amaryllis."

"Would you consider someone like me as a prime candidate?"

He responded with a wide-eyed stare, and then came the question: "Would you consider?"

I knew he could easily think I was his fastest ticket back west, but was he not my best option also? I gave him a flashy smile, hoping to put an end to his questions. Being so blithe didn't come naturally for me, but with Jay, I knew it was appreciated—and, at the moment, very much needed.

But suddenly I hesitated. Was I really ready to commit to this?

For a moment, Jay looked as if he might say more.

The rapid beat of my heart thundered in my ears, my hands shook, and I had the sudden urge to run home to Hilldreth. What had I been thinking to bring up such an idea? Wanting to stop the conversation from going any further, I quickly asked, "I've been meaning to ask you, Jay, what it was like inside the Everstones' private railcar."

"It was like traveling in an elaborate mansion." He exhaled, as if he, too, was relieved I'd brought up a new subject. "Nathan's father had it custom designed as a virtual palace on wheels."

"It was quite beautiful from the outside. Do they keep it at the train station when it isn't in use?" I was still shaken. I couldn't do it. Not yet.

"I believe so. Nathan and Estella took it up to Maine when they left last week." The fact that he called Estella by her given name didn't surprise me—not with the way he'd looked at her at the train station the day I'd met them.

"I do adore trains," I stated, trying to focus my inquiries away from the fact that it was Nathan's railcar in particular that interested me.

"Do you? Most young ladies hardly care one way or another about them. Except for Nathan's sisters—they both prefer travel by train to sailing. They never sail, not even up to Mount Desert Island." Every pleasant sentence was laced with awkwardness from what we'd *almost* discussed.

"Some people simply cannot abide boats. Like me. I get terribly seasick."

"Nathan's sisters must have that same problem. It's unfortunate, for Nathan does love that schooner of his."

Sadly, just as the conversation was truly becoming interesting, Lawry interrupted us as he drove up the path in a small yet elegant-looking buggy. "Here are two of my favorite people, and what a background!" He parked the buggy. "And I have my camera."

"Of course you do." I laughed at his easygoing manner, as did Jay.

Within minutes, Lawry had his camera set up before us. He loved taking photographs of anything and everything, and had money enough to pursue his hobby. I was unsure if it was appropriate to have my photo taken with Jay, but I'd discovered while living with Claudine and Lawry that strict propriety wasn't something they concerned themselves with. And there really was no arguing with Lawry. He was much too amusing to discourage.

"Stay as you are, except I need a brighter smile from you, Amaryllis. I refuse to take one more photograph of a stoic-looking person. There are too many such photographs in the world already."

I remembered the photograph that was still in my Bible, and the smile on Nathan's face that made me peek at it every morning.

Lawry took a few photographs from different angles, which, I gathered from Jay, was the norm. Once he was satisfied, Lawry grabbed my book from my hands. "I meant to ask you before, Amaryllis, did Nathan suggest this book to you?"

I almost laughed out loud but covered it by clearing my throat. "Jay asked me the same question, but no, he did not."

"How odd," Lawry answered, offering no explanation.

Jay seemed almost too quiet as we seated ourselves on a bench and watched the sun make its way from behind the clouds. "Crawford, you should come for dinner. I'm positive Claudine would love to include you, not to mention Amaryllis."

"I've already been invited by Miss Abernathy herself," Jay smiled knowlingly my way.

I smiled halfheartedly back, unsure of what exactly I'd just begun.

TEN

The DeLagrange Ball

"Is not general incivility the very essence of love?"
—Jane Austen, *Pride and Prejudice*

Upon his return a mere three weeks after leaving for Bar Harbor, Nathan did not come back to stay at Hilldreth, as Claudine had hoped. Instead, he stayed with Estella at his aunt Miriam's house, informing her in a letter that he'd soon be back under her care once the DeLagrange Ball had come and gone.

It had been my understanding that he didn't attend balls, and I sincerely hoped he wouldn't be attending the one at the DeLagrange residence. Actually, I wished he would stay away from Lawry and Hilldreth altogether, but that was not going to happen, no matter how selfishly I desired it.

To my happy surprise, Nathan did not tread the threshold of Hilldreth even once during those few days between his return to town and the day of the ball. I was sadly disappointed, however, when, at the last possible moment, Lawry informed me that he had invited Nathan and his sister, as well as Meredyth and Jay, to Hilldreth in order for us all to ride to the ball together in the Everstones' crimson red landau.

Despite feeling ill and unable to attend, Claudine had insisted on helping me get ready for the ball. I was dressed in a deep red evening gown with white lace and yellow silk roses accentuating the ruffles off my shoulders, as well as the train. The style was much more daring than I would have preferred, and I wasn't relishing the thought of Nathan seeing me in it. I hardly knew what he thought of me, but even I had to admit, despite his somewhat brusque treatment of me at times, he was very good at acting as if he couldn't keep his eyes off me.

I tried to calm my heart when he walked through the door of the parlor. His well-defined brows were already drawn together, yet that did nothing to keep him from looking wickedly dashing in his black-and-white evening finery. When he and his sister, along with Jay and Meredyth, came into the room, I immediately latched myself to the nearest person—which was Jay Crawford. He looked nice, too, with his tussled dark hair; but unfortunately, the sight of him did nothing to send my heart racing out of control.

I produced the happiest, most unaffected smile I could muster. This unmistakable show of preference for Jay earned me a stern scowl from Nathan.

Things had not changed a bit.

Jay smiled down at me, acting amazingly delighted at my singling him out. "I'm looking forward to attending the DeLagrange Ball in particular, Amaryllis, for I've been planning something very special for tonight."

"Oh, have you?" I asked with another unmistakably sincere smile. "Is it some sort of surprise for someone?"

"I'm sure there will be lots of people who are surprised, actually." Jay's obvious delight in speaking to me seemed to make Nathan more annoyed by the second.

He was such a strange man. Estella stood next to him, looking as if she'd not wanted to come and could stand to be in the same room with us only if she stayed close by his side. Actually, they were both rather strange.

Of course, Meredyth and Lawry were having a grand time. Those two couldn't have an unpleasant moment if they tried. With one quick look to Nathan, Lawry grabbed Meredyth by the arm and swung her out to the hallway. "We have time before the ball— let's practice our waltzing."

Lawry winked at Estella, who followed them with blatant reluctance. Nathan continued to stand across the room, unmoved.

"Nathan," Meredyth sang, "you must come and dance with me. Your sister has already stolen my partner!"

He hesitantly walked to the pocket doors and scrutinized me for several moments before pulling them closed.

I suddenly realized I'd hardly been able to keep my eyes off of Nathan since I'd clutched on to Jay's arm. With his perfect symmetry, he'd held my attention so rapturously, I hadn't noticed, until it was too late, that I had been left completely alone with Jay.

Taking my hands in his, Jay knelt on the floor. "Amaryllis, will you marry me and join me in my service to the people of Aberdeen, Washington?" The hope-filled look in his brown eyes told me he expected me to accept joyously.

However, my first reaction was not joy, not even gratefulness. It was shock, followed by revulsion. I couldn't help but pull my hands from his.

I'd tried to like Jay. I had. But everything in me cringed at the thought of marrying him, even if he would provide the easiest way for me to accomplish my dreams. I could not bear to think of attaching myself so entirely to anyone, to give up all personal rights. Even if I somehow managed to convince myself it was for the best.

Would I ever like anyone enough that such an idea would not repulse me?

"Jay, please..." I whispered, trying to sound empathetic. "You barely know me."

"I've known since first speaking with you that you were perfectly suited to be my wife." By the steadiness of his voice, he was still entirely confident in himself. And why wouldn't he be, after what I'd so foolishly said to him in the park?

I was at a loss for anything else to say to dissuade him...besides no, which seemed too final of an answer.

"Amaryllis, surely you must know how I feel." He stood and gripped my hands in his again. "Listen, Lawry's told me all about your desire to move back to Washington. By marrying me, you'd gain your inheritance. Do you not see that this is the perfect solution for both of us?"

"I know it is, but—"

"You need more time?"

What I needed was a ticket to Washington. Why couldn't I just take it?

"July. Can I give you my answer in July?" Surely I'd be able to convince myself to marry him by then.

"That is perfectly acceptable. Forgive me for acting so hastily. I should have known better. It's only...you see, I need to get back, and I didn't want to waste time if I didn't need to." He quickly crossed the room and opened the double pocket doors. "I'll go inform the others."

"What will you tell them?"

"That we are not engaged. Not yet, that is." That he already assumed what my answer would be disturbed me more than anything he'd said during our short interview.

"Did Lawry and Meredyth know you were—"

"They all knew." He left, closing the doors behind him without another word.

I sat on the sofa and stared blankly out the front window. I did not like how the conversation had ended. I would not be accepting his proposal. Now or in July. If I did, I'd never be able to live with myself.

Having led such a lonely, boring existence until arriving at Hilldreth, I wondered how my life since then could have been described as anything but. It was as if a veil had been lifted from around me. As if everyone now saw a totally different person.

And why, when presented with everything I needed and I thought I wanted, had I been unable to accept it? If I married Jay, I would gain my inheritance. And I would be able to found my music academy in Aberdeen. With ease, in fact. Not that Aberdeen, Washington, was likely to be anything like Whidbey Island, from what little Jay had told me about it.

I was still sitting, staring out the window when Nathan came into the room.

"Excuse me, Miss Brigham. Do you still want to attend the party tonight?" He was again so very courteous. I twisted to face him and saw that his sister stood close beside him. "The rest of our party has left in Claudine's carriage. You may come with us, if you still plan to attend."

"Oh yes, I'm coming." I glanced out the window again, still unable to focus on anything but the scene with Jay.

"Where are the rest—"

"As I said, they decided at the last minute to take Claudine's carriage." He swallowed nervously, which was actually rather an interesting thing to witness. That was when I realized Estella looked as if she were on the verge of tears.

I looked to the grandfather clock. "I do suppose we should be on our way." Then I stood, gathered my things, and followed them out of the parlor to their immaculate closed carriage parked on the street in front of Hilldreth. Every little detail about the Everstones' landau intimated wealth. Having the fact that I felt so out of place in my aunt's social world made so blatantly obvious brought my mood down even farther. I did not belong in such a fine carriage. It was only a bizarre coincidence I was seated across from Nathan and his sister.

As we stopped in front of the DeLagrange mansion, I was again surprised by Nathan's politeness as he took my hand, helped me out, and kept a possessive hold of my arm. What had happened to the vexed look in his eyes? He suddenly seemed so relieved.

And I couldn't help but notice how everyone in the room watched us as we went through the receiving line.

When I was at last able to leave his side, I glanced about in an effort to find Meredyth. She was descending the grand marble staircase. As she took my arm and led me across the grand hall, all I could think of was the shock and revolt that had coursed through me as Jay had uttered his dreadful request.

⌣

After the ball commenced, my dance card was minus two names in particular: Jay Crawford and Nathan Everstone. The latter had evidently wanted to make sure everyone knew perfectly well it hadn't been his intention to escort me to the ball, that it was merely something he'd been forced into doing by circumstance.

Oddly, this was the very opposite of what I thought he was supposed to be doing for my benefit. It was, however, perfectly fine by me. How disappointed Claudine would be in the morning when she read the gossip pages and learned that Nathan had failed to do his job beyond escorting me to the ball. Surely, everyone had noticed he wanted nothing to do with me, by his avoidance of me from the moment we left the receiving line.

When I realized Wyatt Harden was walking straight for me, I steeled my back in preparation for something unpleasant. I didn't like Wyatt, and not only because I'd recently learned that he had been the young man with Nathan's father that day at The Cleft Stone. There had been something about the stance of his large, broad frame and the hard look in his power-hungry blue eyes that had frightened me.

"So, what do you think of our friend Nathan?" Wyatt smirked as he stood next to me at the perimeter of the ballroom. I was just thankful he hadn't asked me to dance.

"I hardly know him, nor do I particularly care to. Nathan Everstone is nothing but a thorn in my side." I could barely hear my own voice over the orchestra playing in the balcony above us.

"I noticed he escorted you to the ball tonight." He gave me a look that told me he didn't believe a word I'd said.

"He did have that honor, yes." I searched the crowd for Meredyth's face. If only she would see my need to be rescued and come save me. "However, Mr. Harden, as I've already alluded to, he is not my friend but Lawry's. And I'm completely uninterested in anything having to do with him."

"Ah, but I've seen him speak with you, and I can tell that quite the opposite is true. I can also tell that he's most decided upon having you."

My ears burned at his words. The idea that Nathan wanted me, for any reason, seemed preposterous.

"He created quite a reputation for himself before leaving Boston two years ago, Miss Brigham, and he's quite good at what he does, if you know what I mean. I can only guess what he's been doing for enjoyment out West." Wyatt smiled as he caught my eye.

I had to fight to keep my mouth from falling open, not just at what he was saying, but that he was actually saying such shocking things to me.

After a few moments of sorting through his puzzling comments, I answered, "And is this the reason he's avoided me so carefully all evening? The gentleman in question hasn't asked for one dance of me tonight. I hardly see how that constitutes his wanting me."

"He has your attention now, does he not?" Wyatt's words raked the air between us.

"I assure you, I'm quite immune to the charms of Nathan Everstone."

"And I assure you"—his eyes narrowed—"Nathan always gets what he wants, just like his father. I do hope you understand. I'm simply trying to protect you. I'd be very careful in my associations with him if I were you."

"Because his father wouldn't like it?"

"I'm fairly certain Bram could not care less what Nathan wants to do with you, as long as it has nothing to do with matrimony." With that last word hanging in the air between us, Lawry moved in next to me, as if to steal me away for the next dance.

I threaded my arm through his willingly. He was so much like a comforting older brother, and I looked forward to the silence I could enjoy with him.

However, in that silence, my mind obsessed about everything Wyatt had told me concerning Nathan. I knew Lawry would tell me the truth if I asked him, but doing so would be incredibly awkward, and I didn't want him to know it mattered so much to me. What would Lawry think of my asking such questions about his closest friend?

And what on earth would Nathan think if he ever found out?

⌒

Jay spent most of the evening hidden in the card room with Nathan, who danced only twice—once with Nicholette and once with Meredyth.

Jay, for some odd reason, did not dance at all.

Nicholette managed to fasten herself to Nathan's arm every time he ventured into the ballroom that night. With her dazzling smile and radiant beauty, it was obvious she was trying her best to captivate him. But by the grim look on his face, I could tell none of her tricks would work on him.

To get my mind off Nicholette and her relationship with Nathan, I forced my mind to reflect on all the ways Nathan had frustrated me since the day we'd met. It wasn't difficult. He seemed to have quite a knack for it.

Just as I was reprimanding myself for allowing my thoughts to stray back to the moment his hand had held mine, I found him standing directly before me. It was as if he'd done it intentionally, as if he knew I'd been trying to remove him from my thoughts, and he simply would not permit it.

"It seems you've found your ticket back to Washington. Crawford's quite confident in what your answer will be come July." His eyes burned with anger.

This brash comment, combined with the anxious look on his face, made me smile. I'd assumed his nasty attitude toward me earlier at Hilldreth had something to do with Jay's proposal. His snide comment now confirmed my suspicion. Was he angry because I seemed to think I was too good for his friend? And did he really believe I would be so easily won?

I looked up at him, with a little more fortitude than I'd achieved the last time I'd been faced with his abruptness. However, before I could form a response, he whirled around and stalked away. Wyatt's conclusions about Nathan's "plans for me" streamed through my mind, and I smiled.

No matter what Wyatt had said, Nathan most definitely did not want me, nor was he intent upon "having" me for any reason.

ELEVEN

The Musicale Benefit

"If music be the food of love, play on."
—William Shakespeare, *Twelfth Night*

I'd known the day was coming almost from the moment Claudine had returned to Boston. The Musicale Benefit for the Boston Inland Mission Society at The Boston Conservatory had been advertised all over town. And since Claudine had no idea why or how much it would pain me to have to go back there since she was still under the impression that I'd quit of my own accord, she insisted upon my playing twice.

Being in the auditorium of The Boston Conservatory again made me light-headed, even as I was hidden backstage, praying to God no one from the institution would see me and recognize me.

Of course, I knew it was a ridiculous and practically impossible prayer for God to answer. Still, it was all I could do.

God help me. God help me. God help me.

Surely, if anyone did recognize me, taking note of either my name or my playing, he would ignore my existence. Surely, he wouldn't dare cause a scene.

I was scheduled to begin the night's entertainment by playing Claudine's very favorite piece, Mozart's *Sonata No. 11 in A*. For weeks, I'd prayed that the building would be burnt to the ground by the time the dreaded day arrived. However, that prayer remained unanswered, and I was forced to contend with all the emotions driving through my veins merely by hiding backstage.

Dr. Wellesley was nearby. Although he was a gruff old man, I knew he liked me. And I liked him, simply because most people did not. He came up beside me directly after I watched the lights dim in a smooth wave of darkness.

"Miss Brigham, you have the Lord on your side, and the talent He has blessed you with. You will be fine, and you'll do fine."

No matter his encouraging words, my stomach tightened at the thought of walking steadily out to the grand piano at center stage.

The very same piano I'd played hundreds of times before.

Five long minutes after focusing entirely on the graceful movements of my fingers, my musical selection was complete, and I was still alive. There was no gang of angry Amaryllis-haters awaiting me as I exited the stage. The auditorium appeared so packed that even if one person purposed to take a public jab at me, his finding me would have been next to impossible. I was certain there wasn't a single seat left for me to take, and I was happy to resign myself to remaining backstage until the end of the evening, staying as far away from the crowd as possible.

While Nicholette performed a particularly awful rendition of Pachelbel's *Canon in D*, Meredyth came looking for me. Without a word, she grabbed my hand and led me straight through the dark, cramped corridors behind the stage, up the dimly lit far left aisle, to a seat at the end of a row—directly next to Nathan Everstone.

Apparently, she had a very different idea of how I needed to spend the evening.

"With such a crush, I'm certain Nicholette will understand if you take her seat, Amaryllis. Don't you agree, Nathan?"

Nathan cleared his throat as an odd look of surprised delight crept across his face. "Of course."

I'd been fully prepared to face the angry version of him from the end of the DeLagrange Ball, but obviously, Mr. Civility was back again.

I turned and noticed that Meredyth had taken a seat behind us with her family, as well as with Lawry and Claudine. Turning back to the stage, I realized Nicholette had finished playing, and in her place, a small orchestra was playing Vivaldi's *Four Seasons.* And no matter how entranced I was by the actions of the musicians as they created their music, I had to force myself to not look at the man seated beside me.

During intermission, and my first chance to escape Nathan's close proximity, I was unable to leave my seat. So long as he was still sitting beside me, my legs refused to move.

After a few minutes, when all the seats surrounding us had been abandoned, I heard Nathan say, gently, without even turning my way, "Have you had an enjoyable time staying with Claudine, Miss Brigham?" He said it so quickly, and without any movement, I almost thought I'd imagined the words. For I'd wanted very much for him to say something to me, to acknowledge I was indeed there sitting beside him, no matter how foolish the prospect was. He turned his head slightly, as if waiting for an answer.

I realized right away that the reply I was going to give him was far different from the replies I'd given the countless other men I'd met who'd asked me the same mundane question. Nor did I begrudge him for asking it of me, as I had all the others. Every single one of those other gentlemen, including Jay, had asked me the question almost as soon as they'd made my acquaintance. Only Nathan had not.

"I enjoy attending the opera and the ballet and concerts. At least the ones in which I have no part in performing."

"In short, you enjoy anything pertaining to music?"

"For the most part. Many of the other 'entertainments' are much too crowded and vain for my taste."

He laughed under his breath. He must have thought I was referring to him. And I very well could have been.

He quickly turned to me. "Do you miss living on Whidbey Island so very much?"

I thought it a strange question for him to finally ask after all the subterfuge from him and Lawry about their travels to Washington. However, instead of dwelling on his reasons for asking, my heart flooded with reminiscences of the first fourteen years of my life and what it had meant for me to leave the house and horses I loved so much. Vivid memories of rich emerald-green meadows and rolling hills that seemed to stretch in every direction.... My life had been perfection with my mother, my father, and our horses—actually, one horse in particular. But, most of all, "I miss the life I had while my mother was alive."

"As do I." The tenderness in his voice startled me.

"And my horse," I added, desperate to turn the conversation away from the topic of my mother. "We left her when we came east, never imagining we would not be back. I never found out what happened to her, or any of the other horses." Saying the words aloud cut deep into my heart. I'd been so good at burying those thoughts. Why were they all coming out now?

Why hadn't I left my seat as soon as the intermission had begun?

"What was her name?" Nathan met my gaze.

"Elinorah."

"No, I meant your horse."

"Oh, of course. Her name was Chariot. My father bred Shires for the lumber companies in Washington before doing so in Maine."

"Why did your parents come east that summer? Do you know?"

"My grandfather died, and I think Mother wanted to make amends—"

"Did she?"

"No."

"And I suppose you would take off for Washington in a heartbeat if you had the chance." His voice sounded deep, smooth, and strangely interested. I couldn't help but answer him.

"I would."

"And what of Crawford? Is he is not a suitable enough... chance?"

"Contrary to what nearly everyone in Boston seems to think, Mr. Everstone, finding a husband is not my first priority."

Nicholette glared at us from across the room. Did she believe the same things as Wyatt? Nathan looked in her direction and seemed amused by her attention. I'd forgotten to whom I was speaking. He was so good at making me feel as if I should trust him.

"Men, in my opinion, are entirely too inconsistent, and consistency is something I value very highly."

"And money is not."

"I cannot lie—it would be nice to have the inheritance. But not if the price is my freedom."

He didn't urge me to reveal more but actually looked as if he'd completely lost interest in what we were discussing.

After a few silent moments, Nathan reached over to finger the corners of the rolled sheet music I held firmly in my lap. The name of the piece was clearly seen—it was a duet of Felix Mendelssohn's *Hebrides Overture.*

"Are you playing this piece tonight?"

"Yes."

"With?"

"Nicholette." It was a wonder he didn't already know. Nicholette and I had been practicing together at Faircourt for weeks.

"It was Claudine's brilliant idea when it was obvious we weren't becoming as close as she would have liked."

Not that playing the piano together could accomplish such a miracle. In fact, it had only proved to make things worse between us. Nicholette could not deny the fact that I played the instrument with far more skill than she did, despite my efforts to seem as though I struggled at finding the notes as I stared blankly at the music. Would this fluent talent of mine ever bring about anything good?

"Might we perhaps play it together some evening at Hilldreth? *Hebrides* was my mother's favorite. She taught me to play it alongside my twin sister, Natalia."

The one thing I knew I did not need was to sit at a piano alongside Nathan Everstone, having his fingers brush against mine for eight or more long minutes.

"I do not participate in such blatant acts of flirtation, Mr. Everstone. Perhaps you should ask Nicholette? I'm certain she would be delighted." I stiffened against the back of my chair.

"You could go far with talent like yours. Have you ever considered using it as—"

"It was a possibility once, as you well know, Mr. Everstone. But now that I have nothing—"

"So says the heiress of the Landreth fortune."

"You hardly understand. I have no way of—" I wanted to tell him everything, hoping he would understand. However, with a quick look at the kind expression on his face, I wondered if he just might. "I do not plan to inherit anything, so long as it involves marrying. Even if it someday provided the chance of my founding my own—" I hardly knew why I'd told him as much as I had, or why he was trying to have such a conversation in the most unexpected of places.

"Founding your own what?"

I debated whether to go on, but there was something in me that wanted to tell someone. Who better than Nathan Everstone, who, in all likelihood, didn't care one way or another?

"I would found a music school if I could. But I can't. I can't even acquire a teaching position at one." The reasons why came glaringly back as I stared up at the high ceiling of the auditorium.

The crowds were beginning to shuffle back to their seats, and Nathan must have understood the subject was closed, for he ceased asking me questions. During most of the second set of performances, he did well to hardly glance in my direction, even when I slipped away at the end of the evening to play the *Hebrides Overture* with Nicholette.

As I sat at the grand piano, facing her at the second piano, playing one of my favorite pieces in the world with hardly a thought, I realized what Nathan had done by speaking with me so exclusively during the intermission. By remaining seated together while everyone else mingled around us and took their refreshment, we'd practically been on display. And he'd been making up for his treatment of me at the DeLagrange Ball, doing Claudine a considerable favor in showing a high percentage of the people who mattered that he thought I was acceptable.

Why it bothered me so much that he had done so, I could not tell.

Had I not been living in expectation of it?

TWELVE

Games

> *"She generally gave herself very good advice*
> *(though she very seldom followed it)."*
> —Lewis Carroll, *Alice's Adventures in Wonderland*

Nathan slipped in beside me at church that Sunday, and as we waited for the service to begin, he rotated toward me ever so slightly.

I cut a glance his way, but only for a moment.

"Amaryllis," Nathan whispered, "do you not want to be my friend?"

"I am quite certain you have plenty of *friends*, Mr. Everstone," I whispered back. "Please, feel no need to add me to the list."

"And you may believe that if you wish, but I know from personal experience that most of the people who think they are my friend have no idea what I'm really like."

"And just what are you really like? Cynical and glaringly arrogant, or engaging with unparalleled charm? You switch back and forth so often, I can hardly keep up."

"I guarantee that if anyone ever figures that out, it will be you, my dear."

I turned from him to face the empty middle aisle, ignoring the rather misplaced term of endearment. That was when I noticed

Nicholette glaring at us from her seat. That she considered me serious competition for his attention astounded me.

I did not speak to him again, but I did catch him smiling down at me as we stood to sing every verse of "Be Thou My Vision." Claudine and Lawry forced me to share my hymnal with Nathan, and it was impossible to ignore his smooth, deep voice as he sang with what seemed like something akin to sincerity.

We continued to stand after the hymn and opened our Bibles to Romans chapter one. The congregation read aloud together, starting with verse eight: *"First, I thank my God through Jesus Christ for you all, that your faith is spoken of throughout the whole world. For God is my witness, whom I serve with my spirit in the gospel of his Son, that without ceasing I make mention of you always in my prayers; making request, if by any means now at length I might have a prosperous journey by the will of God to come unto you. For I long to see you...."*

I couldn't help but lift my eyes to meet Nathan's smiling green ones.

As we found our seats, the photograph of him and Lawry hiking on Whidbey Island fell out of my Bible and landed on the floor between our feet. He bent down to retrieve it, then handed it to me with a rakish grin. I grabbed it from his hand and hid it away, my face burning.

"You carry a photograph of me in your Bible? How fascinating. Tell me, did you steal it from Lawry in order to view whenever you like?" he whispered under his breath.

I was guilty as charged, at least about the viewing part. But I wouldn't admit that to him. I couldn't believe his arrogance.

"I didn't steal it. Lawry gave it to me."

"You don't deny viewing it often. How very interesting."

"Why would I need to?" I whispered back. "You're everywhere I turn, in the flesh. I have no need of a photograph to see—"

Claudine shushed us.

I wanted very much to finish my sentence with *"your haughty countenance."* Instead, I silently glared at him. But he was faced forward by then, seemingly absorbed in what the preacher was saying about the apostle Paul.

⁓

Nathan sat across from me, staring, in Claudine's open carriage on our way home from church. Breaking the silence between the four of us, he said, "During church, you suggested, Miss Brigham—with quite an alarming amount of pert, I might add—that you have no need of a photograph…to see what, exactly?"

That moment, the carriage rumbled noisily over an extremely rough part of the cobblestone street, and I was relieved for the respite. I hoped Lawry would realize what I had to put up with from his friend whenever we were together.

"Is that what you were whispering about, Amaryllis—a photograph? Whatever for? And in the middle of church?" Claudine put out her hand. "Let me see it."

I reluctantly took the photograph from my Bible and handed it to her.

"I remember one like this, only Nathan was pictured alone," she said as she studied it. "I was sorely disappointed that neither one of you were in very many of the photographs." She handed the photograph to Lawry. "Was this taken somewhere in Washington?"

"It was taken on Amaryllis's Whidbey Island," Nathan admitted as he took the photograph and looked at it for a moment.

"When was the last time you smiled as you did in this photograph, Nathan? You're always so serious." Claudine seemed to have taken him by surprise, for he waited a moment before answering.

"I believe the lovely Miss Brigham may know the answer to that riddle. She makes me smile more than anyone I've ever had a chance to meet. She's an amusing young lady, is she not? And so amusing to watch."

"So happy you're entertained, Mr. Everstone." I cut him a sharp glance. I didn't like that he spoke of me as if I wasn't there. Did he say similar things when I wasn't around?

"I'm so happy you're pleased with her, Nathan." Claudine wrapped her arm around my shoulders.

I took my torture in silence. I felt like a baby being cooed over. I was just glad they had moved on from the topic of the photograph. Nathan handed it back to me, and I tucked it inside my Bible.

"Where is your family's home in Back Bay, Mr. Everstone? Have I ever seen it?" I asked, trying to divert the topic of conversation away from me.

"We'll pass it soon. It's at the corner of Commonwealth and Dartmouth."

As we neared an intersection, Claudine exclaimed, "There it is, the pride of Back Bay."

I hardly know what I expected, but the profligate seven-story brick mansion, with an elaborate amount of exaggerated detail on the many gables and turrets, was not it.

"Do you see Everwood, Amaryllis?" my aunt asked.

Yes, I saw it. It was rather hard to miss.

I'd actually seen it many times before that instance, as it was located a mere two blocks from Hilldreth. I'd thought perhaps the Rockefellers or the Vanderbilts had constructed the opulent mansion, desiring to have a house in every major city throughout New England.

Why ever would Nathan Everstone settle for living with us at Hilldreth while Everwood was an option?

"Do you not want to live there?" I asked, truly curious.

"Not particularly. I prefer living at Hilldreth, especially since Estella is content to stay with our aunt."

"We prefer that you stay at Hilldreth, as well," Claudine told him. "You're welcome for as long as you like." She patted his knee, which turned out to be rather diverting, and precisely the opposite of what I'd been trying to achieve by bringing up Everwood in the first place.

Once at Hilldreth, I went straight to my bedchamber and took the photograph out of my Bible. On the way home, in the midst of that terribly embarrassing conversation, I'd resolved that the only safe place for it was the drawer of my bedside table.

And that was where it would stay.

The following afternoon, Lawry and I met Meredyth and Jay a few blocks from Hilldreth at the Common. We were situated upon one of Claudine's quilts along the edge of a grouping of oak trees. I was beginning to suspect that Lawry and Meredyth were trying to encourage a relationship between Jay and me.

"Are you prepared, Lawry Hampton, to play Twenty-one against the likes of me?" Meredyth pulled a deck of cards from her reticule. "I'm sure you're well practiced, having spent so much time out West. But I'll have you know, so am I."

She wasn't flirting. She was simply being herself, which made me like her all the more. There was a very fine line between being friends with a man and flirting with him, and Meredyth balanced that line with perfect ease.

"I didn't stay out West to drink and gamble, Mere. Jay can vouch for me on that count."

"It's the truth," Jay added impassively.

Lawry reached over her, smiling, and snatched her reticule away. Looking inside, he pulled out a small cribbage board and held it up. "I wouldn't be surprised if you had a pair of dice in here, as well. Who taught you to be so unladylike by carrying games about in your bag?" Lawry shot her a look, and her cheeks flamed red.

"The same friends and relatives who taught you to be a gentleman." She stole the reticule back and held it to her chest. "A gentleman would never search a lady's personal belongings."

Shuffling the cards, Lawry turned a quick glance to Jay, who, like me, had yet to take part in the conversation.

Jay looked miserable. His stature was stiff, his face was frozen in a perpetual frown, and his eyes continually avoided me. Forcing him to endure my company was beyond anything I'd ever wished, but what could I do? I'd hardly seen him since the DeLagrange Ball. What did that mean? Had he changed his mind about wanting to marry me?

I followed his chocolate-brown gaze across the lawn to see Nathan walking up to our little gathering with Nicholette on his arm.

It surprised me that he'd sought out her company so soon after speaking of her with such condescension. But then again, what I knew of most men proved they were all inconsistent.

Why ever would I think Nathan Everstone was any different?

"Hello, all." He took off his hat, then added pointedly, "Amaryllis Brigham." After helping Nicholette take a seat, he lowered himself to the quilt across from me.

Lawry took up the cards he'd just dealt and kept them.

The game was over, apparently.

"We were just speaking about your trip to Washington, Nathan," Meredyth began. "And I'm confused—what was your reason in going?" Did she realize she was asking the question I was certain was still on everyone's mind?

"Has not all of Boston been discussing the reasons these last two years? I'm sure *someone* has figured it out by now." Nathan was facing Meredyth but quickly turned his eyes to me. "Perhaps it's Miss Brigham?"

I arched an eyebrow. "Perhaps it is." I felt fairly certain the reason was the snide young woman seated to his left, who, at the time, must have been around sixteen years old.

His only reply was a mischievous smile, much like the one in the photograph I had of him at Deception Pass.

"Well, are you in Boston for good?" Meredyth seemed not to notice that Nicholette's eyes were blazing with anger. "Or do you plan to take up your father's example and move from place to place to place? He seems to have become quite obsessed with traveling lately. Have you also caught the bug?"

"Definitely not." Whether he meant he was definitely not staying in Boston or definitely not obsessed with travel, he left unanswered.

"That answers for nothing. What do you mean?"

"I'm still considering." He stared at me from across the quilt.

Meredyth reached over and shoved his shoulder. He laughed aloud as he stretched out on his side. He really was much too attractive for his own good.

"And just what are you considering now, Nathan?" Nicholette asked him.

"Lots of things." He continued to stare at me.

I tried not to let his presence affect me, but I couldn't help the defensiveness I felt in my bones. I sat up straight and maneuvered myself so as not to have to look at him, preferring to give my full attention to Jay. I picked up the cards Lawry had set down. "Jay, would you like to play a game of cribbage with me?"

Shockingly, he agreed.

"Let's all play," Lawry suggested.

"And why not?" Nathan sat up. "We'll have to play on teams of two." He reached over and gathered the pegs from the quilt in front of me.

"What are you doing?" I asked him.

"Designating partners," he answered matter-of-factly. "Lawry, you'll be blue, along with Meredyth. Crawford, trade places with me."

"If you stay where you are, you can be on my team, Nathan," Nicholette almost purred.

"No, thank you. We'll all be better off if you're on the green team with Crawford." He stood and waited patiently for Jay to switch places.

As Nathan sat beside me, Nicholette shot daggers in our direction with her beautiful hazel eyes. He seemed not to notice, for he simply held the white peg out to me with two fingers and a smile, waiting for me to take it.

I did so, making sure not to touch him.

The cribbage game took an excruciating length of time to finish, since I was seated so close to Nathan. And afterward, as soon as we finished picking up the game, he insisted upon walking me back to Hilldreth, which only made the flutters in my midsection all the more impossible to ignore.

It wasn't a long walk, but, as I was fastened to his well-built arm for the length of it, it seemed never ending. Not to mention I had sensed Nicholette's fury when Nathan had practically forced Jay to escort her home.

Nathan didn't speak until we were halfway across the park.

"What are you, about five and twenty?"

"Last December."

"I still don't see how you've made it this far without marrying."

"Very carefully, Mr. Everstone." I focused my eyes on Hilldreth, which was now in view. Would he insist on spending the rest of the afternoon there? I hoped not. Surely, he had more important things to do with his time than to have afternoon tea with Claudine and me.

"Have I ever told you how much I value the high degree of pragmatism you're so able to sustain?"

"Thank you." I was sincerely pleased to hear that someone else valued such a trait. Even if it was Bram Everstone's son.

"You're so unflustered, so objective. But do you know what else I've noticed behind your guarded wall of detached emotions? I believe, behind this front of purposeful severity, you—"

"Purposeful severity?" I couldn't help but look up at him, despite how close we were to each other. He was smiling down, as if he'd known his words would provoke such a reaction.

"You save your softer, more lighthearted side for only your closest of friends. You cannot help but be wholeheartedly loyal to those you trust and love." We'd made it to Hilldreth by that point. He stopped me at the bottom of the steps and rested his elbow on the wrought-iron stair rail. "Since meeting you, Amaryllis, I've been thinking about what it would be like to receive such undying devotion from someone who guards herself so entirely. It would be quite something, would it not?" No sooner had he said the words than he took my hand and bowed, then quickly tipped his hat and strolled back down the sidewalk from whence we'd come, walking away as if he, indeed, owned all the world.

I watched him go.

I couldn't help it.

He was able to captivate me so easily, and I had no idea how he did it. Or why.

Never had anyone affected my nerves the way Nathan Everstone did when he looked my way with those watchful green eyes. Truth be told, I found him fascinating, and almost irresistible to gaze upon whenever we were together. And I could tell that he purposefully calculated his every word in order to make me lose my self-possession. He was quite good at that.

THIRTEEN

Nahant Island

*"Life is a storm, my young friend.
You will bask in the sunlight one moment,
be shattered on the rocks the next."*
—Alexandre Dumas, *The Count of Monte Cristo*

My vivid nightmares of reliving my mother's death and provoking Bram Everstone's wrath had only worsened since meeting Nathan Everstone. But the night after he walked me home from the Common, I was startled awake by a new dream.

One that was more disturbing than any nightmare I'd ever had.

The scene refused to leave my mind.

Instead of stumbling blindly through the darkness with Bram Everstone coming after me through the dense fog, there was something new. I was still surrounded by huge stone walls, but the fog was rolling away.

I was no longer running, and I was no longer lost.

There were large, ancient trees growing inside of the giant stone room, and the dusky sky overhead was hardly visible through the dark green canopy of leaves. Everything had seemed so eerily calm; I just stood there, unable to move, staring at a tall figure in an arched passageway in the limestone wall.

Relief flooded my soul when I recognized him.

Nathan Everstone stood with the sunlight shining behind him, his stunning features mere shadows in his silhouette. And when I ran hastily into his open arms...he kissed me.

But oh, how I'd wanted that kiss!

And it was with that horrifying notion pervading every fiber of my being that I awoke.

The fact that I'd dreamt such a thing alarmed me more than any nightmare ever had. For Bram Everstone pursuing me unendingly made perfect sense to me. A dream about Nathan Everstone kissing me did not.

Not in the least.

⌒

Later that morning, Meredyth came to Hilldreth quite early, fluttering about the parlor restlessly with me following in her wake. "Amaryllis, do you know, I don't think Nathan's the only one who's changed from being out West all those years. Lawry is different, too. Have you noticed?"

"I hardly knew him, Mere; we spent only a month together in the summer of seventy-nine. He seems much the same to me." I still had no idea why she'd come, but I suddenly had a strong suspicion that the nervous way she was acting had much to do with the prospect of seeing my cousin again.

"Oh, he's the same as ever, only he's...what's the word for it? Better." Meredyth plopped into one of the chairs next to the fireplace.

"Better than how he used to be?" I still stood, now in the center of the room, wondering if it was at all wise trying to get Meredyth to admit the real matter at hand.

"No...he's just better than...everyone else." Meredyth wasn't one to give information willingly, and it surprised me she'd already said as much as she had. "I hardly thought of him while he was away all those years; never once did it occur to me that he could be so good—" She'd been almost whispering, and she stopped mid-sentence, as if she'd just realized how much she'd divulged.

"There you are." Lawry stood in the open doorway. "Meredyth, have you told her yet?"

Meredyth stood; her face pale with a strange mixture of horror and awe. "No, I haven't told her anything."

Lawry walked into the room. "We've planned a special outing with you in mind, Amaryllis. We're taking you north of Boston to a place called Nahant Island." Without waiting for my reply, Lawry slipped an arm through one of mine and one of Meredyth's and led us out the front door. As I reached for my reticule, he said, "You won't need that. Everything's been planned and provided for, and it's better to not be hindered by such personal items today."

I really didn't want to go to Nahant Island...until we walked down the steps to the sidewalk and I saw the Everstones' red landau parked on the street. Nathan, Estella, and Jay were all standing nearby, waiting for us to join them.

"Nathan's called ahead to his father's resort on Nahant Island in order to have a lunch provided for us," Meredyth explained as we entered the carriage. "The plan is to picnic on the edge of the coast near a place called Forty Steps."

"How lovely." I was determined to enjoy myself, even if the day would involve setting foot on a boat and heading straight for the island where my mother's ship had wrecked nearly eleven years prior.

Once we reached the harbor, I stood and stared out at the calm, glassy sea before me. Fortunately, no one had ever thought of taking me to the shore, and I had a feeling that it had been quite purposeful. I did not like the sea, and my soul hurt to dwell on all that it had robbed of me: my mother, my home, my security, my peace....

And boats had never done me any favors. Even before Mother had died in the shipwreck, I'd never been able to withstand being aboard a sea vessel without becoming sick. That was one reason I'd hardly ever left Whidbey Island in the fourteen years I'd lived there. And it was the only reason my mother had left me at Truesdale that fateful day, instead of taking me with her.

I'd made it to the edge of the harbor when Meredyth walked up behind me.

"Are you feeling all right, Amaryllis? You look pale."

"I've never been fond of water." I said it quietly so only she could hear.

"Would you rather not go? We can send you home."

"No, I want to come."

Satisfied with my answer, she moved on to say something to Lawry.

"Are you feeling unwell, Miss Brigham?" Nathan was suddenly standing beside me. He'd hardly said a word to me from the moment I'd walked up to the group before entering the landau.

"No," I answered courageously. "I'll be fine."

I had quickly come to understand, during the drive to the harbor, that Nathan and I were to be enjoying the day together. It was extremely obvious that Lawry intended to spend his time with Meredyth. And Jay seemed to have made his choice. When forced to choose between me and Estella, he chose her.

Even with an unanswered proposal dangling between us, who was I when compared to Estella Everstone? Had he changed his mind about me? Was he now focusing his efforts upon wooing her? His gaze did seem to always gravitate to her whenever she was around; it had done so even before he'd asked me to marry him.

But I couldn't imagine Nathan's sister moving to the West Coast for any reason—especially not to become a missionary— even if she had the misfortune of falling madly in love with Jay. Surely, Bram Everstone would never allow such a thing.

Trying to think of something else, I again noticed the fine-cut suit Jay wore. His wardrobe continually surprised me. How was it that a missionary could afford to wear the same quality of clothing as Nathan Everstone?

I looked up to see Nathan smiling down at me, though the expression didn't quite reach his eyes. I stared at him for a moment before turning away, then caught a glimpse of a schooner rocking gently in the water.

Painted in deep red was the name "Elinorah."

"Is that your schooner?" I asked. "The one named *Elinorah?*"

"It was my father's when he was young. He gave it to me when I turned nineteen," he replied, and then strode away—which bothered me more than I wanted to admit. I should have been happy he was hardly speaking to me. That was what I wanted, wasn't it?

Once we were aboard the schooner, I found I wasn't nearly as fine as I'd insisted.

I'd made it to the point of standing securely, holding on to the railing. My legs were a bit wobbly, but it was nothing that couldn't be hidden from my friends. However, as soon as Nathan had the schooner making its way through the waves, my knees gave way completely.

One minute, I was standing; the next, blackness had come upon me from all sides.

When I regained consciousness, Nathan held me against his lap while he massaged my wrists.

"Amaryllis," he said softly. "Amaryllis, wake up."

"Amaryllis, oh, please, open your eyes." Meredyth was lightly patting my face with her soft hands. I felt the touch of Nathan's hands burn through the bodice of my dress. Trying to push them away, I struggled to stand on my own. I ended up managing only to crawl away before his hands were on me again, lifting me to my feet.

Once I finally stood on my own, I couldn't help but notice the water again, and the turbulence. Before I knew what was happening, my stomach heaved, and I lost my breakfast on the wooden deck right where Nathan stood. Meredyth was right beside me with her handkerchief, wiping my face.

I was mortified. Could the day get any worse?

"Forgive me, Miss Brigham, but—" Nathan lifted me into his arms. "Crawford, take over. I might be a while." With my arms wrapped around his neck, he carried me down some steep steps and then through a tight hall to a cramped room with a small bunk. Meredyth followed us. Once Nathan laid me on the bed, I quickly rolled over to face the wall.

Immediately my nightmare came to mind, and there was nothing I could do to convince myself that the boat would not be sinking soon, and that I would be lying there when the waters came, unable to do anything but let God take me just as He'd taken my mother…my debilitating nightmare come to life.

"Oh, Amaryllis!" I felt the weight of Meredyth seated next to me on the mattress. "You should have told me you were prone to seasickness. We didn't have to come. We could have done something else instead."

"I wanted to come." It was all I could manage. Even as the words were said, I wondered what could have produced such an outlandish desire that I would willingly put myself through all that had happened within the ten minutes of setting foot on that boat.

I remembered how happy and carefree my friends had been for the short while before the motion of the boat had turned my world upside down. Meredyth had been smiling and laughing, hanging over the railing, as Jay and Lawry had hoisted the sails and Nathan had begun to put the boat in motion.

Nathan and Estella had both seemed rather quiet, but Estella almost always seemed dismal whenever I was around. And there was never any logic to explain Nathan's behavior.

When I was finally back on wonderful, unmoving dry land, I felt incredibly idiotic for having been so traumatized by the short voyage. I wondered if I would need to go through the whole thing again on the way home. I was not looking forward to that, and it was an ever-present concern of mine as we walked up the embankment to the Bailey Hill Hotel.

The hotel was a huge, sprawling building, but not what I would have expected of anything owned by Bram Everstone. I was fully prepared for the hotel to have the same kind of austere arrogance and stuffiness as Everwood. In actuality, the Bailey Hill Hotel looked more like an oversized cottage with walls of windows overlooking the coast.

It was past lunchtime when we took one of the hotel carriages down to the rocky bit of coast called Forty Steps. I was delighted to find the cliffs much like those I remembered seeing and enjoying on Mount Desert Island with Lawry and Nathan's twin sister, Natalia.

Nathan walked me out to a giant, flat-topped boulder protruding into the ocean, which was where he chose to picnic with me. We were surrounded by the waves of the tide reaching their highest point, crashing all around us. The roaring sound unnerved me a bit, but I knew that as long as I stayed upon the high boulders, I would be safe from the rushing waters.

The food he'd ordered from the hotel restaurant was marvelous, and I was starving. I felt much better by this point, but my embarrassment from the situation on the boat prevented my wanting to especially speak with him.

He didn't say much. He looked my way only if he thought I wouldn't notice, which seemed somewhat strange to me. He was always looking at me for some reason. That I didn't know the reason hardly mattered. It was simply something I had grown accustomed to.

"This is called Castle Rock." He pointed to a boulder jutting farther out into the ocean than the one on which we sat. "Did you know the word *nahant* means 'almost an island'?"

"This isn't an island?"

"There's a large sandbar connecting it to the mainland...." His response seemed so stifled. What had happened to the ease that usually permeated the conversations between us?

"I'm sorry you had to go to so much trouble on your boat." I focused upon his forest-green cravat, which matched his eyes almost to perfection.

"It was nothing, Miss Brigham. I took the trouble most gladly." He said nothing for some moments, just stared back at me with those dark green eyes.

It was curiously comforting to sit so tranquilly with him.

"Did you know my mother died in a shipwreck?" Once it was out, I realized it was the first time I'd ever begun a conversation between the two of us, and that it was the first time I'd ever been willing to speak to anyone of the details concerning my mother's death. Why I thought he would care, I hardly knew.

"I didn't know that." He had a sad sort of look in his eyes.

"I have awful nightmares of drowning...."

"Why is that?"

"You don't often take your boat up to Mount Desert Island, do you?" I quickly took my chance to change the subject. "Jay told me you often take the railcar, when you'd rather...not."

At the quizzical look on Nathan's face, I immediately regretted mentioning Jay.

He didn't answer right away. He simply continued to stare at me as he took a bite of his apple, likely pondering what a ridiculous person I was. I was rambling on like a child. What was wrong with me?

"I do enjoy conquering the vast ocean with a little wood and sail. However, it is true that my sisters both prefer the train. That's why we make use of the railcars so often."

"Your family has more than one?"

"When I so unexpectedly took the one to Washington, my father—" His speech seemed a trifle halted. "Father ordered another one for Natalia and Estella to make use of while I was traveling." He stood up. "If you'll excuse me."

I watched as he walked across the boulders to where Lawry and Meredyth sat on some rocks along the shore. What on earth caused his moods to change so drastically from one day—one moment—to the next? I was happy he was being taciturn, though. Maybe if he kept it up, I would forget all about the existence of those green eyes and that gorgeous smile.

Sitting alone, I couldn't help my gaze from wandering out to the ocean's surface. So this was where my mother had died, along the jagged coast of this island.

I couldn't look away, and I wouldn't allow myself to cry, though the tears burning my eyes were putting up a good fight. Before I had the help of the photograph Claudine had given me, I'd hardly been able to remember what my mother looked like.

Nathan returned to me sooner than I'd expected. Honestly, I'd figured he'd had enough of my company. He'd certainly been acting that way.

"I am going to hike out onto Castle Rock. Would you care to join me?" There was a strange, eager look in his eyes, so different from the shielded one that had been there before.

And why he thought to ask me such a nonsensical question, I could hardly tell. But since he was the one doing the asking, I couldn't help but answer, "Of course." I stood to my feet.

I found it almost impossible to refuse anything he asked.

He shrugged his jacket off and threw it upon the rocks, pulled off his cravat, and unfastened the top buttons of his shirt. Then he looked at me and smiled.

I hadn't moved. I just stood there, captivated by the sight of him.

"You'll want to take off your boots." He crouched down to unlace and remove his shoes. Once he was barefoot and had his trousers rolled to his ankles, he looked up. "Do you need my help?"

"If you wouldn't mind." I had no qualms about removing my boots, though I knew it was socially inappropriate—especially since he was helping me do so.

"I wouldn't mind at all, actually."

Nathan held my hand as I removed my boots with the other. He kept hold of me as he led me to the low areas of the rocks close to the water's surface, then up to the large boulder. The sharp rocks dug into the tender bottoms of my feet, but I made a point not to look as if it affected me.

He let go of my hand once I was standing safely atop Castle Rock, facing the ocean. He circled around me, over and over, walking just as easily as if he were on level land.

"You're standing so very still," he remarked.

"It's safest that way." Truthfully, I hardly trusted myself to walk without using him for balance.

"Are you enjoying yourself now that we're not aboard a boat?"

"Mostly." I caught his eye as he turned to pace around me again. I wished to see a glimpse of that eager look in his eyes from before, but it was long gone. "Believe me, I'm just as astonished as you are." The sound of my own laughter surprised me and made him smile.

"And just why do you suppose you're enjoying yourself so much?"

"I believe it has to do with these rocks."

By the expression on his face, that was clearly not how he'd expected me to answer.

"They make me feel safe." I wished I knew what he did expect from me.

"Why is that?"

"They're unmovable, constant. No matter how the tide tries to reach them, it can't."

He stopped circling and stood before me, near enough to lean into…if I wanted to.

"You always seem to see things in such a unique way."

The breadth of his shoulders, so close and covered only by a white shirt, blocked my view of the ocean entirely, and I suddenly had the unreasonable desire to feel his arms around me again.

My gaze darted from his chest to his face. "Most people simply don't stop to analyze what is going on before their very eyes."

"And yet, you're so blind." He resumed circling slowly around me.

"On the contrary, I'm extremely perceptive."

"As you say, Amaryllis, but how have you perceived me? In truth?"

"I hardly think that has anything to do with what we're speaking about." I was unwilling to verbally respond to such a question, so I asked, "And why do you keep calling me 'Amaryllis'? I haven't—"

"Why do you, Amaryllis, stubbornly insist upon calling me 'Mr. Everstone,' when I've asked you not to?" He was behind me again. I was about to turn to him when I was stopped by his next sentence. "If I could have the great fortune of having everyone in the world forget I was ever born into the Everstone family, I would begin with you."

"And I would be the first to eagerly consent!"

"Well, that's a start, I suppose," I barely heard him say behind me. "Before I get off subject, I need to tell you something. But you have to promise me...."

He stood before me again, holding my hands in his. Without warning, he led me down to where the tide licked the rocks at the edge of the water. I couldn't see anyone from where we stood, and I was certain no one could see us either. What on earth would the others think we were doing?

And what *were* we doing, exactly?

Standing before me with his hands now upon my shoulders, Nathan again blocked my view of the water. "I need you to trust me, Amaryllis."

And for the first time, I realized that I did.

Nathan had been the reason I'd boarded the schooner, and he was the reason I was standing on the edge of the treacherous ocean—two things I'd adamantly refused to do for most of my life. When I didn't answer audibly, Nathan let go of my shoulders and paced along the rocks behind me.

"I want you, of all people, to know the truth."

Fascinated by his words, I turned to face him, but something snagged my dress, and I completely lost my footing. As I reached for his arm, I just missed and barely grazed the fine material of his shirtsleeve. Since he was facing the other direction, he didn't realize what was happening—until it was too late.

The last thing I saw before tumbling off the edge of the rocks and into the frigid ocean was the look upon his face as he realized he could do nothing but watch as I did so.

I was stunned, first by that look, and then by the cold, salty water as it enveloped me, just as I'd imagined it would do in my never-ending nightmares.

My head broke the surface, and I gasped for air, my chest constricting with a suffocating tightness. My lungs felt full, and I was certain I knew just what my mother had felt in her last moments before death had overtaken her.

The water was deeper than I'd imagined. I kicked desperately to find something to vault my feet off of, but the sharp rocks under the water's surface only scraped into my shins through my dress as it twisted about my legs, making my every movement cumbersome. The heaviness of the soaked material threatened to pull me under as the waves pushed me into the rocks, then turned to pull me out to sea. Struggling to stay afloat, I clawed at the rocks in hopes of gaining a grip on something...anything.

When I finally had a firm hold, I quickly realized it was of Nathan as he knelt over the edge of the water. His hands held my upper arms with a viselike grip, but all I could focus on was the fact that he was kneeling on the sharp rocks, in all likeliness ruining his trousers, for my sake. I kept trying to climb out of the water, feebly trying to grab anything except for him, but it seemed impossible.

"Hold on to me, Amaryllis! Keep holding on!" he demanded. I heard Meredyth scream my name and then Nathan's name. And then mine again. All the while, it was as if time stood still. My arms and legs were numb, and my eyes and nose burned as I gagged on the salty water. Something deep inside felt as if it was squeezing the life from me, and it kept tightening about my chest, preventing me from taking another breath.

Why was I still in the water? Did Nathan truly have ahold of me? Was he going to save me, or was he going to let me drown? And which would I prefer?

I felt so weak, so faint. I just wanted to let go of everything.

As those morbid thoughts crossed my mind, Nathan at last pulled me from the bitterly cold water. But, oh, if I'd been cold before! The breeze, which had felt so marvelously refreshing during lunch, now whipped around me like painful icicles. My teeth chattered loudly, and there was nothing I could do to stop my whole body from shaking uncontrollably against Nathan as my arms again clung to his neck.

FOURTEEN

The Bailey Hill Hotel

"What do girls do who haven't any mothers
to help them through their troubles?"
—Louisa May Alcott, *Little Women*

The short ride back to the Bailey Hill Hotel took forever with Meredyth pressed in close, hugging me. Fortunately, the woolen blanket she'd wrapped around me was thick enough to protect her dress from also becoming soaked through.

Once we made it to the hotel, Nathan situated Meredyth and me in a hotel room on the first floor.

"Elle, she's already had the worst day imaginable," I heard Nathan say as they left the room. "We really must do all we are able...." And the door closed behind them.

Meredyth started a bath for me in the large claw-foot tub in the private washroom while I sat upon the tall cherry four-poster bed, still cold, dripping wet, and wrapped in the wool blanket.

My gaze went from Meredyth to the stunning magnificence of the bedchamber. The molding, the marble fireplace, the silk sheets, the elaborate wallpaper...everything about the decor was quite the opposite of what I'd expected from the quaint exterior of the hotel.

I stood and walked across the room to the mirror above the bureau. My hair had come completely undone and was a stringy, tangled mess down my back.

Before long, Nathan returned to the room carrying a small trunk. He placed it gently on the floor before me and then left again. Estella, who had entered behind him, remained.

"There should be something in here that fits you." She opened the lock to the trunk with a tiny key attached to a hotel key ring. "We often leave trunks of personal items at our father's hotels, in case we're in the neighborhood and find ourselves in need of something."

I hardly cared that it was the longest string of words she'd ever said to me, or that she looked as if she didn't really want to loan me any of her personal garments. I was simply thankful to have something dry to change into, no matter whose it was.

After my hot bath, Meredyth and Estella helped me into the blue and white striped dress that Estella had selected for me to wear.

"Amaryllis, on account of everything you've been through today, Nathan wants us to take the train home from Lynn." I felt immense relief at Meredyth's words and tried not to dwell on Nathan's involvement in the plan.

Estella immediately left the room, most likely to have a word with her brother about the plans for the remainder of the day.

As soon as the door closed, Meredyth sat upon a chair and had me sit on an ottoman in front of her. Taking ahold of my hair, she attempted to comb out the wet tangles with a brush from Estella's trunk. But then she asked, "Amaryllis, are you truly interested in marrying Jay Crawford?"

"Oh, I see. Are you worried that Estella's in love with him?" I let her jerk my head about. I wasn't about to turn and face her.

"I know Estella's in love with him. She has been for years."

The news brought to mind all the covert glances I'd witnessed between Jay and Estella since the moment I'd first met them at the train station in March.

Meredyth tugged at my hair again. "And I don't think you are."

I was unaccustomed to hearing such straightforward proclamations from blithe Meredyth Summercourt.

"Does it matter?" I asked.

"It does if you want someone else."

I didn't like the implications of her statement, and I thought long and hard about how to put an end to the unwelcome conversation. I realized suddenly the reason I'd always liked Meredyth so much: She was usually content to let people keep their inner struggles to themselves. Just like I was.

"And who do you think I want?" I couldn't help but feel defensive, betrayed. This was Meredyth, after all. One of the very few women in my life I thought I could trust.

"It's quite obvious who you want, Amaryllis, and that he wants you just as badly."

"You're talking nonsense. I don't want any man, but I'll settle for Jay because...." I couldn't believe the words were making their way out of my mouth, out of my heart. "I will delight in the Lord, and He shall give me the desires of my heart. He will create the desires of my heart, Meredyth. Not the other way around."

"Trust in Him, and He shall bring it to pass," she finished the couplet of verses for me. "You don't trust anyone, Amaryllis, let alone God." She'd given up on my hair. It was still too much of a wet mess to fix with the few hairpins we'd been able to salvage.

Exasperated with the conversation, I crossed the room and took a mug from the coffee tray that had been delivered by the hotel staff while I'd been bathing. I poured the now lukewarm coffee and downed it in one gulp. Putting the mug down, I turned back to Meredyth. "And what are the desires of your heart, Meredyth? What do you want? Or *who*, should I ask? Are you dragging Lawry's heart all around town while you're pining away for your Mr. Mysterious?"

"Lawry's heart is hardly involved when it comes to me, Amaryllis. Not like that. And stop changing the subject." She stood from her chair. "I know it's your favorite thing to do. We're talking about what you want right now, because it's of the utmost importance you recognize that you can't marry Crawford if you're in love with—"

A loud pounding sounded on the door, and it didn't stop until I hurried across the room and opened it. Nathan stood there, his hand still poised, ready to knock once more. He, too, had put on dry clothes, since rescuing me and carrying me around afterward had soaked his attire.

"Are you—" He smiled down at me, taller than ever. Beginning with my unshod feet, his eyes traveled upward until I could tell he was taking in the sight of my long, loose, dark hair. And then his gaze met mine. I couldn't help but take in a deep breath. He cleared his throat. "I've called the station in Lynn. We'll need to leave soon to make the earliest train."

"Where's Lawry?"

"He and Crawford are sailing my boat down to Boston. You girls are stuck with me."

"Nathan Everstone." Meredyth came to stand behind me, making a point to finish the sentence he'd interrupted so perfectly.

"What?" he asked.

"Nothing." Meredyth shrugged. She took my hand from the door and gently started to push it closed. Speaking to Nathan through the crack, she added, "We'll be right out. As you can see, Amaryllis is still only half dressed." She closed the door the rest of the way.

"I am not half dressed. I'm just missing my boots."

"It's a wonder you have no idea how appealing you are, Amaryllis. Clearly, you don't know how a man thinks. Especially that one."

When Meredyth and I walked to the lobby, she was strangely quiet. Perhaps she'd realized she'd overstepped the boundaries of our friendship. In the past, we'd both held back. That's just how we were. And up until that afternoon, it had seemed perfectly fine.

Nathan was nowhere in sight, and I couldn't help but wonder where he'd disappeared to. Not that I needed or wanted to see any more of him after such a day.

If I thought the man confounded me before, I hardly knew what to think after such an afternoon. Was this all part of his game? Was he trying to fool me so completely? Why would he do such a thing? Did it have something to do with Claudine's request? Or something to do with his father? Was Meredyth seriously so blind to what Nathan was up to?

And did she really believe I wanted anything to do with him?

I suddenly wanted to know just what Nathan thought of Jay's marriage proposal. His rude words from the DeLagrange Ball still bothered me, and I was convinced that my hearing even more of his overconfident arrogance would benefit me more than anything else.

Meredyth, who seemed satisfied to wait for Nathan to come looking for us, took a seat in the lobby next to Estella, while I left the building in search of him.

As I crossed the yard, I spotted Nathan walking straight for me. He seemed distracted, for he was staring at the ground and didn't see me until he'd practically passed me by. Finally looking up, he stopped about four feet away from me. "I need to have a word with you."

"Certainly, Mr. Everstone. Have you not yet had your fill of my company today?"

"Far from it," he said dryly as he guided me to the stables, his hand holding firmly to my elbow.

We walked into the nearly empty stable, and I stopped in front of one of the stalls.

"It's too bad we didn't have time for riding while we were here," I said. "I ride my horse through the Common every morning, while you're busy slaving away at your father's offices." I stepped up onto the slotted gate of a stall, gripped the top bar, and rested my chin on my hands. I kissed the air a few times, trying to gain the attention of the flaxen beauty inside the stall, but she kept eating her hay, refusing to acknowledge my existence.

"Do you often notice how busy I am?"

"No," I stated, again becoming frustrated with him...and with myself. "Lawry mentions it almost every day."

"You're so good at—"

"I'm not good, Mr. Everstone." I turned to him sharply. I had no idea what he'd been about to say, but I took my chance to steer the conversation back to where I needed it to go. "Take my apprehension about marrying Jay, for example. It was heartless of me. I should have gladly accepted."

His expression startled me. All the color had drained from his face, and he looked as if I'd kicked him in the stomach. But he recovered himself quickly.

"Crawford needs to take care. I don't know what he was doing, asking you such a thing."

His sudden moodiness surprised me, but this was the reason I'd wanted to speak to him again in the first place. We were becoming much too friendly with each other. For supposedly being such good friends with Jay, Nathan continually astonished me by always seeming to spit his friend's name. Did it perhaps have something to do with Meredyth's being convinced that Estella was in love with Jay?

"I'm sorry you're disappointed about your friend's proposed affiliations with me, Mr. Everstone—if that is the case. Truthfully, I have no idea why you should care so much one way or the other...."

He shook his head, and my stomach contracted. He looked at me steadily, wordlessly. Then he motioned with his eyes to the other side of the stables, where a groom had come in and was leading out a carriage horse.

He stepped closer and whispered, "How is it that you can take everything I've ever said to you and twist it around until it seems I meant something entirely different?"

The groom had taken the carriage horse outside by then, leaving us alone. I stepped down from the stall door, intent on heading back to the hotel without him, when Nathan gently took hold of my shoulders and turned me to face him. I tried to back away, only to press myself against the stall.

"If you'll allow me, Amaryllis, to tell you just what I think of you, I believe you may be somewhat surprised. I'd like you to know what I've come to find over the last month or so." His eyes continually scanned my face, as if trying to read me. "It is, in fact, that I've never admired anyone as much as I admire you. I have such a strong affinity for you. And only God knows why, for you're the most irritatingly self-protective young lady I've ever met." He leaned in closer, and I was unable to breathe. "And your constant frankness in giving your opinion proves to me you're an extremely honest person, which I value immensely." His fingers grazed the bridge of my nose, then trailed down my cheek to my jaw. "And, of course, there's this face...and your amazingly expressive eyes. You can't help but display, to anyone willing to take note, exactly what you're thinking at all times."

I couldn't think of a word to say. My poor heart wasn't experienced enough to handle the way Nathan Everstone caused it to tumble around in my chest, and I was quite ready for our conversation to be finished. His face was much too close to mine, and all I could think of was my horribly intense dream...and how badly I had wanted him to kiss me.

"Please, Mr. Everstone. We really don't need to press our luck and have your father come home to find we actually like each other." I tried to sound as unyielding as possible as I pressed my hands to his hard chest. He refused to move.

"That we like each other?" He took one of my hands and pressed it to the stall door with his, palm to palm. "No, I suppose that wouldn't do at all."

"You agree."

"It sounds like a terrible idea." He allowed me to finally push him away, but he didn't let go of the hand he'd been holding against the wall.

Still grasping my hand, he situated it at the crook of his arm and headed toward the hotel, as if we were merely taking a pleasant stroll together through the yard to meet Meredyth and Estella, who were standing near the carriage waiting to take us to Lynn.

FIFTEEN

A Ride

"*It would be so nice if something made sense for a change.*"
—Lewis Carroll, *Alice's Adventures in Wonderland*

Amaryllis, what do you think of Nathan?" Lawry asked as we walked toward the stable at Hilldreth a few days later. "I hardly know him." My words reminded me of what Nathan had said to me at the library about Nicholette. In almost the same way that she'd convinced herself she was in love with him, I'd convinced myself I couldn't stand him—which really wasn't the truth at all. I had a strong suspicion that neither one of us truly knew him.

"You must be pleased with him. How could you not be? Every woman in Boston under the age of thirty wants to marry him."

"Or marry his inheritance."

"Do you really find him to be so entirely disagreeable?" Lawry looked at me as if I'd lost my mind.

"Oh, don't get me wrong—I can't deny he's an extremely attractive man, Lawry. But he's much too arrogant and overbearing for my taste." As I finished my little speech, I hoped Lawry would repeat my every embellished word to his friend.

The sight of a Shire horse with the same rare black-and-white tobiano markings as my horse caught my eye. My father had worked for years to create such an uncommon look for his Shires, something I knew only because of one of the few letters he'd written me over the years. "Do you know whose horse that is?"

"That's Thunder; Nathan's horse. He just had him shipped down from his family's cottage on Mount Desert Island this week. It's rather similar to yours, isn't it?"

That Nathan Everstone had known of my father and his horse farm in Maine was one thing, but the thought that he might have actually been there was quite upsetting.

I'd never even been there.

Resisting my desire to ask more questions, I turned to greet Meredyth, who'd ridden up to us alongside her older brother Garrett. They both rode stunning white Arabians. As I smiled a greeting at them both, I caught a glimpse of Nathan coming out of the stable, staring at me with an unyielding gaze.

I quickly averted my eyes to the young groom struggling to lead my horse from the stable behind Nathan. Truelove immediately recognized the other Shire horse and headed straight for him.

When it became evident the groom wasn't used to handling such a large horse, I hastily walked over and took Truelove's reins, leading her to where Nathan's horse was tied. Thunder had noticed her by then and had begun nodding his head.

Then the giant horse nuzzled me with his head, causing me to step back against something solid. I quickly turned to discover it was Nathan's chest. His hands gently gripped my arms, and for a moment, I was unable to move, stunned by the unexpected contact. I managed to free myself most ungracefully, only to turn around and find Nathan looking down at me with an exquisite, crooked smile.

"Not many young ladies have the courage to ride a draft horse around the fashionable streets of Boston."

I refused to respond, letting him silently help me onto Truelove, before he mounted his own horse.

The exasperating dream of his kissing me, and my original childhood nightmare of my mother's death and being chased by Nathan's father, seemed to take turns occupying my mind at night to the point that trying to balance my fears and desires during my waking hours was beginning to wear on me. I hardly understood them and didn't know what to do about them. The only thing I did know, without a doubt, was that they were clouding my judgment concerning Nathan. And it didn't help my efforts that I was forced—by my own horse, no less—to ride uncomfortably close to him as we headed down the street behind Lawry and Meredyth. I'm sure they looked a sight—two black-and-white tobiano-marked Shire draft horses trotting side by side down the streets of Boston.

We reached the Common without a word having passed between us.

"How is it—" I began, and then stopped myself. I waited a few seconds before continuing with a more direct tactic. "You bought your horse from my father."

He smiled but didn't answer. We guided our horses down the well-manicured trail.

"Are you not going to answer me?"

"I don't remember a specific question, Miss Brigham. I do recall an observation, though, and now I will supply my own. Your mare's name is Truelove."

"Yes, it is."

"Did you name her yourself?"

"Yes," I admitted, feeling incredibly uncomfortable. It was such a foolish name for a horse. I had been as shocked as anyone when my father had sent her to The Boston Conservatory's stables for me just as I was beginning my classes. I would be the first to admit I'd named her while in an uncharacteristically euphoric state, so happy was I to have a horse of my own again after so many years without one.

I turned away from Nathan, focusing on the new leaves on the trees surrounding us. If he wasn't going to tell me what I wanted to know, then I simply wasn't going to speak to him.

My gaze traveled from Lawry and Meredyth, who were riding ahead of us, to a nearby bench where Nicholette Fairbanks sat with two other young women. Her eyes locked with mine, and I saw the same evident hatred as always. It didn't help that every time I saw her, I seemed to be with Nathan.

The thought of him being married to her made my stomach churn.

I had to admit, though, they would look utterly astonishing together. I groaned inwardly when my thoughts drifted toward the many aspects that marriage entailed. They would, no doubt, create beautiful, angelic-looking children.

I swiftly decided not to dwell on the likelihood of Nathan's marrying Nicholette, or anyone else, for that matter. The thought seemed to cause a streak of jealousy to race through my veins. I made myself stop staring at her and glanced back at Nathan. He was still looking at me, still smiling his irresistibly gorgeous smile. It was such an effective weapon. And that was a fact he clearly knew all too well.

"I've never seen a sidesaddle made for such a broad horse," he said, ignoring the fact that I was ignoring him. What I couldn't ignore, when I looked his way again, was how his eyes matched our lush green surroundings at the park.

"My father sent it along with Truelove while I was attending The Boston Conservatory."

"Your father was British, wasn't he?"

"Yes," I said. But I found myself unwilling to stop with that tiny bit of information. "I hardly knew him, though. After my mother died, I suppose all he could see in me was a living reminder of her." I hated that Nathan Everstone, of all people, was the one and only person able to compel me to say more than I wanted to, simply by being beside me.

"That's not true."

"And what would you know about it, Mr. Everstone?"

"If I answer your questions, will you allow yourself to act as if you enjoy my company?"

I wanted so badly to agree but instead replied, "That would be unwise."

"Why?" He looked at me sternly, his brows furrowed. It was at that precise moment I realized I'd forgotten to look up the word *inordinately*.

The sentence he'd quoted to me from my own book came crashing through my mind. "*Whensoever a man desireth anything inordinately, he becomes restless in himself.*"

"I hope you realize, Miss Brigham, that even if you keep presenting this brick wall you've constructed about yourself, I will eventually find a way to climb it. I have my ways, you know."

Wyatt Harden's warnings came to mind, and I felt extremely uncomfortable visualizing just what Nathan implied. Not that I was certain what that was.

As I looked past him again, Garrett Summercourt rode up beside us. We greeted each other, and then Garrett was the one riding alongside me instead of Nathan.

Garrett had called upon me during my "at homes" a few times, but I noticed that he, like Nathan, was never at the society events Claudine insisted Lawry and I attend. I often wondered what Nathan and his friends did with all their spare time while I was trapped in society's web of fashion and manners.

"I heard you postponed answering Crawford's proposal," Garrett said.

I nudged Truelove into a canter in order to put some distance between us and Nathan. He was still riding close behind, and I preferred that he not overhear this particular conversation. I also wondered if anything was sacred between Lawry and his close-knit circle of friends and why none of them seemed to have any hesitation to bring up the most inappropriate subjects with me. Did they speak to all young ladies with such candor?

"Are you going to tell me that by so doing, I've likely thrown away my best chance of inheriting the Landreth fortune?"

He laughed to himself before answering me. "Surely, you don't believe that. There are plenty of young men who are in love with you already. Crawford was simply the first to act. It only surprised me you didn't accept. I thought you seemed well suited. You're originally from Washington, are you not?"

"I am," I answered with a sly smile. "But about plenty of young men being in love with me, you must be jesting. No one loves me."

Garrett certainly wasn't in love with me, that much was clear. He wouldn't have started such a conversation if he were.

"What about Wyatt Harden?"

"An opportunist of the highest order," I said with utmost confidence. "Being as he's Claudine's attorney, I'm sure he knows all about the details of my inheritance."

Garrett brought his horse a little closer, leaned in toward me, and whispered with all seriousness, "What of Nathan Everstone, then? You could say no such thing of him."

I glanced at Garrett's smiling face and then looked straight ahead, unable to believe my ears.

I could hear the hoofbeats of Nathan's horse still following close behind us, so I answered Garrett quietly, "That you would even suggest such a thing makes me fear you are in grave danger of losing your senses. That gentleman is definitely not in love with me."

"Are you so certain? I've never seen him conduct himself in such an unwarranted manner in all the years I've known him." His words set off a jumbled mess of scattered thoughts concerning

Bram Everstone and his eldest son—two men who, I was beginning to realize, seemed nothing at all alike.

"If you must know, it is all a farce. The only reason he's been playing at giving me his undivided attention at all is because Claudine asked him to do so in order to ensure my popularity." It sounded like such a silly excuse, but I knew it to be true.

"You really think so?"

"I know so. In fact, we are barely able to tolerate one another."

Garrett seemed genuinely preoccupied by my answer, but he said no more.

I was unable to see Lawry or Meredyth anywhere. How strange. I stole a glance behind me to find Nathan watching intently. Turning again to Garrett, I asked, "May I ask a question that may sound rather odd?"

"You may ask me anything you wish, Amaryllis."

"Do you happen to know what the word *inordinately* means?"

"I believe it is used to describe a state of being unrestrained or unreasonable, for example, in one's conduct or feelings."

Somehow that made sense to me. It was true—Nathan seemed to act quite inordinately every time he was near me.

I knew my thoughts regarding him were anything but consistent. He made me constantly question my opinion of him. Had he truly become a Christian while in Washington? Or had he been telling me only what I wanted to hear? Despite all my questions and all the rumors I'd heard about what he was like, there was something that made me want to keep seeing him...to keep talking to him.

I didn't want him to be like his father. I wanted to hope, for some preposterous reason, that he was indeed the person Lawry and Meredyth both believed him to be—even if it did seem highly improbable.

A few moments later, Nathan took his place beside me again, and Garrett wandered off on his own. My mind was still trying to grasp Garrett's definition of *inordinately*. What had Nathan meant by quoting a sentence using that word to me?

And that was when I realized where I was.

We were nearing the north side of the park that bordered the Granary Burial Ground, where my mother had been laid to rest. I'd tried hard not to think about the place during the years I'd been in Boston. No one had ever thought to take me there, and I'd never found the nerve to ask to go...until that moment.

It was an irrational idea, but I was suddenly determined.

"Is something on your mind?" Nathan asked as he turned to face me.

"Do you happen to know where the Landreth burial plots are located in that burial ground?" I asked him quickly before I could think of all the reasons I should not. He alone had that amazing effect on me, making me more courageous than I ever thought I could be.

"I do." He looked both surprised and glad to be of service. "Would you like me to take you to them? They're actually not far from the street."

I didn't care that it was Nathan Everstone who had finally been the one to ask me. I simply answered, "Yes."

SIXTEEN

The Granary Burial Ground

"There are moments when,
whatever be the attitude of the body,
the soul is on its knees."
—Victor Hugo

It did not take Nathan long to lead me to the one place in Boston I wished to see above all others. I hadn't realized it until that moment, but it was true. There, against the background of a small gathering of pine trees, not far from Hilldreth, I found what was left of my mother's family.

In between the gravestones of my mother and my grandfather was my grandmother's:

Marielle Abernathy Landreth,
Wife of Jasper Landreth III
Died October the 1st, 1888, in the 69th year of her age

What I hadn't noticed eleven years prior was a small gravestone beside them that read:

Jasper Landreth IV, 1842–1843

Standing before the graves, I realized my mother was the only child of theirs who had survived infancy. And yet, they'd disowned her because she hadn't married Bram Everstone, as they'd wished.

Nathan watched me closely with another one of those indecipherable looks.

I noticed many of the elaborate gravestones behind him had the name "Everstone" engraved on them. "Is this where your family is buried, also?"

"Everyone save for my mother. She's buried on Mount Desert Island near Rockwood." He surprised me with such a sincere answer. "Your mother died the same...." His voice faltered as he took a step closer to my mother's grave.

"Yes, the same summer I visited Mount Desert Island and met your father."

He retraced his steps, his perfectly fitted suit jacket outlining his broad shoulders—and keeping my attention for far too long. Turning to the gravestone, I ran my fingers over my mother's name. *Elinorah Landreth*. The name "Brigham" was forever missing, as if she'd never even met my father, let alone married him.

My eyes roamed across the rows of gravestones as I sat before my mother's grave, unconcerned about what might become of my riding habit as a result.

Everything looked the same, even the gravel path down the hill where I'd been mercilessly shoved into the Everstone carriage and completely severed from the only life I'd ever known. My eyes searched the towering branches of the trees. They were much bigger now.

I tried to remember what my mother had been like, but the only thing that came to mind, as always, was the empty hole she'd left behind by dying...all because of my rebellious actions one day.

I shook my head to dispel the thoughts. I would not think of them. It was better not to. It was easier not to. I glanced up to see Nathan pacing circles around a centrally located towerlike monument, seemingly deep in thought.

It was so strange that I was there with him, of all people.

I stood and leaned against a nearby gravestone. He started toward me.

"Will you join me?" The determined set of his brows caught me off guard, and I simply stared at him for a moment. It really wasn't that difficult to do, as I kept proving.

I hardly looked forward to hearing what he might want to say to me, since he was acting in such a strangely subdued manner. The last time he'd spoken to me, touched me, was still so fresh in my mind, even though it had been over a week ago.

What if he tried to kiss me again? Would I be strong enough to resist?

I noticed our horses nuzzling together under the shade tree we'd tethered them to. It was heartbreaking to think they would soon be separated once again. But, regardless of what their future held, the affectionate display made me smile.

"I wish I could make you do that." Nathan's voice startled me. He'd walked up beside the gravestone I was leaning upon. He propped himself against it, supported by his left hand.

"Smile? I smile all the time."

"I've noticed. And at times, you even laugh...only never for me. Do you do that on purpose?"

"You do frustrate me," I admitted.

"May I clear up a few of your frustrations, then?" He leaned in closer.

"That is not very likely." I turned my face from his. "I'm sure your efforts to clear things up will only prove to make you seem all the more puzzling."

"Do I puzzle you, as well as frustrate you?"

I did not want to answer any such question, and I did not like the fact he'd dared to ask it of me. Or that he was so close.

"And here, I'd hoped you'd figure me out so easily. I am doing everything I know to help you along without being too blatantly obvious. But perhaps that's what you need."

I stood up and headed to my horse.

"Wait." Nathan raced up beside me and grabbed the inside of my elbow. The earnest look in his eyes made my breath catch. When I sat upon the closest gravestone, he began pacing again, raking his fingers through his hair. "Yes, I bought my horse from your father, years ago, in fact."

"You've been to my father's farm in Maine?" Hearing the truth created even more jealousy within me. When had I become so covetous?

"I used to have a large role in purchasing the horses for Greaghan Lumber. I'm even the one who convinced your father to send you Truelove when he did."

"You knew him so well?"

"I did. And when I left Boston two years ago, Amaryllis, it was with an agreement to lease his place in Washington."

I stood, unable to comprehend the possibility.

His place...meaning my place.

"On my Whidbey Island?" A torrent of tears threatened to break through, but I held them back.

"Amaryllis, I've wanted to tell you everything ever since learning of your stance regarding my father, but I need you to promise me...I need your utmost secrecy."

"You know you have it." I was stunned by how much I wanted his trust.

He began walking back and forth before me once more.

Did he always do that when he had something difficult to communicate?

"When my mother died, Natalia and I were given a letter that had been written the summer before we were born." He looked up, and when he saw my gaze following him, he continued. "As far as I know, no one knew anything about it until the day we opened the seal to her will." He ran his hands over his face. "Natalia and I have always known that we were born a mere six months after our mother married Bram Everstone. It really isn't as uncommon a problem as it should be...once a marriage takes place, society has a way of overlooking such things. In the letter, she disclosed an account of what exactly happened the summer before I was born."

I sat back down, feeling the blood drain from my face.

"My mother had been engaged to a man named Axel Olander. He was killed in some sort of accident while inspecting a lumber camp for my mother's father, whom he happened to work for."

Nathan's brows were drawn together, while his eyes focused on my boots sticking out from under the hem of my dress. The sincerity in his voice riveted me. I could have listened to the deep sound, edged with such sincerity, for the rest of my life. "My mother was already pregnant when she married Bram Everstone. She married him because your mother didn't."

He knew. He knew all about it. But what did it mean for him to bring it up to me so openly?

Nathan walked forward slowly, reaching out to the gravestone I sat upon, his eyes never leaving my face. As he came closer, the truth of what he was saying pierced me like an arrow through my heart.

"Bram Everstone isn't truly your father." For a fraction of a second, the thought seemed oddly liberating.

"No, he's not."

"Did you ever find out anything more of Axel Olander?"

"I've done some investigating, but there was little to find out. He was from Sweden, I believe. I imagine I must resemble him. Just look at me."

I did, for what turned out to be a rather long, suspended moment, before I was able to speak. "But Bram Everstone obviously loves you like a son and wants the best for you." I didn't move an inch. There was such a war inside me concerning Nathan Everstone and his astonishing revelations. Such confessions from him grew my trust beyond what I thought was reasonable.

"He isn't a bad man, Amaryllis. Not like you think. What do you think he's done that you hate him so? That you fight everything in you telling you that we're—"

"Mr. Everstone." Suddenly his formal name sounded so rigid upon my lips, and I wondered for the first time what it would be like to give in to the friendship, and, quite possibly, to so much more...whatever it was he'd been trying to form between us for weeks on end.

He remained standing there, so close, staring at me without a word. If only he knew it would take just a few more words before he was scaling those walls he'd alluded to before. If only he knew to finish that last sentence.

Could I believe he wanted nothing of his share of the Everstone family's twenty-million-dollar inheritance? In the end, it would surely sway any deciding factors against doing what Bram Everstone wanted—which was for Nathan to marry Nicholette. How could it not?

"Did you like living on Whidbey Island?" I took my chance to divert the conversation. It was an irrational question, and I was shocked by how much I desired to hear an affirmative answer. Would Nathan end up going back to Washington with Lawry someday? How bleak my world would become if those two particular gentlemen left for the West Coast together, and I was never able to follow.

"I'd return in a heartbeat." He stepped closer.

"Are you planning to go back with Lawry?" I looked away, determined to ignore his proximity.

He leaned in, moving his hand along the gravestone in my direction. "Would you come with me?" The hint of yearning in his smooth, calm voice sent shivers up my spine. I closed my eyes for a brief moment, feeling almost light-headed.

When I looked up again, I was stunned to see he seemed to be in earnest. Where was the cocksure arrogance I believed he attained in spades? Fighting the desire to stay right where he had me, I slipped from where his arms were so close to being wrapped around me and quickly walked toward our horses.

"Are you still afraid of trusting me?" Nathan sounded as if the notion astonished him.

I walked on, fighting against the strong sense of camaraderie our serious discussion had stirred in my heart.

He followed me down the stony trail, the rocks crunching loudly under our feet.

I faced him again. "What, because no one can resist you? Is that it?"

"No one, it seems, but you. And you're the only one I want."

I stood motionless, stunned by how his words were crushing my stern reservations. They were crumbled at my feet. I lifted my eyes to his and saw that they'd lost the standard, concealed look I was used to seeing. He suddenly seemed like an entirely different person. "Mr. Everstone, I need—"

He cupped my shoulders with his hands—one of his favorite things to do, it seemed.

"We need to go…find the others." I tried to dart away.

He released me as I was about to say something more—heaven only knew what. Without another word, only a rumbled groan from deep inside his chest, he stalked past me toward the horses.

As we rode to the entrance of the cemetery, I tried to put distance between us—a difficult feat, as our horses were still intent on being as close to each other as possible. My previous feelings of disdain and intolerance were entirely gone. It seemed as if every harsh thought I'd ever had of Nathan was forgotten and replaced with a rather odd feeling I hardly recognized.

Before urging Truelove to canter down the street ahead of him, toward my friends, I glanced up at him and winced at the hard, hurt look upon his face. And at the sight of that one awful, heartrending expression, I felt something in me shift.

I ignored it, of course. It was nothing.

Nothing I needed to dwell on, at least.

SEVENTEEN

Rumors and the Truth

"Hatred, by a gradual and quiet process,
will even be transformed to love...."
—Nathaniel Hawthorne, *The Scarlet Letter*

A few days later, Lawry invited Jay Crawford to join us for dinner.

I was beginning to realize what it was about Jay that bothered me. Even though he'd already proposed to me, he'd not once, before or since, tried to flirt with me. At least, not like Nathan insisted upon doing. Nor did he act obtuse, like Wyatt Harden did every time he came to Hilldreth. Jay had such a reserved nature, an almost statuesque poise to him, that I'd never been able to get behind.

Was he hiding something? I wasn't really sure what I thought of Jay, beyond that he was a welcome distraction to keep my mind off the fact that every time I found myself alone with Nathan I nearly allowed him to kiss me.

Surely, the dream I kept having was at fault.

I hated that in my dreams, I unwittingly allowed myself to delight in him. How could my mind so completely betray me? Or was it my heart? I could not tell. All I knew was that I needed to put a stop to the uncontrollable thoughts creating such rebellious feelings.

"If you want her, you have to tell her, Nathan. Don't leave her hanging, wondering what's wrong with you." Lawry's voice echoed loudly through the crack between the pocket doors of the study.

"You hardly understand. I've tried everything," Nathan's velvety voice answered, oblivious to my prying ears. "She's still annoyed with me. She hardly believes a word I say."

I stood perfectly still before the doors, hoping to figure out whom they were speaking of. Surely, it was Nicholette.

"You haven't tried everything."

"I've tried everything save for kissing her senseless. Not that I haven't wanted to."

"Well then, now you know what you must do. When does your father return? You have until then, correct?"

My heart plummeted to the floor. It had to be Nicholette. She was likely disgruntled by the fact that he'd practically ignored her existence since returning to Boston, and now she was obviously playing hard to get.

"Trust me, Lawry, this is the most difficult task I've ever taken up in my life...and he wants me to announce the engagement upon his arrival."

Nathan's words caught me off guard, and I backed away from the door. I couldn't stand to hear any more of the conversation. I shouldn't have tarried outside the door as long as I had.

His words, and the implications, nearly made it impossible for me to breathe.

As I finally took a breath and turned to make my way down the hall, the pocket doors opened.

"Amaryllis! We were wondering what was keeping you. Where's Jay?" Lawry ushered me into the room, as if the secrets shared a few moments earlier were not still hanging in the air.

"He's waiting in the drawing room." I stood at the threshold, refusing to go in. My mind raced with questions I would never dare ask.

Was Nathan, indeed, going to be engaged soon? Was he going to marry Nicholette? And did she deserve him?

I noticed a few of the photographs of Jay and me at the Common spread out on a rectangular white marble-topped table. Nathan held one of them in his hand. His brows were furrowed as he slowly lifted his gaze, meeting mine. There was something alarmingly heated about the look that made me want to dash from the room.

I suddenly felt as if I hardly knew him. It surprised me that he even recognized my existence. Not that he had acknowledged me much after the afternoon we'd spent together in the cemetery.

After that most enlightening conversation, he'd reverted to treating me as he most likely had wished to treat me all along—by ignoring me completely. But it finally made sense. He could not very well pretend to be interested in me when he was soon to announce his intention of marrying someone else.

⌒

As had become our habit, Claudine, Lawry, Nathan, and I, along with Jay, congregated in the drawing room after dinner for music and cards. It had become a comfortable routine to which I looked forward. However, Claudine had decided to retire early that evening, leaving me to entertain the three gentlemen all on my own.

"Amaryllis, may I turn your sheet music for you?" Jay asked from close beside me as I stood near the piano. He was acting oddly, and I wasn't sure I liked it. However, I couldn't be uncivil with him. I couldn't treat him as I'd treated Nathan on numerous occasions.

Nathan, who was so tough and arrogant...not much got through that hard exterior of his, whether good or bad. His confidence in himself baffled me. He simply went on as if he were invincible and could do anything and have whatever he wanted.

"That would be delightful." I intentionally looked across the room at Nathan, who smiled cynically back at me. And I knew why. He'd been almost exclusively the one to stand next to me, turning the pages of my sheet music unnecessarily, as I played by memory, since he'd returned to Hilldreth. I knew he'd been looking for the perfect opportunity to reveal to Claudine that I did not need the music.

It was undeniable that Nathan had not liked Jay's attentions toward me at dinner. I'd seen the covert looks they'd been giving each other. They were not at all amiable, and I was certain Estella was the reason. I thought it best to not make things worse between them, but then, who was Nathan to advise me whom I could and could not befriend? I certainly could not be friends with him. That much was certain.

And I was no one to him, which was even more certain.

When I'd finished playing, I headed to the other side of the room to sit with Lawry and Nathan, but Jay had other plans. He pulled out Felix Mendelssohn's *Hebrides Overture.* "Would you like to play a duet with me, Amaryllis? I remember you played this with Nicholette at a musicale a while back."

"Were you there? I don't remember seeing you."

"Yes, I was there. I was backstage most of the evening."

I looked up to find Nathan staring at me. I really didn't want to play a duet with Jay, nor did I want Jay to think I did. But I wanted very much for Nathan to think so.

He made me do the strangest things.

I'd played duets exclusively with my female classmates over the years, with the exception of Nicholette. And we'd played on two separate pianos.

I did not have the luxury of my own piano now, and I was far from prepared for the extreme awkwardness I knew I'd feel as Jay sat beside me on the bench. Especially when his fingers grazed mine as we played the rather long piece together. I was glad I'd never agreed to do such a thing with Nathan. My self-composure would have hardly survived.

After we finished, Jay led me to the sofa, where we both sat down.

Nathan and Lawry were seated across from us on the chairs near the fireplace.

No one said a word, so I smiled happily at Jay, with the intent of saying something ridiculously feminine. Looking about the room, I caught Nathan glaring at me.

The fact that I had done something to provoke such a horrible reaction from him made my heart sink. In all our conversations, he'd never once exhibited toward me such a striking glimpse of emotion, and I wasn't so sure I liked it.

It was clear he felt something very strong toward me, and for a second, I believed it to be hatred. Not just a vague inclination but pure and unfiltered hatred. I didn't like the feelings it caused in me at all. I would rather have liked to believe he cared nothing than that he hated me so. I looked cautiously at Jay again, who didn't seem to sense anything amiss.

I stood, crossed the room, took up the playing cards from the table, and began to shuffle them. I needed a distraction. Having Jay and Nathan in the same room was too unsettling.

Jay was my partner at cards that evening, and he sat across the table from me, which I suddenly, heartily welcomed. Watching Nathan hate me from across the table would have been more than I could stand. It was awful enough to have to sit next to him, knowing his eyes were on my every move.

I'd partnered with him only once, the evening before, and every time I'd looked up at him, he'd given me a strange, undecipherable look that caused tingles to run up my back. He seemed so discomposed all of a sudden. What had happened to the cool, collected Nathan Everstone from the cemetery?

And why did it make any difference to me?

I had plenty of proof he was, in essence, a womanizing flirt, and that I'd been nothing more to him than some sort of conquest fueled by Claudine's desire to have him pretend to be in love with me.

I was immediately ashamed of such bitter thoughts. Who was I, after all, but the daughter of the famously disinherited Elinorah Landreth and a father who had wanted nothing to do with me? I was no one.

And who was Nathan Everstone?

Oh, yes...only one of the richest, most-sought-after young men in all of New England. The most eligible bachelor Boston had to offer. Having him stay with us at Hilldreth had almost made me forget. He seemed so normal most of the time. He so easily fooled me.

"Amaryllis, Nathan and I were speaking earlier today about our time in Washington. You must have loved living out West as much as we did," Lawry said as he waited for Jay to take his turn.

"I did, and I've missed so much about it over the years." I glanced at Nathan, sitting to my left. His brows were furrowed as he studied his cards intently. "Mr. Everstone." He still didn't look up. "I didn't have a chance to ask you the last time we spoke, but how did my mother's house at Bruckerdale look when you were there last?"

I thought he'd not heard. But then he turned to me, just long enough to say, "Everything was still there, and extremely well taken care of."

Surely, he didn't mean everything of my mother's. That would have been impossible.

I knew that if I ended up returning to Washington one day, everything would be different. My life, in every sense, was vastly altered from what it had been back then. Everywhere since, I had been merely surviving. At least until recently, it seemed.

"Was it soon after you came east that your mother passed away?" Jay asked.

"Less than a month," I responded tersely. How was it that I attained more enjoyment out of sparring with Nathan Everstone than spending any amount of time in even pleasant conversation with Jay Crawford?

"You believe, if your family had stayed out West, that she would still be alive." Nathan's unexpected yet touching reply was absolutely correct. I'd never put it into words, yet I realized that it was exactly what I'd believed for almost eleven years. How appropriate that he would be the one to clarify my own feelings for me.

"Yes, I suppose I have, deep down."

"It was unquestionably God's will for you to come to the East Coast when you did, Amaryllis, no matter what the outcome of the trip was," Jay added mechanically.

I did not like his comment, and suddenly I didn't like him, either. I looked down at my cards and played my turn in silence. I then glanced at Nathan. It was his turn again.

It was at that precise moment I realized there were certain qualities I'd not found in most men that I'd begun to find in him. Of all people.

All I'd ever seemed to do was compare everyone to Nathan Everstone. And why? Because he was perfectly suited for me? That was preposterous—ridiculous, even.

But as I tried to convince myself I was utterly mistaken, I couldn't bring myself to pull my gaze from his face as he played his turn.

How was it that Nathan Everstone was the only man who'd even come close to being what I wanted or needed from a man?

Although it was now Jay's turn, my eyes refused to leave Nathan until he caught me staring. However, the look on his face had changed since the last time he'd looked up.

It was as if he knew exactly what I'd just been thinking.

That night, I awoke with a start, my heart beating wildly in my chest, my breathing ragged. Everything about the nightmare was familiar: the heat, the foggy mistiness surrounding me, the fear. But something was different. I was still deathly afraid, but of what, I didn't know. And it was only when I stopped trying to run that I was able to move. But again and again, I collided with huge, dark, damp stone walls. They were everywhere I turned.

Bram Everstone was somewhere in the distance, yelling, farther away than before. I looked around frantically and finally found the arched stone passageway where Nathan had been standing. It was closed in with jagged stones mortared in place, blocking the way.

Where had Nathan gone? Was he trapped on the other side of the wall? With his father?

Or was he with Nicholette?

My heart wrenched at the thought.

I tried to stop thinking of him, but it was impossible. It always had been. Instead, I thought of every inscrutable look he'd given me the night before. There had most definitely been hatred in some of those glances, but there was also something else. Suddenly when I thought of all the things he'd ever said to me, I doubted everything I'd thought I was sure of.

Sitting on the edge of my bed, I stared blankly into the mirror across the room. The dreamy haze began to clear from my mind, and for the first time in my life, I felt as if I hardly knew myself. I was powerless against the unrecognizable emotions suddenly racing through me.

The awful truth was that I'd fallen in love with him.

Nathan Everstone.

I quickly realized how truly dreadful it was to have such a profound awareness of another person. He would never be mine.

The prospect alone haunted me, creating a physical pain inside my chest.

How had I allowed such a thing to happen?

Was I not simply a game to him?

A game that he was winning quite effortlessly?

I knew, considering how well he could read me, that I was going to have to begin working very hard at not being myself. What that meant, I wasn't quite certain.

How had he described me? Frank, honest, and expressive?

Well then, it was time for me to be closed, careful, and unmoved. Three things I thought I'd mastered long before ever meeting Nathan Everstone.

EIGHTEEN

Winning

"Girls are so queer you never know what they mean.
They say no when they mean yes,
and drive a man out of his wits...."
—Louisa May Alcott, *Little Women*

I t wasn't often I had Hilldreth so blissfully to myself.

I'd purposefully declined Claudine's invitation to go calling down the street at Summerton, and I didn't have a clue where Lawry and Nathan had gone that morning.

Nor did I care.

Ever since the evening Jay had come to dinner, I'd successfully avoided associating with Nathan altogether. The more I kept away from him, the easier it was to avoid my treacherous feelings for him.

It turned out to be a dreary, rainy day. The house was overcome with steep shadows by the early afternoon, and it was probable that every one of my friends would wait until the rain had subsided before returning home. Taking this into consideration, I headed down to the study, which was one of my favorite rooms at Hilldreth. I sat in the comfy chair at the huge, ornately carved library desk at the end of the room to finish reading *Les Misérables*.

I'd read for only a short while when I heard the front door open, then Higgins welcome someone with familiarity. I stopped and listened to try to discern who it was. But all I heard was the front door slam shut, most likely from a gust of wind. Since I'd heard neither Aunt Claudine's nor Lawry's loud, energetic voice echoing through the hall, I knew it was likely Nathan. The pocket doors opened, and he stood there, putting my suspicions to rest. With his back to me, he closed the doors, shoved off his soaking-wet jacket, and ran his fingers through his hair. He finally noticed me when he turned around. He gave me a quick smirk as he whipped his cravat from his collar and tossed it over the back of a chair.

"What are you doing, sitting in a dark room on an already gloomy afternoon?" He crossed the room and lit the lamp on the table nearest me as he unbuttoned his collar.

"It's not that dark in here, Mr. Everstone. I had enough light coming in through the windows."

He sat down in one of the large leather chairs facing me. "Have I ever told you I adore how opinionated you are?" He paused, giving me that rare, radiant smile of his, looking as if he were measuring his next words. "And how beautiful, yet quaint, you look sitting there at that huge desk of your grandfather's."

Before I could respond, he continued, "I thought you'd be out with Claudine today, perhaps visiting Meredyth."

"Is that where you've been, calling upon Meredyth? Was Nicholette there?"

"I did stop when I saw Claudine's carriage, but I didn't stay long. And yes, Nicholette was there. Why do you ask?"

"Oh, no reason. Did you walk here from Summerton?" I asked quickly, recalling how thoroughly soaked his jacket had been when he'd entered the room.

"I did. I left my landau there, blocking everyone in."

"Why did you do such a thing?"

"You really ought to know the answer to that question by now, Amaryllis." He did not push the subject, so I let it drop. "Do you know what else I adore? That you're not afraid of being alone."

"There's nothing wrong with being alone."

"Most women hate it, you know. But then again, you're like no other woman I've ever met."

"Something very much to do with the fact that I was born and raised on a horse farm in Washington, Mr. Everstone, and not here in this glittering world of yours."

"My ever-sensible Amaryllis, you do have an answer for everything, don't you? Truly, have you not noticed that most women are in constant need of being seen at every opportune moment of the day? And when they are seen, they say the most nonsensical things imaginable. Take Nicholette, for example—"

"Yes, I've noticed."

"And here you are, dearest of all, Amaryllis Brigham, who would rather hide away alone than be seen at all."

I lifted my face and found his eyes fixed upon me with an intensity that made my stomach flip. How I wished it wasn't all an act.

"Not that I mind finding you entirely alone. No, I am far from disappointed." His words matched the look in his eyes, both of which prevented me from looking away. "What is on your mind at this moment, I wonder? You seem rather preoccupied."

"I am reading this daunting book." I held up the abnormally large volume, as if he'd not seen it already.

"That you are."

I was not comfortable with the situation I'd helped create. It felt so much safer to argue with him than not—I'd learned that much in the last few weeks. "I never gave you my permission to use my Christian name, so—"

"Are we not friends by now?" He stood and walked over to the window. The rain was still beating against the panes, so much so that all he really could have been looking at was the water streaming down in front of him.

I didn't answer.

"How about we figure it out over a game of chess?" He continued to stare at the window.

"Fine." I forced my eyes off of him as he turned around to face me, and added, trying to be vague, "Did you come to Hilldreth looking for Lawry?"

"No, I left him at Summerton. He's there visiting, as well. While we were there, Claudine told us you were here...and so, here I am, also."

I tried hard to focus all my attention on the book in my hand, but Marius Pontmercy doing absolutely nothing more than stare longingly at Cosette Fauchelevent in the park day after day came to mind, reminding me, oddly, of the perplexing man standing before me.

"May I ask you something?" he asked.

"Of course. You have no need to ask permission. You must know by now I will tell you whatever it is you wish to know."

"Is that so?" He crossed his arms over his chest, seeming to be genuinely astonished.

I stood from my chair behind the desk.

"Well then, I have one burning question for you. Why are you still resisting me?"

"Excuse me?"

He stepped closer, the desk still between us. "Wait. Before you answer, let me. Perhaps I already know."

"Go ahead. I'm quite interested in hearing your hypothesis."

"You, Amaryllis Brigham, believe you never even had a chance; and therefore, you determined not to be judged as a miserable failure by not trying and then, of course, not failing. One cannot fail when one isn't even playing the game." He placed the chess set on the small marble-topped table between two leather chairs and then sat down.

It infuriated me that he knew me so well. "If that is indeed the case, we will all be miserable failures, save for one."

"Yes, save for one. And do you know who she might be?" He wasn't looking at me when he spoke, his attention primarily on setting up his chest pieces.

"Mr. Everstone, look at me."

His eyes slowly and steadily took in every detail of my burgundy jacquard dress edged with white lace. And then he looked into my face for a very long time.

It was a while before I was able to gather my thoughts.

"Don't you trust me by now, Amaryllis?"

"I admit I trust you...a little. But I do not believe most of the words that come out of your mouth." With my loosened stays, I was able to curl up in the deep, overstuffed leather chair across the table from him. Taking the white chess pieces out of a satin bag, I began setting them up on my side of the board.

"You trust me a little? I could ask for nothing more." He barely looked my way while he finished setting out his pawns. "However, if you were to perhaps let your guard down—if you could believe me a little—do you know what would happen?"

"No, and we're not going to find out." I began the game, moving a pawn to the center of the board.

"No one gets through that fortress of yours, do they? Is it because you're afraid to find out that you're just like everyone else—ruled by passions, taking no consideration for what might be the logical thing to do?"

"But I'm not like everyone else."

"I know."

"And, unlike every other young lady you're acquainted with, I have absolutely no desire to marry you."

"Indeed?" He looked taken aback. "I thought, perhaps, you might at least be persuaded! As I've heard told, I am quite the catch."

"You are a rake...who has entirely too much money."

"Too much money? Is that even possible? Well then, I'll rectify the situation with haste!" His eyebrows were raised high. "To whom shall I give it all? An orphanage I know of in Seattle? Or, I know—how about I give it all to the Boston Inland Mission Society? I do believe that would be a fair trade for your heart."

I was beyond exasperated. "That's not even taking into consideration what your father would think," I continued in an effort to ignore the words he insisted on tormenting me with.

"I've already told you, Amaryllis, he's not my father, and you have no reason to fear what he thinks about you, or me. And we do get on fabulously, do we not?"

"Is this us getting on fabulously?" I asked, trying my best to contain the emotions produced by his insufferable remarks.

"It's called attraction, my dear," he responded coolly. "Which reminds me, I wanted to ask you something about Crawford. Has he provided you with any amount of this sort of attraction?"

"Answering that question would hardly be prudent."

He laughed, and I knew why. I'd never once cared about being prudent during any of our conversations.

Both of us silently focused our attention on the chess board for some minutes before Nathan added cryptically, "I think the odds of your winning this game are quite good."

"You admit it, then? That it's a game?"

"Chess? Why, yes, it's a game. My favorite game, in fact."

"I— You are— That is—"

"Tell me this, Amaryllis." He leaned in, resting his forearms on the small table. "What exactly would you be looking for in a husband, if perchance you ever found yourself wanting one?"

"Consistency and dependability, Mr. Everstone." I sat up straight in my chair, preparing to tell him an outright lie. "Like I've said before—there is no man on earth consistent enough or dependable enough to make me fall in love with him."

He wasn't smiling anymore. He actually looked offended.

As I moved my queen into position, I solemnly declared, "Check."

"Fair enough. As I, too, am beginning to be a strong advocate of marrying…for love," he said slowly, his voice deep and intimate as he leaned over the practically empty board. "However, I have one final, yet very important, question for you." There was a surprising amount of humility in his facial expression, something I was quite certain I'd never seen there before.

"Yes?" I was ready to wage war.

"I would do, would I not?"

I fought against the hope welling up in my chest. What on earth was he asking?

"Impossible," I said, hardly above a whisper, praying that he'd believe me. My eyes were focused on my white queen, and winning the game.

When I did finally dare to look up, his eyes were locked onto mine, and I saw something that told me there was a strategic battle going on inside his mind, and that it had much more to do with me than the chess game.

"What do you think would happen, Amaryllis, if you actually took a chance and opened your heart to me?"

"I hardly know." I felt positively spellbound.

"Then what's stopping you from admitting—"

"Admitting what? That I'm in love with you?" I forced myself to laugh at him, when all I really wanted to do was cry. "I must say, as you've acknowledged, you are fairly tolerable, Mr. Everstone. But I assure you—"

"I want nothing more in this life than to see you every morning when you wake—beside me." The words were said with absolutely no emotion at all, his own fortress up without a moment's hesitation.

I looked at him for a solid minute before replying, my last move of the game entirely forgotten. What possible reason could he have for saying such things? Was he truly in earnest?

I ground out my next words. "You're lying."

"I've never spoken with more truth in all my life. Why will you not believe me?"

"I believe one thing concerning you, Mr. Everstone: that most of the words you've ever said to me, including these latest ones, are meant only to shock me for your own amusement." I was hardly certain what I truly believed about Nathan, but I did know it was best not to dwell on it.

He surprised me by laughing out loud. "Shock you? For my own amusement?"

"You know perfectly well—" I could barely go on. Somewhere deep inside, my heart revolted against every word. I knew it was best—what I was doing, what I was saying. I knew they were lies, and that he probably knew it, too.

He'd probably known the truth all along, even before I had discovered it.

"I suppose that's my answer, then." He smiled as I knocked over his queen and won the game. Then he paused, looking at me for a long time. "Perhaps I should carry on as if I weren't dreadfully in love with you. Would that be better? Saying fewer of the *shocking* words I so often say?"

"Fewer words in general would be quite novel," I said quickly, exasperated by his perseverance.

"Consider it done. You will receive no more shocking words from me...unless you change your mind, of course. You will inform me if you change your mind, won't you?" He stood and walked over to the chair where he'd draped his coat earlier.

I allowed his each and every graceful movement to captivate my attention, just so long as his back was turned.

"Of course." Feeling miserable, I stood and walked to the desk.

He'd seemed to have been getting ready to leave the room only moments before, but then he stood next to the pocket door he'd opened, waiting for me to collect my book.

I didn't end up heading toward the staircase once we were in the foyer, though all I wanted was to run up to my bedchamber to escape his searing green eyes.

I stood, unwilling to take the first step. I certainly didn't need to give him the chance to follow behind me as I went up the stairs. It seemed so improper to me that he was even allowed to do such a thing, but as long as he was Claudine's guest, it was entirely permissible. Seeming to have noticed my reservations about the staircase, he held back.

With a sudden blaze of courage, I turned and grabbed the ornate newel post, praying to God Nathan would not follow. I took a few steps up and then, despite all my fears, looked back.

He was still staring at me, yet he most definitely was not following. He had the most indeterminate look on his face.

I knew I was helplessly in love with him, and that the intense conversation he'd just inflicted on me was merely part of a game to him. However, hearing such words, even in jest, had created a distinct hollowness in my chest I'd never noticed before.

If only he were in earnest, and I could be happy.

"Have you changed your mind already?" He walked forward and put his hand on the rail next to mine.

"No, Mr. Everstone. But thank you for asking."

NINETEEN

The Invitation

"*I would be friends with you and have your love.*"
—William Shakespeare, *The Merchant of Venice*

Directly following our frustrating conversation over chess, Nathan had his belongings packed and removed from Hilldreth before Claudine or Lawry returned from the Summercourts'. He moved into his family's town home, Everwood, even though it would be only a few weeks before he'd be packing again to head to Rockwood on Mount Desert Island.

I was told on multiple occasions during that week, by different people, that the move was surely for his father's sake—Bram Everstone would be arriving home soon, and everyone knew he preferred Everwood to any of his other elaborate estates.

It had been over a week since I'd last seen Nathan when he showed up at a soiree hosted by Nicholette's parents. I was seated on a sofa next to Mrs. Summercourt, listening to her explanation of Nathan's supposed intentions to move into Everwood, when the man himself strode into the room. Lawry caught my eye, as we were the only ones there not looking at Nathan Everstone.

Lawry winked at me.

As if I knew what that meant.

If it meant he thought I needed to seek out Nathan's attention, Lawry was going to be infinitely disappointed.

Mr. and Mrs. Fairbanks both seemed extremely pleased that Nathan had decided to break from his normal routine of ignoring invitations in order to attend their last soiree of the season. They were obviously delighted by every minute Nicholette was able to share with Nathan, standing in the corner as they were, laughing and smiling at each other. Why had I never seen them do so in all the months I'd been in Boston?

And would it even have helped?

I didn't know what I would do if I had to stay in New England forever and watch Nathan marry Nicholette. If I didn't say yes to Jay's proposal, would I have no further prospects?

I quickly turned to Lawry. "I should have devoted more time to finding a position somewhere." I'd hardly even looked for one, to tell the truth. And then I realized I'd never told Lawry of my ultimate plans. By the sudden frown upon his face, my poorly timed comment had disturbed him.

When he did answer me, he did so very quietly. "I wondered about that."

He took my arm and stood, intent on leaving the room, I guessed. When we reached the hall, he stopped cold, looking down at me as if there was an entirely new idea dawning in his mind. I could still see Nathan from where I stood. "I know of a school in California with a position that might be of interest to you," he told me.

"Why did you never mention it to me before?" The question spilled out without forethought. I caught Nathan glancing at us from his corner as he continued his very thorough conversation with Nicholette.

Lawry guided me farther down the hall. "I thought you and…I thought things would work out differently. And I promised… someone…that I wouldn't mention the specifics to you."

"It was Nathan, wasn't it?" I was unsure if it was at all wise to just come out and ask such a question, but my patience concerning that particular man was coming to a short end.

"It's unimportant now who it was." From the look in Lawry's eyes, I could tell I'd guessed correctly. "I am confident God will work things out the way He sees fit." Such a proclamation of faith from him stunned me. How could Lawry so calmly wait on God, when all I wanted to do was pack my bags and head west, whether I had somewhere to go or not?

"Do you think they would hire me without references?" I asked, feigning a sense of serenity that I most certainly did not feel.

"Based on what I know of your character, Amaryllis, you'd be hired on the spot."

About a week later, after filling in a final time as pianist for the mission society's prayer meeting before heading to Bar Harbor with Claudine, I overheard a young woman in the hall say to her friend, "I just saw Nathan Everstone and Lawrence Hampton walk into the auditorium. Can you imagine why?"

I could.

I had little regard for what anyone thought of me as I hurried through the crowded hall looking for Meredyth, who'd uncharacteristically decided to come with me that week to help with my music class.

The double doors at the back of the auditorium were still propped open wide, and the first person I saw was Nathan, as he was taller than everyone else surrounding him. He was standing on the stage, speaking with someone, while leaning against the piano his father had given to the mission in honor of his late mother.

The piano I'd forced myself to play every week for the prayer meetings.

Fortunately, Nathan and the man he was speaking to were both facing the other direction. I made a quick survey of the spacious room but didn't see Meredyth or Lawry anywhere.

I knew it was best to simply turn around and look for them, who surely were together somewhere. But I couldn't move when I realized Nathan was speaking to Dr. Wellesley, and doing so with a brilliant smile upon his face. My heart skipped at the thought of how easy it was for Nathan to win everyone's favor without trying. Even mine.

Just as I was about to turn in search of Meredyth, Nathan turned around and looked directly at me, as if he'd been watching for me. He said something quickly to Dr. Wellesley, then stepped down from the stage and started walking up the aisle in my direction.

I turned around and headed up a nearby staircase.

As I hurried through the upper hall, I heard him coming up the stairs two or three steps at a time and knew my flight was pointless. Still, I made it to my favorite music room, my "office," at the far end of the hall and closed the door behind me, wishing the small rooms had locks on them, or that I knew where Meredyth was hiding.

I sat down at the piano, which almost filled the tiny room, and dove right into playing my favorite part of Chopin's *Raindrop* as loudly as I possibly could. I knew Nathan would eventually find me, anyway. I also knew perfectly well the reason I was so afraid of seeing him face-to-face and alone. He had an odd way of always knowing what I was thinking, and I could not allow him to read my heart.

Not considering how I felt about him.

The music room door finally creaked slowly open. He stood, leaning against the doorjamb, watching me, until I came to a good place to stop. "What are you doing here?" I asked, still sitting at the piano, staring at the keys.

"I came to see you."

He'd barely said a single thing to me in the last few weeks of attending the same social functions, so that was definitely not what I'd expected to hear. I'd actually resigned myself to the belief that the game between us was most definitely over. He'd won, and we both knew it.

"You knew I would be here?" I stood, my fingers nervously fiddling with the keys of the seventh octave, my eyes still glued to the piano.

He moved into the room. "I wanted to tell you that I'll be traveling to Bangor during the next week or so; my father is selling one of his hotels and wants Will and I to be there. I've already told Claudine. Both Lawry and Garrett are coming with me. From what I gather, Claudine's already preparing to take you up to Maine for the summer, and you'll likely be there by the time we're finished taking care of business."

"Oh, you know all that, do you?" I pretended not to be too interested.

He stepped forward, resting his left hand on the first octave. As he stepped closer, his fingers trailed loudly along the keys until they reached mine. He took hold of my hand and held it between us.

"I've noticed for a while now, Amaryllis, that your heightened frustrations can be accurately measured by the passion with which you play the piano. Your piano playing has become alarmingly turbulent as the months have gone by." He smiled down at me, caressing my palm with his thumb. "Not once have you played anything as calm and relaxing as Beethoven's *Moonlight Sonata* since the night of Claudine's dinner party back in March."

"And I suppose you think there's some lesson for me to learn by such an observation?" I finally allowed my eyes to meet his. My breath caught in my lungs—he stood so stoically, so seriously. Oh, why wouldn't he simply leave me alone?

"That there is." He took a step forward, backing me to the window, keeping hold of my hand—as if I truly wanted to get away. "The very same lesson I've been trying to get through to you for months now."

He stood there a moment, staring down at me, before letting go of my hand and reaching into his coat. He produced a small white envelope sealed with a red wax letter *E*. He held it before my face with two fingers, brushing the edge of it against the bridge of my nose.

I cautiously took it from him.

He leaned in, his eyes clearly focused on my mouth. I held my breath as he bent even closer and whispered next to my ear, "Be prepared, Amaryllis, for those fewer words…since that is what you seem to want so badly."

He backed slowly away and left the room. I heard his steps as he walked along the tiled hall and then down the stairs. I looked at the envelope again. It was addressed to the household of Hilldreth.

Why had he not sent it to Hilldreth in the post or by messenger, like all the others? Or even simply given it to Lawry, for that matter?

As I walked down the narrow hall toward the stairs, I broke the seal on the envelope.

It was an invitation to a party to be held on the nineteenth of June at his family's cottage on Mount Desert Island. I knew of only one reason that Nathan, who hardly ever made a practice of attending any kind of party or ball, would host one at his family's summer house.

He was engaged to Nicholette, and he was going to announce it to the world.

The notion did nothing to appease the uncontrollable sensations that were stirred up inside me by the fact that he'd soon be making Nicholette so extremely happy.

Oh, such a thought! Did I actually believe being married to Nathan Everstone would make me happy?

Of course I did.

When I arrived home from the mission, Lawry had already left for Bangor with Nathan, and Claudine had the whole household of Hilldreth in an uproar. She'd sent a messenger to the train station to secure our passage for the following morning. She also had every servant in the house pulling things from the cabinets, drawers, and wardrobes in an effort to make the train with everything we could possibly need for the entire summer.

I was thankful that Claudine understood my aversion to sailing and had made plans to take the train up to Mount Desert Island without a word from me. I didn't need the added stress. Everything that had occurred in the last few weeks was enough to put me on edge, likely for the rest of the summer. Escaping to Truesdale seemed like a most welcome idea, though I never would have expected to reach such a conclusion in all my life.

TWENTY

The Engagement

"Nothing is less in our power than the heart,
and far from commanding, we are forced to obey it."
—Jean-Jacques Rousseau

I t didn't take long after arriving in Bar Harbor for me to realize
that Truesdale Cottage was still a most exasperating place for
me to live by far.

There were simply too many women living in the house. I felt
terribly sorry for Uncle Edward, trapped as he was in the house
with four rather silly women and, of course, with me. Lawry's
family was not happy that he had yet to see them since his return
from Washington months before; but as I'd learned quite well
since he and his friends had come back east, they did as they chose
most of the time.

I wandered down the extravagantly carved wooden staircase of my family's vacation cottage the next morning in search
of Claudine, but absolutely no one was about. The mansion
seemed eerily empty. In finding myself alone, I walked out to the
large veranda that led to the garden facing the rocky shore of the
Atlantic.

The yard between the house and the ocean was still a beautifully maintained garden with benches, shrubs, and pergolas—the
perfect setup for outdoor parties of all kinds.

It was more beautiful than I remembered. The great stone wall I had been held prisoner behind for a month eleven years ago was now merely a quaint fence-like structure with flowers and ivy growing from the planters built atop it.

Truesdale was just as elaborate as Hilldreth, situated in somewhat of a cove surrounded by thousands of evergreens. It all looked so familiar and so different at the same time.

Looking up and down the coast, I could see the terra-cotta roof of the neighboring limestone mansion, which was built high up on a hill above a rocky cliff overlooking the ocean.

Rockwood.

"Hello, Amaryllis!" Claudine shouted from somewhere above me. "Up here!" Turning my back to the sun, I looked up the hill to the grand mansion my family had the audacity to call a cottage. Claudine waved from a balcony off the attic level. "Come and join us!"

"I'll be right up!"

I could hear them all talking and laughing before I actually saw them.

At a table, set as if it was completely natural to eat breakfast on the roof, Claudine sat with Aunt Lizabeth, Uncle Edward, and my younger cousin, Ainsley.

They'd finished breakfast a long time ago and were simply enjoying themselves and the view. Had I not been so focused on safely ascending the two steep flights of stairs off the side of the house, I would have thought to look out at the breathtaking view.

As it was, I did not think to look until my feet were firmly planted on the level balcony with the sturdy railing to hold on to.

I'd forgotten all about that balcony and the view.

Ainsley got up from the table to stand by my side. She was a rather shy girl, who, at the age of seventeen, still hadn't been introduced into society. I was under the impression that my waiting until the "old" age of five-and-twenty to take my place in my family's society gave her much hope.

When Ainsley failed to speak, I continued to take in the vista over the tops of many of the trees. I could see neighboring mansions in every direction, and the bigger-than-ever ocean. Looking to the north, I could see much more of the castle-like mansion on the cliff. It was even more impressive from three stories up.

Aunt Lizabeth, who had noticed me staring at it, said, "It's extraordinary, is it not?"

"I've never seen another house like it."

"Nor a man comparable to the one who had it built," Uncle Edward supplied. I realized then that they must not remember that I'd witnessed the altercations between Bram Everstone and my mother long ago, right there on the edge of those coastal rocks between Truesdale and Rockwood.

"The Everstones have been friends of ours for generations, but I must admit, Bram is a peculiar man," Aunt Lizabeth said as she walked up behind me. "He's not been back to Mount Desert Island in precisely eleven years. His daughter Natalia lives at Rockwood with her husband, Dr. George Livingston. Her twin brother, Nathan, has been Lawry's closest friend since they were children. I heard he was kept busy while his father was in Europe, having the hotel fire to deal with and all." I nodded, taking it all in, as if it were the first time I'd ever heard of them.

"Did you happen to see much of him in Boston, Amaryllis?" Ainsley asked.

My stomach turned into a tight knot. "A little."

"You'll probably meet him again—if he bothers to come up, that is," Uncle Edward added.

"Nathan did come up for a few days in the spring, but we hardly saw him. He seemed all out of sorts. He's so like his father," Ainsley commented, sounding surprisingly like her mother.

I suppose they were both trying to impress me with their vast knowledge of him, but I was having a hard time not thinking how correct Nathan had been in his interpretation of how well people "knew" him.

No one really knew him at all.

"Nathan will be back." Aunt Lizabeth returned to the table where her husband sat reading his newspaper. "George had to arrange for someone to collect his horse the other day."

"Thunder is at Rockwood?" I blurted out. The thought of seeing the horse again thrilled me.

"You've heard of his beast of a horse, have you?" Uncle Edward asked from behind his newspaper. He must not have paid much attention when we'd arrived the day before with Truelove—she was virtually a "beast of a horse" herself.

Ainsley asked, with sudden, overflowing excitement, "Amaryllis, is it true Nathan is finally on the lookout for a—"

"Good morning, everyone!" announced Lawry's widowed sister, Daphne, as she exited the house from a door on the attic level.

"Good morning, Daphne. Did you sleep well last night?" Uncle Edward asked, still concealed behind his newspaper.

"As always, Papa," she answered almost too sweetly. "Oh, hello, Amaryllis. I forgot you had come." She gave me the slightest nod of acknowledgment. "Who is on the lookout, and for what?"

"Nathan Everstone, dear," Aunt Lizabeth said. "It seems his father is again pushing for him to marry."

"Oh, is he?" Daphne pulled her light brown hair around to the front of her right shoulder. "How wonderful. I do hope he comes up for the summer. I've just begun the hunt for my next husband. He'd do fabulously, would he not, Mother? 'Mrs. Daphne Everstone' sounds much preferable to 'Mrs. Daphne Langenwalter.' And I must say, I'd never complain about how *he* looks by my side."

"It sounds beautiful, dear." Aunt Lizabeth smiled at her daughter. "He'll come, at least for the Independence Day Festival."

Evidently she, too, was interested in seeing something develop between her eldest daughter and Nathan.

I tried my best to seem completely uninterested in and unaffected by their conversation. After all, to everyone concerned, save for Claudine, Nathan was practically a stranger to me.

Claudine sat across the table from Uncle Edward, looking troubled. But then, with a smile in my direction, she said, "Nathan will be sure to come as soon as he's finished with his business in Bangor. He told me as much before he left Boston."

I walked over to the farthest edge of the balcony and stared at Rockwood. Far below the great limestone mansion on the cliffs, I could barely see some rocks jutting out into the ocean a ways down the coast. It looked like a small peninsula made completely out of jagged rocks, much like Castle Rock on Nahant Island. Was that The Cleft Stone?

I remembered so vividly sitting upon it with Lawry and Natalia that day when we were younger.

It didn't make sense to me why I'd always remembered it with such fondness. It was where I had met Bram Everstone for the first and the final time, and practically the last place I'd ever seen my mother alive.

Then I realized why: The Cleft Stone was the last place I ever remembered feeling truly safe before everything about my life had fallen apart.

"Do you enjoy sailing, Amaryllis?" Daphne came up behind me. "Nathan has the most gorgeous schooner you've ever seen. He always takes us out, at least once a week."

"Oh, no, I don't believe I'll go near the water much this summer. I don't really like it. And I most definitely don't like boats. They make me seasick."

"That is too bad," she said with a pretend smile. "His boat parties are so much fun."

Soon after this piece of information had been shared, everyone headed down the stairs, leaving me alone.

What on earth was I to do? I was stuck in a house where Nathan Everstone was everyone's favorite topic.

⌒

As the week progressed, I found it was customary for the entire Truesdale household to gather each afternoon for tea on the veranda facing the ocean. This was usually the worst time of day for me, for I would invariably find myself in the midst of lengthy and rather uninformed conversations about Nathan Everstone.

I never said much. What could I say without possibly giving my heart away?

On one afternoon a few days later, Natalia and Estella joined us.

"Amaryllis, I am so happy to see you again!" Natalia exclaimed, disregarding protocol as she flew to my side.

Did she really remember me so well after eleven years? Did she remember how her father had treated me that day on The Cleft Stone? Or had her father's ill manners been an everyday occurrence for her as a child?

Daphne focused on attaching herself to Estella, acting as if they were the closest of friends. And I knew exactly why. From the moment I'd met the adult version of Daphne Hampton, I knew she had one goal for the summer, and that was to become Mrs. Nathan Everstone. Not that I believed she would succeed. Someone else had already done that.

With the newcomers came a split in the company. Daphne led Estella and Ainsley to the west end of the veranda, closest to the house, where they seemed content to gossip about all the heirs and heiresses soon to bombard Bar Harbor in time for the Everstone Ball.

Natalia, who'd taken a seat next to me, turned and said, "All week I've been looking forward to seeing you again, but I've been so very busy, what with getting the house prepared for the ball, that I haven't had a single moment of rest, let alone time to get away!"

"That's quite all right, Mrs. Livingston."

"Oh, please, you must call me Natalia."

From across the veranda, Daphne gasped loudly and cried, "Are you absolutely certain?"

Estella glanced nervously from Daphne to me and then back again. Natalia frowned at her sister, fire blazing from her green eyes.

Daphne stood and came directly over to her mother, announcing unabashedly, "Nathan Everstone is engaged to Nicholette Fairbanks!"

And with those words, it felt as if a heavy blackness was draped over me.

"He is not," Natalia said forcefully.

I had no idea why she would argue the case as she did. Would she really know whether it was so?

"Estella says your father and Nathan were on their way to Newport from their business in Bangor to arrange everything days ago," Daphne expounded to her.

At this, Uncle Edward stood up and walked into the house, obviously wanting to steer clear of the drama that was quickly unfolding.

"I'll not sit here and listen to idle gossip about my own brother," Natalia declared, looking deliberately at me.

My breathing threatened to accelerate, but I tried desperately to calm myself. It was best to seem as uninterested in their conversation as possible.

"Natalia, I assure you, everyone will know soon enough," Estella added wearily.

"Well," Natalia said, "since there's been no formal announcement, for I certainly knew nothing of it, I suggest we keep this information to ourselves. We do not need everyone in Bar Harbor involved."

Although Natalia had said these words with a coolness I would never have been able to achieve, I could tell she was disturbed by what had been disclosed.

About ten minutes later, Claudine, Aunt Lizabeth, Natalia, Estella, and Ainsley all went into the house. Daphne alone held back, seeming intent on speaking with me.

What I wanted most was to go off and be alone, but I allowed her to loop arms with me, just as she had done with Estella earlier. We descended the stairs and started along the path toward the sea.

She turned to me sharply, almost stopping our progress. "It's hardly fair that Nicholette should get to marry Nathan. He undoubtedly doesn't want her. Was she not the reason he left two years ago for Washington, taking my brother with him?"

I couldn't bear staying quiet one moment longer. "Perhaps he was simply waiting for Nicholette to grow up," I suggested. "She was only sixteen at the time, after all. And I've heard he's changed his ways quite drastically since then."

"Did you see much of Nathan in Boston?" She glanced my way, as if she suspected me of hiding something.

"He really didn't come around much." I stopped walking as we reached the edge of the lawn. "He spent most of his time with Lawry and also taking care of his father's affairs."

"Do you believe he's reformed? Do you think he's truly put his past ways behind him?"

"I hardly know. He's a virtual mystery to me, Daphne. I highly doubt that any of my best guesses about what his intentions were all spring could even come close to reality."

When at last I was able to separate myself from Daphne, I circled around the sprawling cottage in hopes of finding some form of distraction. What I did not expect to find was Ainsley sitting on a bench swing suspended from a large oak tree along the edge of the woods. She appeared to be waiting for a turn to speak with me.

"Guess who we heard has arrived on the island this morning?" Ainsley slid to one side of the swing, making room for me. After days of hearing every female in the house speak incessantly of Nathan, I'd finally given up hope that they would ever choose another topic.

"Nathan Everstone?" I asked as I sat next to her in the breezy shade.

"No. Who cares about Nathan? I'm talking about Dr. Jayson Castleman!"

I smiled at her with relief, perfectly prepared to hear all about the man. Anything to keep my mind off Nathan's engagement to Nicholette.

"Oh? And what is Dr. Castleman like?"

"Jayson's family is from Concord, New Hampshire, and they own a multitude of different companies, much like Estella's father does."

"So he's one of the heirs soon to bombard Bar Harbor, then?"

"He used to come every summer with his family, at least while he attended Dartmouth. They all attended there together, you know."

"They?"

"Lawry and Nathan and Jayson. However, Jayson went on to get his doctorate in medicine."

"What does this Dr. Castleman look like, Ainsley?"

"He has dark curly hair and the prettiest brown eyes you've ever seen on a man. Oh! But I hope Estella doesn't still have her claws in him."

This bit of information was what finally convinced me that Ainsley was indeed speaking of the man I knew as Jay Crawford. But what did it mean? Everyone in Boston who'd known him as

Jay—all my friends—had they all been lying for him? And to me? Why had he been going by an alias? And why had he been living in a boardinghouse downtown if he came from such a wealthy family? And why had he never told me? Was this what he'd meant when he'd told me of a surprise he'd planned for the DeLagrange Ball? And why he'd spent the entire evening hidden away?

"Has Estella had his heart for very long?" I asked, feeling as if I'd stumbled on a treasure trove of knowledge only waiting to be found out.

"Let me see," Ainsley said, tilting her head and using her fingers to count back the years. "They've known each other ever since Lawry brought him home from college their freshman year. Heavens! But he never noticed Estella until about four years ago, when he came back from England after finishing his doctorate at Oxford. She would've just turned sixteen. I remember quite vividly, because I was there. I saw her kiss him."

"How did you come to see such a thing?" Oh, I felt like such a gossip. I detested gossip, but never before had I been so interested in something that did not directly involve me.

Yet it did involve me, didn't it? Had he not asked me to marry him? Was I not supposed to give him an answer by July?

Ainsley pointed to a corner of the garden. "It happened right over there, under that trellis."

"Oh, Ainsley! Were you spying on them?"

"I was quite young at the time and, of course, not allowed to attend parties. So I snuck out here to watch from outside the ballroom. It was hardly my fault he followed her out here. I hardly had time to make myself scarce before I realized what they were doing."

I couldn't help but smile at Ainsley's simple honesty. She really was the best part about staying at Truesdale.

"What happened after they kissed?" I asked further, wanting to know exactly what was going on between the two of them. They had, together, confounded me all spring.

"He kissed her for the longest time, while I was stuck watching from so close by. I was embarrassed, but I couldn't move! They spoke to each other quietly for a bit, and then she seemed upset and slapped him. I think she was mad because he was going away again, and he wouldn't marry her and take her with him, for that was the last we saw of him. He's only just newly arrived...back from Washington, I believe."

"Do you think her father kept them apart?"

"I believe Jayson felt the direction of his life and future wouldn't be good enough for her, being as he wants to practice medicine. You see, Natalia's husband is a physician, as well, and her father hasn't been back to Mount Desert Island since Natalia married him."

"But surely, Natalia's marriage isn't the reason Bram Everstone hasn't come back."

"I don't know the real reason. No one does. But it's been rumored that Jayson wants to practice medicine in the mission field and that his family is against the idea. Oh, but could you imagine Estella living in China or India?"

No, I couldn't. Not even in Aberdeen, Washington.

But a good many things I'd never dreamed possible were quickly becoming a reality. Starting with the fact that within the three months I'd known Nathan Everstone, he'd effectively transformed the toughness of heart I'd spent years perfecting into nothing more than a fragile shell of heartbreaking loneliness.

TWENTY-ONE

The Everstone Ball

"*Love is a burning forgetfulness of everything else.*"
—Victor Hugo, *Les Misérables*

Ainsley and Claudine stood behind me as the three of us stared at my reflection in the mirror. My hair was parted to the side and pinned up high at the back of my head. I didn't know how Ainsley had done it, but in all the months I'd been held captive by Claudine's "polite society," not once had anyone striven to make me feel comfortable in my coiffed hair and evening garb. Only Ainsley.

She truly had a knack for sensing what a person was all about.

About every twenty seconds for the whole extent of the last several weeks, I had found myself thinking of Nathan and wondering what I was supposed to do, how I was supposed to act whenever I saw him again.

My only inclination so far was that I would hide. All night long. Away from him. And away from Nicholette.

Away from everyone, if at all possible.

～

From the moment I walked through the large wooden double doors of Rockwood, the only thing I was aware of, in truth, was the misery that was quickly filling my soul at the prospect of seeing Nathan again.

The ornate decoration of the foyer, staircase, and great hall didn't help.

I could already see Nathan standing at the other end of the grand hall with both of his sisters and a young man, who I assumed was his youngest brother, William. The sight of him brought a flush of heat up my neck. William Everstone looked strikingly like Bram Everstone had almost eleven years before.

Would Bram Everstone be there? I hadn't heard much of him while I'd been staying at Truesdale with Lawry's family. I was shocked that my fears of having to face him again had been so easily overshadowed by my thoughts and anxieties concerning his son.

As Lawry, his family, Claudine, and I were slowly prodded through the receiving line, I saw Natalia smile at me, and I realized it reminded me very much of Nathan's smile from the photograph of him and Lawry overlooking Deception Pass. And a hundred other times.

He had that amazing, crooked grin on his face as he looked down, standing so close before me, taking my hand. "Miss Brigham." His eyes didn't leave mine.

I hated how he was able to turn my mind to mush. And I hated that he somehow knew it. Staring at him was much preferable, though, to gawking at every ornamental detail of the large ballroom I was about to enter.

"Miss Brigham, meet my brother Will. He's just graduated from Harvard—"

"Yes, I've heard."

"Ah, Miss Amaryllis Brigham, it is so good to finally meet you. I've heard so much," Will Everstone greeted me, his cold, dark eyes raking down from my head to my toes.

"Unfortunately," Nathan said with a knowing smile, "my father was unable to come to the party tonight, and Vance, of course, is still in Europe." Will had already moved on from our introduction and was speaking to Daphne and Ainsley, but Nathan still held my hand in greeting.

The time anyone was afforded in the line was short because of the mass of people behind us still wanting to get into the party. I was quickly pushed along by the crush and felt my hand slip from his. Was it my imagination that he had held on as long as possible?

It seemed that all of Bar Harbor was at the doorstep. Meredyth and her family were even there, newly arrived to the island that very morning. And, of course, the entire Fairbanks family was present. I felt sick at the sight of Nicholette looking so perfect and uncharacteristically cheerful.

For days prior, I had claimed I was sick and expressed doubts about being able to attend the Everstones' party. But in the end, I'd been virtually forced into accepting the invitation by Claudine, not to mention the entire Hampton family, no matter how I felt.

After all, they said, how could anyone refuse an invitation to attend a party at Rockwood?

I had more reasons than any of them knew.

That it was held at Bram Everstone's house was, first of all, one very good reason not to attend.

After the ball had officially begun, and I'd spent the first half hour hiding in the ladies' room, I finally allowed myself to dance with Lawry, who'd made it into town just that morning. And while in his arms, I caught a glimpse of Nathan waltzing with Nicholette, and my heart sank.

Had everything Nathan said about disliking her been only for the purpose of deceiving me? Had he been playing with both of us, paying attention to me in order to taunt her? I watched as Nicholette's stunning blonde ringlets bounced against her perfectly sculpted neck.

Just imagining what it would be like to be held in Nathan's arms put dancing with Lawry in stark contrast. Nathan was so stunning. I wondered again, for the hundredth time, how Nathan could have ever described me as beautiful when compared to Nicholette Fairbanks.

Suddenly, I felt like someone had hit me in the stomach. How was it that he'd so effortlessly strutted into my composed little world and turned everything so topsy-turvy?

"Is something troubling you, Amaryllis?" Lawry asked, proving that I still needed to work on not being quite so transparent.

"No, I'm merely tired," I lied. It was becoming something I did entirely too easily.

Over his shoulder, I continued to watch Nathan waltz with Nicholette. My eyes would not stop going back to them, no matter how much it hurt. Nathan would eventually marry her, and my heart would indeed break, if it wasn't irreparably broken already.

It was what Bram Everstone wanted—for Nathan to marry a properly bred heiress of Boston's elite society. And he was the sort of man who always got what he wanted.

⁓

"He's here! Look! Jayson Castleman has arrived!" Ainsley pulled my virtually empty dance card out of my hand and grabbed my arm. "Come and look!" She led me to a balcony that overlooked the ballroom. We leaned slightly over the edge. "There he is."

There he was, indeed. Jay Crawford.

He looked around the grand room and smiled the same boyish grin I was used to seeing upon his face. Was he looking for Estella? Or perhaps for me?

"What do you think, Amaryllis? Is he not incredibly handsome?"

"That he is, Ainsley," I said truthfully, but mostly for her sake. However, when I turned, I realized she was already headed down the hall toward the stairs without me.

I spun back around to look at Jay again. I found him standing, looking straight up at me, as if waiting for me to notice him.

He seemed different as he smiled and gave me a salute, which I returned bashfully. I suddenly realized that the man I'd known in Boston had been a mere shadow of the man he really was.

As I went down the grand marble staircase of Rockwood, eager to be reintroduced to him, I could only wish to God that I had succeeded in convincing myself to accept the offer of marriage he'd made back in April. Perhaps then Nathan Everstone would have left me alone all spring instead of making me fall in love with him.

There was nothing left in my heart to give anyone now.

Nothing compared to the hopelessly impenetrable feelings I had for Nathan, whether he was engaged to Nicholette or not.

⌒

When I entered the ballroom, I caught sight of Nathan and watched as his gaze traveled over the many faces in the room until it rested upon mine. I glanced away and turned in the direction of the grand staircase.

He found me mere seconds later, as I was about to head back up the stairs with the aim of hiding from him in the ladies' room.

He stopped me with three words: "Miss Brigham, please."

I turned, my whole body drawn involuntarily to him, my insides twisted into knots.

"May I see your dance card?" he asked abruptly, apparently not having liked my reaction to seeing him. I extended my wrist to him without a word as I heard the music begin for the next dance. I wondered what he thought of all the empty lines on the card. Save for the names of Jay, Lawry, and Garrett, who had also made it to Bar Harbor just in time for the party, it was still mostly blank. "May I have the next waltz?"

Oh, why did he insist upon torturing me so?

"Of course," I answered as he finished writing his name with the attached pencil, then placed the folded card carefully back in my hand. I said nothing more, and he quickly excused himself and left my side.

I made my way back to the ballroom to stand next to Claudine. There was no point in hiding from him now. He'd claimed me for the very next dance.

From where I stood, I caught a glimpse of Lawry dancing with Estella. I also saw Will Everstone and Nicholette standing with her parents. I saw her spy Nathan as he walked into the room. No sooner had she seen him than she left the group to claim one of the three crystal glasses he carried.

If I were smart, if I had any sense of self-preservation, I would have made sure that my dance card was filled before Nathan had had a chance to claim that waltz. However, during those few months of living with Claudine, having a full dance card seemed an impossibility.

Perhaps, like Garrett had once said, everyone assumed Nathan was in love with me and therefore wanted to steer clear of getting in his way.

I noticed that Nathan stayed on the opposite side of the room with Nicholette and Mrs. Fairbanks until it was time for the dance to end. He then abruptly left them and began moving toward me with evident purpose.

I was terribly nervous, and I hardly knew how to behave. I was frustrated by my inconsistent emotions regarding him; for while I wished he'd simply ignore that I was there, I could not wait to feel his arms around me.

As the *Waltz of the Sleeping Beauty* began, I focused entirely on my feet as Nathan's left hand held my right, while his right hand rested against my waist. The skin under my bodice burned with awareness as he led me around the room.

With my hands clutched to him, I felt like a trespasser.

He was not mine, nor would he ever be.

I could tell his eyes were focused on me, and that everyone in the room was watching with interest. It was not often Nathan was in attendance at a ball, let alone dancing with someone as insignificant as I.

"Why are most of the dances on your card blank?"

I knew it was incredibly rude of me, but even as he spoke, I kept my eyes fixed on anything but his face. I hardly had the courage to look up while he held me so close.

"I believe you already know the answer to that question, Mr. Everstone. It has everything to do with your agreement with Claudine."

"My agreement with Claudine?"

"It seems to have backfired dreadfully, has it not?" When he declined to answer, I added, "There is no need to pretend you weren't aware that I knew about it. We spoke of it the day we met."

He remained silent as we danced for some moments. "I wish you would have told me as much before tonight," he finally said.

"Please, take my humble apol—"

"It would have made things considerably less complicated had I known you were under the impression—"

"Please. Mr. Everstone, must you keep up this grueling mockery?" I asked, genuinely irritated with him for putting me through such anguish. He had to know how he affected me. "I've already confessed I know all about—"

"You've confessed nothing."

I didn't like the vexed look in his eyes and decided to change the subject. "I wonder why I let you persuade me into dancing with you. I hardly know you."

"You know me better than anyone in this room. And you wouldn't deny me. I know you just as well."

"Well, I really cannot afford to go around declining dance partners when so few come my way." As if that had been the reason I'd agreed.

"If only you would comply so easily with everything I asked of you."

"Hmm, if only," I replied with a tiny smile. I gathered my courage and looked up to face him again, which was a mistake. His eyes were devouring me.

I swallowed, stumbled over his feet, and then completely lost my train of thought as his arms tightened around me for a fraction of a second.

"I'd rather be dancing with you than with anyone else at this dreadful party."

"They all seem rather dreadful, actually," I agreed, completely ignoring the part of his comment that referred to me. "What is the purpose of all these parties? Do you know?"

"This one, in particular, has something very much to do with you."

Heat crept up my neck, and he caught my eyes with a steady gaze.

"Have you seen your father lately?" I asked quickly.

"I have. We met up in Newport last week."

"I heard you had much business to discuss. Is everything settled, then?"

"You have nothing to fear from him, Amaryllis."

It was the first time Nathan had called me by my first name all evening, and I was surprised to feel an odd sense of relief as soon as he had done so.

"What exactly have you heard about my trip to Newport?" he asked.

"Oh, nothing of—" I stumbled again, lurching forward. He caught me and wrapped his arm tighter around my waist, pulling me closer, this time for much longer than should have been allowable. When I looked up again, he gave me his amazing smile. Could he feel the heat between us, too?

"What exactly were you referring to when you mentioned an agreement with Claudine?"

He astounded me. Was he going to continue pretending he knew nothing about it?

"You were— You've been…paying special attention to me."

"How observant you've become."

"But you never wanted— You never meant—"

"I've more than meant every word I've ever said to you. If Claudine wanted me to do something, she never told me. Quite possibly, she found me doing what she liked. And can I blame her if she wants us to be happy?" He ground out the words rather loudly, as if I'd successfully tried his patience to the nth degree.

"Please, Mr. Everstone. People will hear you."

"I hardly care if everyone in Bar Harbor hears what I have to say to you," he stated evenly.

If he'd wanted to render me speechless, he'd found the correct words to do it. I took another long look at him before dragging my gaze away. We danced in silence for a few seconds longer, until the music ended. He then walked me down the hall to where he'd first found me trying to escape him.

"Now, you may hide yourself away, if that's truly what you wish to do," he said with a strained smile, then walked across the sparkling hall to the glass doors leading outside. As I lost sight of him, I doubted myself more than I had in months, probably years.

But by the look on his face as he'd left me, it was already too late to do anything about it.

TWENTY-TWO

The Proposal

"But true love is a durable fire, in the mind ever burning,
never sick, never old, never dead, from itself never turning."
—Sir Walter Raleigh, "As You Came from the Holy Land"

Awhile later, as I endeavored to lose myself in the crowd, Wyatt Harden slinked up to stand next to me. "May I have your next available dance, Miss Brigham?" His ice-blue eyes narrowed approvingly.

I took a good, long look at my dance card, again wishing it were already full. "The next dance is free."

I gave him my hand, and he led me out to the floor. I searched the room and caught a glimpse of Nicholette standing with Will and Nathan, and my heart sank. How could he so easily go back and forth between me and her?

As Wyatt and I began to dance, something suddenly seemed very wrong.

Wyatt had been acting strangely distant and aloof of late, and I'd been wondering what I'd done. After a long and awkward silence, he asked, "Nathan hasn't been bothering you, has he?"

Bothering me? I couldn't think of any man alive who bothered me more.

"No, he's...." I didn't know what he was. Provocative? Charming? Enigmatic?

I gave up. There were no words.

I tried to read Wyatt's look, but it was impossible. His behavior was so bizarre.

"You'll have to be very careful this summer, Miss Brigham, with him being just down the coast and all. Fortunately, I'll be around to protect you—"

"Surely, Mr. Harden, I will be perfectly fine." My hands itched to stop touching him.

"But I want to protect you. I'll be around. I stay at the gatehouse at Rockwood most summers, close to Truesdale. It would be my pleasure." He was being incredibly persistent all of a sudden, and his unwanted, marked attention, I know, made me frown. I couldn't help it, no matter how impolite it was.

As the music ended, I let go of him and quickly began clapping with the rest of the crowd. Without bothering to answer him, I moved away in search of either Meredyth, whom I'd hardly had a chance to see, or Claudine. I spotted them both standing in the midst of a small group across the room, speaking with Jay and Daphne. Everyone seemed to be having an immensely enjoyable time.

Jay caught my eye and gave me a searching look that made my insides churn. By the expression in his eyes, I knew why he'd come to Mount Desert Island. I'd hoped his feelings for Estella had been the real reason he'd come. Not me.

"I believe I'm next in line?" Garrett came up beside me and took my arm with a brotherly smile. It was a generally known fact that all three of Meredyth's brothers had the worst reputations of being horrible, noncommittal flirts. I was also under the impression that it was only because of my ever-growing friendship with Meredyth that he treated me like I was his sister instead of just another conquest.

We walked over to Jay, Daphne, and Ainsley. Meredyth was suddenly nowhere to be seen.

"Ainsley...you were able to come." Garrett stood transfixed, staring at her, as if he'd never seen her before.

But I knew he had. They'd been neighbors every summer their entire lives.

"I'll be beginning my first season this fall, staying at Hilldreth with Lawry and Aunt Claudine." Ainsley, like always, spoke with excitement lacing her every word. Her bright blue eyes sparkled. "I begged Mother all last month, and she finally agreed that I might as well use the Everstone Ball as my debut into society." She smiled at Garrett, completely oblivious to what she seemed to be doing.

Garrett's eyebrows shot up. "How old are you now?"

"I'm nearly eighteen. Why, I've always been seven years younger than you, Garrett. You know that."

"I'm glad you were able to come out...finally." He paused awkwardly, "For Amaryllis's sake."

For my sake? Whatever did he mean by that? He was acting so unusual, I wondered if I'd perhaps missed something.

Daphne, who had never been shy in any instance I'd ever witnessed, said, "Heavens, Garrett, you act as if you've never seen Ainsley before, like she's some strange creature come up from the bottom of the sea!"

Garrett finally pried his attention away from Ainsley.

Jay said, rather awkwardly, "Garrett, may I offer you a very pleasant dancing partner?" He offered Ainsley's hand. "I have been marked in for the next dance. We could trade partners, if you'd like."

After giving Jay a grateful look, Garrett turned to me. "Do you mind, Amaryllis?"

I wasn't at all surprised. Why would he want to dance with me when fresh, young Ainsley Hampton was around?

"Of course not. I have plenty of available dances you can have."

Garrett led Ainsley to the dance floor, and I noticed Daphne move to the other side of the room, where William Everstone stood on a balcony above the ballroom, surrounded by an assembly of ladies and gentlemen.

I could tell that Jay still watched me. I didn't know what to say to him, so I remained silent.

"Would you like some air?"

I placed my hand on Jay's arm with a slight nod of my head, and he led me through the tremendously crowded hall toward the doors to the veranda overlooking the sea.

Bending low, he said, so I alone could hear, "You must think I'm the worst kind of liar to keep you in the dark for the last few months. And even proposing.... I'm sorry I was unable to come clean before now, Amaryllis." Before we reached the doors, Jay led me down a large, empty corridor that was far enough from the crowd but still in plain view of everyone in the great hall.

"Why were you lying?" Truly, there wasn't anything I wanted to hear more from him than the reason he'd been so hot and cold in his regard for me all spring, and how his secret identity was involved.

"I didn't want my family to know what I was planning. My father disapproves of my occupation and would try and stop me."

"And what exactly is your occupation?"

"I am a missionary, Amaryllis. Despite everything I never told you, all of what I did tell you was the truth."

"Ainsley seems to think you're a physician."

"I am. The mission in Aberdeen consists of both a church and a small hospital. And I am in search of a wife." He stood awkwardly beside me but fortunately did not try to touch me. "I was set on finding a good Christian woman who wouldn't mind going west to serve the Lord as a missionary to the lowest of the low...not someone interested in marrying into my well-to-do family. I need someone serious and level-headed, someone who cares nothing for my family's wealth and societal status...in so many ways, as you well know, Amaryllis, someone precisely like you."

Which I'd known all along.

I walked toward the doors to the veranda, Jay trailing behind me. I really did need some air, after all.

It was no wonder to me that I hadn't managed to make myself like Jay Crawford all spring. He was the epitome of inconsistency, lying to me, pretending to be someone he wasn't, thinking he could simply take my life for the asking. As if I could want nothing more than to throw my heart at the first person to ask for it.

There were a few other couples outside, talking quietly, so he led me to a bench at the far end of the veranda, where I reluctantly took a seat.

He gave me a somewhat customary smile and sat beside me.

"For months, I've been positive you're the one, even after you almost turned me down. All spring, I haven't been able to escape the fact that you are the perfect choice. I know I said I would wait until July for your answer, Amaryllis, but I'd like to leave for Aberdeen as soon as possible."

"Are you in love with me?" Even as I asked the question, I knew the answer and highly doubted I'd be hearing the truth from him.

"I should love you," Jay stated quickly, but then he rectified his words: "I mean, yes, I think I do love you...very much."

"And if I don't love you back...does that matter?"

"I know you aren't in love with me, Amaryllis. You've known me as two completely different men, and you hardly know me still. But can't you see that God wants us to be together? That He's been orchestrating our lives to come together for such a time as this?"

Could he know how ridiculous that sounded? Did he really believe that God wanted me to marry him when he was, in all likelihood, in love with someone else?

"Are you not in love with Estella?"

He stared at me, unmoved. "You know me better than I dared hope."

"Do you deny it?"

"I can't marry Estella Everstone. I'm not going to. I just know my father would use her, convince her to somehow change my mind against doing what I am convinced God wants of me. I can't take that chance." He leaned forward, his elbows on his knees, looking defeated, as if his father had already won the battle without even involving Estella. He shook his head.

"You don't believe you deserve her, do you?"

"I have no doubt in my mind Estella would marry me if I asked. She's always...." He paused, and I thought he wasn't going to finish. "She's loved me for almost as long as I've known her. We've shared this bond...born from our mutual concern for Nathan's behavior over the years. And we were engaged once, secretly, but we put an end to that when I left for England, when I knew what God was calling me to. Estella wouldn't belong—"

"But you love her, and she loves you. I'm sure of it."

"I cannot in my right mind take Estella to Aberdeen, Amaryllis! And I need to marry someone. The mission society demands it. Please say you'll come with me, that you'll marry me."

"I've never looked forward to marrying, Jay, let alone to a husband who holds another in his heart."

At first, I'd been rather intent on making my imminent refusal of him as painless as possible. But he was beginning to annoy me.

"As much as I wish I could take you up on your generous offer, Dr. Castleman, I'd only be doing you the same disservice you'd be doing me. So, no, I cannot marry you. I will not, even for all of Washington." I stood and started toward the steps leading to the lawn, then paused to look back once more at Jay.

His head rested in his hands as he stared blankly at the flagstone floor of the veranda. "So, what am I supposed to do now?"

"I don't know, Jay. Perhaps you should marry the young lady you're in love with and trust God with the rest of the details."

I bravely turned my back to him and took a step onto the grass where the yard sloped gently down toward the rocks bordering the ocean. My slippers were immediately dampened, but I really didn't care at that point. There would be no more dancing for me.

What I really wanted was to leave, or at least hide away before I had the chance to hear the culmination of all my fears in one tidy engagement announcement.

I stood in the shifting moonlight at the center of the yard, still contemplating my rejection of Jay's suit, wishing to God that I'd been able to say yes, when I heard footsteps on the grass behind me. I turned around.

It was Estella.

With the help of the glow of the lanterns outlining the yard, I could see she'd been crying. Had she been witness to the awful conversation I'd just had with Jay?

"I wanted to thank you," she began hesitantly as she came to stand beside me. "You could've simply said no, but instead… instead, you stood up for me. I hardly expected that."

I really had no idea what to say in response. I was so accustomed to the awkward silence that usually came from Estella, which I almost preferred.

"It was the least I could do."

"I understand now why he likes you so much."

"Who, Jay?"

She turned to face me for a moment. "No. Nathan."

I wanted to believe her, but wasn't she the one who'd informed everyone at Truesdale that he was engaged to Nicholette? I decided not to respond.

Once again, an uncomfortable silence reigned between Estella and me as we listened to the ocean waves lap across the rocky shore a mere twenty feet away. Yet, I couldn't help but add, "Jay hardly deserves you, you know."

"Yes, I know."

Like most of the parties I attended with Claudine, she went home early and insisted that I stay long into the night and be escorted home by others. Several long hours later, I found Lawry in the deserted billiards room, all by himself. I'd been unable to find Meredyth. In all honesty, I'd expected to eventually find them together.

I said nothing as I walked into the room. I hardly needed to, not with Lawry. I sank into a red velvet chaise longue, and when he'd finished making his shots, he sat beside me. I'd barely seen him all night.

"Has Meredyth already left? I haven't been able to find her anywhere."

"She wasn't feeling well."

"When did she leave?"

"Shortly after the engagement was announced."

I tried to swallow, to breathe, to blink...but nothing seemed to work.

I'd achieved my goal. I'd missed the announcement.

But it still hurt.

And was Lawry just as disappointed in Nathan's decision to marry Nicholette?

After we spent perhaps a total of ten minutes sitting together discussing different people who'd made it a priority to attend the Everstone Ball, Nathan entered the room rather abruptly. I sat up straight at the sight of him. It had been hours since I'd allowed him even a glimpse of me.

"There you are!" He seemed almost angry as he crossed the large room. He didn't clarify exactly whom he meant, but I could only assume he was looking for Lawry.

He walked over and deftly handed us the two crystal goblets he'd brought in, then sat beside me on the chaise longue. Leaning forward with his elbows on his knees, he raked his fingers through his hair. When he sat up again, his tussled appearance affected me more than I wanted to admit.

"You look awful," he said, turning his head and looking right past me, to Lawry.

"It's been one of those evenings."

"That it has."

I couldn't have found a single word to contribute, even if they'd tried to involve me.

Out of boredom, I sipped the beverage Nathan had handed me, then asked, "Should you not be spending the remainder of the evening with your fiancée?"

Nathan finally looked at me as if he couldn't believe I'd dared speak to him.

"I've tried to do just that and have ended up failing quite miserably—yet again."

Was he not engaged? Could Nicholette have actually changed her mind? The sudden thought created a warm feeling of lightheartedness inside my chest, which, in turn, produced a smile on my lips.

In response to this unexpected flash of blitheness from me, Nathan cleared his throat, put both feet firmly on the carpeted floor, and clutched his knees with both hands. He sat like that for a moment.

"Of all the times to make her smile," I barely heard him say under his breath, sounding a bit exasperated. He quickly stood and walked over to the door, but as he was about to leave, he turned back around and strode back to me with a sudden look of determination in his eyes.

He stood before me, his hand outstretched. "Amaryllis, may I have a word with you, apart from Lawry?" His words seemed to come out wearily. He looked frustrated, and I'd never seen his smile look so unconvincing.

How funny he seemed at times.

I hardly knew what possessed me to quickly empty the contents of my beverage down my throat, set the glass on a nearby table, and willingly take his hand.

But that was exactly what I did. And as Nathan guided my hand to the crook of his elbow and held on to it securely, I felt unexpectedly warm...and happy.

TWENTY-THREE

Persistence

"When soul meets soul on lovers' lips...."
—Percy Bysshe Shelley, *Prometheus Unbound*

Nathan led me through the deserted front hallway, quickly glancing into one of the front rooms. I peered in around his right shoulder, and what I saw was the remnant of the crowd that had, hours before, been a thriving party. Most of the guests who remained were unmistakably both tired and quite inebriated. Everyone seemed to be crowded around William and Nicholette, for some reason. And Meredyth was still nowhere to be found.

"Have you seen Meredyth?"

"She's already left," Nathan answered as he pulled me across the great hall into a darkened room, then nearly closed the door behind us.

"Oh yes, I forgot."

He guided me to sit at the end of a deep leather sofa, turned on a nearby dim lamp, and then took a seat next to me.

The moonlight glistened off the walls of leather-bound books surrounding us. It was a huge space, like all the rooms at Rockwood. In addition to housing books, the room was also filled with stuffed eagles and hawks perched on branches stretching diagonally from one wall to another, high above our heads—not to mention mounts of moose, elk, and all kinds of deer hanging from the walls in between the bookcases.

When my attention returned to Nathan, I realized he was staring at me.

And I stared back.

I'd always had such a difficult time not looking at him. It was eerie how it always seemed that I was looking into the eyes of someone who knew me better than anyone else...just like he'd mentioned during the waltz.

That was precisely when I realized how strange I was feeling—so fuzzy around the edges, so delightfully unrestrained. I stood to my feet, but, feeling an unusual rush to my head, I sat back down. I turned my entire body to his.

He was smiling, but even in the moonlight, I could tell the expression seemed unnatural.

"Why do I feel...is this how it feels to be...foxed?"

"Foxed?" Nathan chuckled, the contented sound resonating from his chest. "Yes, that is the word you'd use for it, isn't it? I haven't had any of the punch myself, but my only guess is that someone's added a little something extra to it."

"What do you mean? Don't you know there's Prohibition in Maine?" I spoke slowly and had to deliberately catch each word before uttering it, as it seemed all the words I knew were floating haphazardly through my head. "And now...and now, because of you, I'm breaking the law," I added despairingly.

"Don't worry, I won't tell on you. But I must say, this is rather enjoyable, your being so unrestrained."

"Being restrained is a good thing, and I like being that way," I replied, all the while thinking how amusing it was that he'd used that specific word. *Unrestrained.*

"Self-discipline is a virtue, after all," I finished with an uncharacteristic laugh.

Nathan inched closer. "Not when you abuse it so entirely." His leg brushed against mine, and it felt oddly thrilling, instead of awkward or wrong.

"Must we be alone in this dark room with the door nearly closed? If we're caught together, I'll be absolutely mortified. And what would—"

What would Nicholette think?

"We've been alone before, Amaryllis." He spoke slowly and so very articulately. "And you were alone with Lawry a few moments ago. You weren't mortified when I walked in and joined the two of you."

"Lawry's somehow my cousin...but do you know how? I certainly don't." I knew I was babbling, but for some reason, I couldn't stop, "And, anyhow, he hardly affects me the way—"

"The way I do, Amaryllis?" he asked softly.

I realized he knew already. The awful truth.

"You don't affect me at all, Mr. Everstone," I bluffed.

"Apparently." Nathan looked more appealing than ever as he leaned even closer.

Since my mind seemed thick with fog, and my legs wouldn't work properly, I had no defense left against him, only to lean back against the high end of the sofa.

"What exactly do you want from me, anyway?" I knew those were dangerous words, and I wasn't certain if I was ready to hear the answer.

He remained silent for what seemed like minutes and then said, "I'd like you to say my name."

I closed my eyes.

"Say it...the name you won't allow yoursel—"

"Nathan." By letting go of those two heavily guarded syllables, I felt something at the center of me dissolve—the veil, the wall, the barricade. Whatever it was, it was coming down, and fast. The way was almost clear, and soon, if I wasn't careful, he would no doubt find his way to the center of my foolish heart.

"That wasn't so bad, was it?" he whispered.

I opened my eyes. He was smiling down at me, so close, now with a real smile that reached his eyes.

"Oh! Why must you be so...so unbelievably—"

"Disarming?"

"Yes!"

"And just what do you truly think of me, deep down?"

"I couldn't help but fall—" I couldn't believe the words were escaping my lips.

Nathan let out a long, audible breath, as if the answer he'd been searching for all along was there in those final few words I'd refused to say. His right arm now rested along the back of the sofa, and he moved in closer, captivating me with his eyes.

"What do you think you're doing?" I was still helpless to move, let alone breathe. His strong hands encircled my waist, pulling me close.

"I believe I'm finally going to kiss you."

His words thrilled me to the core, despite the fact that I'd tried to set up every possible guard against him. I really thought I'd built a better wall between us than the one he'd just disassembled so easily.

"You're—"

He gently stopped my words with his lips, and I couldn't remember what I'd been trying to say, or why. Amid the shocking sensations driving through me, I tried to think of the reasons I should have been running away as fast as I could. But there was nothing...only the feel of his lips upon mine.

It was becoming more and more apparent to me that whenever I was faced with just Nathan, everything else simply faded away. Nothing else mattered.

When it was obvious I was kissing him back and telling him everything he wanted to know, he drew me even closer, melding me to his chest. And then, as if that wasn't close enough, he pressed me against the side of the deep sofa, his hands traveling up my back, then down again and then up my sides, as if he wasn't able to touch enough of me to be satisfied.

My own hands stayed timidly clutching his shoulders until they somehow reached the back of his neck and my fingers delved through his hair. I grasped him to me, face-to-face, not wanting to ever let go. I was paralyzed by the sensations coursing through my body. Never had I expected a kiss to do so much, or that I'd be lost so easily in the midst of it.

And this was Nathan Everstone.

When he slowly took his mouth from mine, my hands slid down his chest, and I pulled him back by the lapels. One more.... Oh, but how could one more kiss ever be enough?

I opened my eyes and quickly let go of him, but he hardly moved. He was staring at me as if seeing something completely new. He spread his fingers across my bare collarbone. Of course he knew he was the reason for such a rush within me, and the fact that my breathing was so labored.

I stayed as I was, my back pressed against the leather cushions. My mind raced, trying desperately to make sense of what I had just allowed to happen—what I had just participated in. What kind of person was I turning into, kissing someone else's fiancé? God help me, I was just as bad as everyone else.

"Amaryllis," he whispered. "What are you thinking?"

"I had no idea I could enjoy anything so completely." Again, my words escaped without a coherent forethought. What of the guilt I felt? Why could I not produce the words to describe just how awful a human being I was?

"And I swear I'll never be prepared for anything that comes out of your beautiful mouth." He smiled the biggest smile I'd ever seen on his face.

The fog inside my head was clearing away little by little. I stood up, but then, as before, I had to quickly sit down again. I turned to him, to tell him something, and Nathan drew me close once more.

After a few tense moments, when it seemed as if he was going to kiss me again, my hands again went to his chest. I immediately withdrew them, trying desperately to refrain from touching him anywhere...from being reminded of just how attracted I was to him.

What had I wanted to tell him? And why was it so hard to make sense of everything? Oh, but then I remembered Nicholette...and the shame of what I'd just done came suddenly crashing through.

"Why are you kissing me? Are you not engaged to Nicholette?" I was doing a magnificent job of trying to detach myself from what was going on. I had to look at everything as logically as possible.

"No, I'm not, nor will I ever be, engaged to Nicholette."

"Estella told us—"

"Well, Estella was misinformed at the time."

"You were in Newport discussing the details with your father and Mr. Fairbanks—"

"And William."

"And I heard you tell Lawry. I heard you in the library that last day you and Jay...." I could tell his every answer was the truth, and it was breaking down the last of the walls.

"If you heard me talking about becoming engaged to anyone, Amaryllis, it was to you."

"What about your inheritance?"

"I could ask you the same thing. Would you marry someone you didn't love in order to gain yours?" he asked with furrowed brows. He stood up and began to pace in front of me. "If that were true, you would have been engaged to Crawford months ago and now quite possibly already on your way to Washington."

"I know."

"So what stopped you again tonight?" He stood before me, only now he looked as if he were about to fall at my feet. "What do you want from me, Amaryllis? Ask, and it's yours."

What did I want?

Had I ever even asked myself such a question?

But I knew the answer. I'd known the answer for months—and that it had very much to do with the man standing before me, who, in spite of perplexing me, had succeeded in becoming entirely too important. Suddenly, I wondered if perhaps he'd been sincere in his affections all along, and I'd merely been too afraid to believe it of him.

"If you want, I'll walk out of this room, and you'll never have to see me again...if that's truly what you want."

I jumped up and grasped his arm, worried he'd actually follow through with his appalling threat. "No, don't. I don't want you to do that."

He took my hands, his green eyes displaying just a hint of a smile. "I don't want to do that either, Amaryllis. I want to be with you every day for the rest of my life. I want you to marry me—"

The large pocket door was loudly thrust open, causing a jolt of shock to run through me. I'd let go of Nathan by the time Lawry came striding into the room, evidently in search of us.

"This party is quite finished." Lawry yawned as he squeezed his way between us and sat on the sofa. He hardly seemed surprised to have found us there together, alone. "So, when's the wedding?"

I looked from Lawry to Nathan and quickly back again, hardly believing my ears.

"It will be a summer wedding at Rockwood next June," Nathan replied.

"What wedding?" I asked.

"Didn't you hear, Amaryllis?" Lawry eyed me. "Nicholette's letting Nathan off the hook to marry Will instead." He uttered the words as if they were all perfectly understandable. "Father's left already with Mother and the girls, but Mr. and Mrs. Summercourt are still here and have agreed to escort us home. They've called for the carriage. Are you as ready as I am?"

"Of—of course," I answered Lawry, but I looked to Nathan, wishing my words could have been in response to a much different question.

Nathan offered me his arm, and as we followed Lawry out of the room, he added with a whisper, "Of course?"

"Of course, Mr. Everstone."

As we walked down the deserted great hall, I wondered what I'd been thinking...and doing...and saying. My every word and action had invariably told him, without question, that my heart was truly his, and that, yes, I did believe that he loved me. And that he did, indeed, want to marry me—Amaryllis Brigham.

⌒

When Lawry and I were dropped off at Truesdale, we found that everyone, save for Claudine, was still awake and sitting in the front parlor.

When I had settled myself down next to Ainsley, she said, "Oh, Amaryllis, I almost forgot. Claudine wants to speak to you in her room. I promised her I'd send you up as soon as you returned."

It was an odd request from Claudine, and on my way up the massive staircase, I wondered what she could possibly want to speak to me about. She was not one to broach touchy subjects. She had not brought up my inheritance or my strange behavior concerning Nathan the whole time I had been in Boston, so I hardly knew what to expect.

By the look on Claudine's face when I entered her room, whatever it was that she wanted to say was important.

"What did you think of Rockwood tonight, Amaryllis? It's an impressive house, is it not? I'm so happy Nathan seemed comfortable in his role as host, that he put aside his preferences to stay out of the limelight for the sake of his brother's engagement party."

"It's a beautiful house," I answered. And yes, Nathan had indeed seemed quite comfortable, at least nearer the end of the evening.

"I noticed you were acting rather peculiar all night," Claudine continued. "I know you are not particularly a social butterfly, but you do usually try to have a good time."

"I do try."

Claudine glanced my way with a certain sparkle in her brown eyes. "I also noticed Nathan was still vying for your attention tonight. Has he succeeded yet? He is a charming young man, is he not?" She waited a moment for me to answer, but I could only stare back. "You know, it's been rather entertaining to watch him stare at you from across the room these last few months. I can perfectly understand how Jayson didn't have a chance," she said and then went on quickly, "I have a feeling Nathan may be falling in love with you. Has he said anything to you that might suggest as much?"

I forced myself to smile as if she hadn't just stunned me with every sentence she'd uttered. I really didn't want to have such a conversation with anyone. "I've hardly known how to take anything he's said."

Nathan had said and done all kinds of things in the months I had known him, but my past opinion of them no longer mattered. All I could think of now was how he'd looked at me after I'd kissed him.

"I'm sorry I gave you such a complex about him, Amaryllis. The Nathan Everstone who came back to Boston in March is very different from the one who left two years ago. I'm sure that most of what I said about him is now completely untrue."

"He does seem a little different from how you first painted him," I allowed quietly, giving her a tiny glimpse into my thoughts and feelings concerning him.

"Something he said to me tonight made me want to assure you of something, Amaryllis. I never did tell him I wanted him to pay you special attention. I hardly needed to."

It took me a moment to figure out exactly what she was telling me. My silly heart was doing flips inside my chest.

"I daresay I didn't expect him to even look your way this spring without my having to beg him to do so, let alone to become so entirely enthralled by you."

I knew Claudine wasn't trying to insult me. She simply spoke her mind, as she often did. She was as genuinely shocked as anyone else would have been that Nathan Everstone acted like he was half interested in me.

TWENTY-FOUR

The Question

"Peace overflows from your heart into mine."
—Nathaniel Hawthorne, in a letter

Nathan was expected at Truesdale early the next morning, as he and his sisters needed to leave for Newport to attend some sort of engagement party put on by Nicholette's grandparents. Lawry told us that Natalia and Estella, as well as Nicholette and her parents, were taking the Everstones' private railcar from Ellsworth, while Nathan would sail down on his schooner with William.

No preparation on my part did anything to quell the anxiousness I felt the moment I heard his voice as he walked in the front door with his sisters. My heart pounded frantically in my chest. I was sure Claudine could hear it.

I could do nothing to keep my eyes off him as he filled the doorway of the parlor. Natalia and Estella came in to greet me, while he simply remained standing at the threshold, seeming as if he had no intention of entering the room at all. I was grateful that the rest of Lawry's family, besides Claudine, were all still sleeping, resting after their long night of partying.

I, on the other hand, had hardly been able to sleep and could not fathom being cooped up in my bedchamber all morning. Not while the photograph of Nathan was also in the room with me. I'd held on to it all night, praying, wishing everything he'd said the evening before was indeed real.

Nathan greeted Claudine with a smile and then finally turned his gaze to me. He seemed to be estimating something about me, and once he was finished, I saw the same look in his eyes from the night before. Yes, I was certain he did see something new—something even I didn't recognize.

"Good morning, Amaryllis," he said pointedly. "I trust you had a restful night's sleep after such a long and eventful evening?"

"Yes, thank you...Nathan." I was sure he knew quite well I had not.

He still didn't come into the room, and then he said why: "If you ladies will excuse me, I need to discuss some urgent business with Lawry before he leaves again for Bangor and I set sail."

And then he was gone, too quickly. I felt as if my heart had gone missing. Had it not been thumping loudly in my ears just moments before?

"Amaryllis," Natalia began after we all took our seats, pulling my attention back to other matters, "I was so looking forward to spending more time with you at the party last night, but it seemed everyone in Bar Harbor needed to speak to me. I never had a single chance to get away!"

I liked that she'd not included me in her generalization of "everyone." There was *everyone*, and then there was me. That was exactly how I'd felt my entire life.

"That's quite all right," I told her. "I am sure you had many old friends who wished to see you."

"Not many that we would consider friends, but many who will claim such a friendship exists." She grinned, just like Nathan. "I'm under the impression you've become quite good friends with my brother of late." She was still smiling.

"Oh, they've become very good friends, Natalia," Claudine put in. "He took to her almost immediately after arriving in Boston in March."

I remembered those first moments at the train station, and how he'd practically ignored me during his first week at Hilldreth. Was that what Claudine considered his "immediately taking to me"?

"We really aren't so close," I insisted. But as I said it, the memory of his kiss came to mind, and my breath caught in my lungs. Of course, we were friends...and now so much more. He'd told me as much, so many times. I'd simply never been able to believe it before.

"How delightfully modest you are! That's probably why he likes you so much. He cannot stand when people pretend to be something they're not."

"But I am pretending! I've been pretending all spring. I don't belong in this kind of society at all." I wanted her, above all others, to understand.

"Amaryllis, you fit in perfectly," Claudine assured me. "Like a refreshing breeze in comparison to the general stuffiness the Boston Brahmins strive to create."

"You may feel as though you're pretending, Amaryllis, but I have a feeling you've not been pretending with Nathan," Natalia said. "From what he's told me, he values your friendship very much."

"Yes, he's been quite intent upon having it all spring," Estella finally spoke up.

Every detail from the night before came crashing through my defenses again, refusing to be shoved off. There were new feelings and emotions rolling around inside of me: anticipation, anxiety, and still a little bit of guilt from my own undignified and improper reactions to Nathan's touch.

"Oh, I've tried telling her," Claudine added.

"He does need good friends." Natalia took my hand in hers. "He's always had Lawry, of course, but there have been a few other acquaintances over the years who have not been such a good influence on him. You've met Wyatt Harden, have you not? He used to be one of my father's most cherished attorneys and had a large part in leading Nathan down paths he now regrets."

I suddenly found my heart. It was sinking in my chest.

The excitement of having learned that both Natalia and Estella were seemingly ready to welcome me into their family was taken over by a distinct uneasiness at the reminder of Wyatt's mysterious connection to Bram Everstone. How closely did the man still associate with him? Had Wyatt been informing him about Nathan's attention to me all spring? Had Bram Everstone known everything before even stepping off the ship from Europe?

And how could Claudine have been so careless, allowing Wyatt to see so much of me?

"Uh, yes, we've met." I was unsure of what awful avenues the conversation might take. However, the discussion from there went on to cover more of the ball—who'd come to Bar Harbor specifically for that single night, and who would be staying all summer long.

Not once did any one of them, even Claudine, tread upon the subject of Jayson Castleman. It was almost as if they were purposefully speaking of anyone and everything but him.

"We should be going," Natalia said as she stood up to leave. Estella, Claudine, and I followed suit. "We need to see Nathan off soon. He's taking his schooner down to Newport, and we'll be leaving for Ellsworth shortly. Will you be coming with us to see Nathan and Will off, Amaryllis?"

"No, I probably shouldn't. I try to stay away from harbors… and water in general." I hoped I'd be saved from having to go into my reasons why.

My experience at Nahant Island alone had been enough to keep me away, even if going would mean being in Nathan's presence for another thirty minutes. To see him sail off into the open sea on his schooner…no, I didn't think I'd be able to handle that.

My mind immediately conjured up how devastating it would be if he happened to never come back—if he, too, was taken from me by the sea.

"That's perfectly understandable," was Natalia's only reply as she laid a hand on my arm. And as if on cue, the pocket doors opened, and Nathan appeared, standing next to Lawry.

"Amaryllis, may I have a private word with you?" Nathan didn't even bother to acknowledge anyone else.

Without a thought, I took a step forward, only to have Claudine, Natalia, and Estella rush past Nathan and me into the hall. Lawry shut the doors behind them.

Nathan was immediately at my side. I turned my back to him. I had to collect myself, prepare myself.

I really thought there would be more awkwardness. But instead, there was a new sort of amity between us, which was much deeper than anything I'd ever experienced with anyone before.

As I turned around to face him, I saw in his eyes the same intensity that had always been there, I'd just never understood it. I had no idea what I was supposed to do or say.

He stepped closer. "Nicholette's grandparents are hosting a private dinner tomorrow night in honor of her engagement—"

"Is your father still in Newport?"

"Yes." That single word seemed to bring Bram Everstone all the closer.

The fact that the man was so near unnerved me. I'd not realized that having the Atlantic Ocean between us all spring had provided some sort of barrier, which was exemplified perfectly by the fact that I'd fallen in love with Nathan, despite knowing better than to do so.

Nathan reached out and put his arms around me, bowing his head close to my shoulder, and whispered, "Lord God, I thank You for bringing Amaryllis into my life. Please watch over and protect her while I'm unable to be with her in these coming days.

Strengthen her heart, Lord, that she may trust me as she trusts You. For I've taken Your commands to heart, and I strive to love her as You have. I would do anything for her." He paused and let out a long breath. "I pray these things in Jesus' name. Amen."

He remained unmoved.

I looked up, meeting his eyes, finally seeing him the way he'd wanted me to all along.

"Forgive me for my behavior last night, Amaryllis. In my earnestness to convince you that you are indeed the one I want...that I, indeed, love you very much...." His words, as quickly as he'd uttered them, filled the air between us.

What could I possibly say in response to that? That I believed him? That I loved him, too? Each utterance was stuck in my throat. All I could do was look at him.

"If you can believe it, I've been trying my best to tell you that for weeks. It's just that, put simply, I've never been so unprepared for anything in my life." The serious look on his face was transformed into a smile while his fingers crept up my back, my neck and into my hair. I did everything I could to stay focused on the brown buttons of his exquisite suit jacket.

Then I timidly reached out to grip his arms. My chest tightened, as did my grasp. "I love you too, Nathan."

My words. And such words to Nathan Everstone! I pulled back to get a closer look at his face as my hands moved up his muscled arms and broad shoulders to his starched white collar.

With a huff and a smile, he seemed to remember something. Reaching into an inner pocket of his coat, he pulled out a garnet ring encircled with diamonds. "We never had a chance to properly settle things last night. Will you marry me, Amaryllis?"

So this was what one was supposed to feel instead of shock, instead of revolt: utter happiness I'd never even imagined possible.

I was already nodding my head yes when I finally found my voice and held out my left hand. "Yes—yes, of course I will." With the ring on my finger, I put my arms around him and finally felt I was home.

"It was my mother's ring, and her mother's before that." I held up my left hand to look at the ring on my finger. Its tiny circumference made the garnet look absolutely enormous against my small hand.

"What will Bram do?" I asked as I pressed my cheek to his warm chest, his heart beating against my ear. No matter what Nathan had ever said about Bram Everstone, or how convinced I was that Nathan loved me, I could not forget.

"Will you tell me now why you're so afraid of him? What do you think he's done to deserve such fear?" I could hear his words echo through his chest.

"You told me yourself that he's been responsible for funding my way through every school since my mother died," I said, still cuddled close.

"But why do you assume that's a bad thing? Without his provision, where would you be? You certainly wouldn't be here in my arms."

I still wasn't sure how I was ever going to tell Nathan about the letter from Bram Everstone to Professor Silvious, or how I really didn't know how I would ever forgive him for doing such a thing. Getting off the subject entirely, I pulled back a few inches and asked, "You never planned to come back and marry Nicholette, did you?"

"I never wanted to set foot in Boston again, to tell you the truth." He smiled down, caressing the bridge of my nose with his fingers. "At least, not until I saw you walk up to the train with Claudine, smiling radiantly. Till that point, my plans had been set. I was going to head straight up here to Rockwood with Estella and Crawford, convince them it was best that they marry, and then convince Natalia and George to move to Washington with us permanently."

"Were you unable to persuade Natalia and her husband when you came in March?"

"I never even brought it up. All I could think of was seeing you again. I knew so much about you already from what your father had said about you and from your entertaining letters to Lawry. But until I saw you, I suppose I had always conjured up the image of a child, not a beautiful young woman—especially not one who was quite decidedly against having anything to do with me." Nathan draped an arm around my shoulders, bringing me nearer once again. "And I had no idea you would be so beguiling."

"I am no such thing!"

"You are. How else do you explain this clutch you have on my soul? And may I inform you that you were the first?" Nathan put his arm farther around me still. "You were the first to ever *not* want me, which, in essence, caused you to get under my skin almost immediately. I swear, by the time I left you at the library that day, I was lost. You were the first to utterly make me forget myself."

"You've really wanted me from the very beginning?"

"I hardly know how you think I didn't! I was acting like a love-sick fool. I hardly knew what to do with myself!" He loosened his arms until his hands rested at my waist.

"Is that why you always seemed so frustrated?"

"'Frustrated' is a mild term for what you've put me through in the last few months. I had the hardest time drawing the line between wanting to help you see that I wasn't the ogre you thought"—he had a rakish look in his eyes—"and just plain wanting you altogether."

"But whenever you looked at me, you looked—"

"As I've said...frustrated," he answered with a smile.

"You tormented me with that book! And *inordinately?*"

"I spoke only the truth."

"You were always so angry with me. I could see it in your eyes."

"Because, my dear, I've never had to work so hard for anyone's attention in all my life."

"You were angry with me that morning in the parlor! You grabbed my hand."

"I wanted to kiss you."

Those words dangled in the air between us as the doors opened and Lawry poked his head in the room. "We'd better be off."

A moment later, Lawry opened the doors fully, revealing the fact that Natalia, Claudine, and Estella were deep in conversation with one another in the foyer. They were obviously ready to leave. As Nathan led me down the hall to join them, I made certain none of them—particularly Claudine—saw the garnet ring.

However, from the look they gave us, they all knew what sort of conversation we'd been having, and about the ring, too.

After Nathan's sisters, Claudine, and Lawry had walked out the door, Nathan quickly came back through one last time and closed it behind him. He pulled me to him, bent low, and kissed my lips. "I couldn't leave without doing that." He smiled and kissed me again, only this time the short, sweet brush quickly turned into a lingering, urgent pull that left us breathless. "I love you, Amaryllis," he said between kisses. "And I miss you already...so dreadfully."

"You'll be back as soon as you can?" I asked wistfully, still pressed to him, his back against the wall.

"As soon as I possibly can." Nathan wrenched himself from my grasp. "I've really got to go." The door was suddenly opened, and he was down the steps. I watched as he climbed into the carriage where the others patiently waited, probably well aware of exactly what we'd just been doing behind that closed door.

TWENTY-FIVE

The Cleft Stone

"He felt now that he was not simply close to her,
but that he did not know where he ended and she began."
—Leo Tolstoy, *Anna Karenina*

Claudine rushed into my bedchamber just as I finished dressing for the day. I was still smoothing out the thin material of the simple old white day dress I'd chosen to wear. It had been exactly two weeks since Nathan had left for Newport with his siblings, and also of my hiding our engagement from everyone.

"Amaryllis, I have something for you that I believe will cheer you up," Claudine informed me. "Lawry will be back from Bangor today, in time for the Cove Party tonight. He's taking a break from the research he's been doing for his father's firm, since he'll likely be—"

"I don't need cheering up. I'm perfectly fine," I said, trying to ignore the reason she believed I would need to be cheered.

It was the Fourth of July. And I was all ready to head down to The Cleft Stone for the first time in exactly eleven years.

"You can't fool me. You've been moping about ever since Nathan left for Newport. And I know why." She pulled a small envelope from her pocket and held it out to me. "You received a letter from him today, disguised as a letter to me from Natalia, of course."

When I didn't willingly take the letter from her, she shoved it into my hand. My name was scrawled across the small envelope in a bold, neat hand. And still, I waited a moment before deciding whether to open it. I was terrified of what it might say. What if his father had found out about us and wanted Nathan to take the ring back and never see me again?

I handed it back to Claudine. "I can't."

"Amaryllis, you are engaged to Nathan Everstone, are you not? Natalia said he gave you their mother's ring." She took my hand, and I realized I'd forgotten to remove the engagement ring after waking up. "If your fiancé sends you a secret missive, you are under obligation to read it!" She pressed it back into my hand. "I'll leave the room, if privacy is what you want."

Once she'd gone, I carefully tore open the envelope and unfolded the letter inside.

My dearest Amaryllis,

I know you will probably see me before even receiving this letter, but I could not pass up the chance to send you my love when I found Natalia was intent on writing Claudine. I'll be able to return to Mount Desert Island in time for the Summercourts' annual Cove Party during the Independence Day Festival. Newport is dreadfully full already, and the engagement celebrations just keep coming. I miss the seclusion of Rockwood...and I miss you even more. I cannot wait to see you again...to be in your arms...to see your smile. I want to announce our engagement at the Cove Party. What do you say?

With all my love,
Nathan Lander Everstone

When I was finished reading, I opened the door of my bedchamber. Claudine was standing there, evidently waiting to hear whatever news the letter contained.

"He'll be back in time for the party tonight, if he's not arrived already."

⌒

A little later, I walked across the lawn from Truesdale to the rocks bordering the coast. I wasn't looking forward to seeing The Cleft Stone up close again after so many years, but there were simply things a person needed to do, whether she wanted to or not.

I crept all the way down to the hidden edge of the boulder facing the ocean, to the exact place I'd sat with Lawry and Natalia right before my world had spiraled out of control. Reveling in the peacefulness of the sound of the tide coming in, my mind went back eleven years to the only other day I'd ever stood upon that rocky bit of shore. Straight ahead, I could see the Porcupine Islands, and farther south was the corner of Mount Desert Island on which Bar Harbor was situated, the scene all so familiar.

Had the devastating outcome of that day's events really been my fault?

No matter how many times I went through the sequence of events in my memory, it always remained the same. If I hadn't disregarded the rules put in place by my aunt and uncle and hadn't left the grounds of Truesdale that day, my mother would still be alive.

It was that simple. Every single time.

Mother never would have gone looking for me, and she never would have found herself face-to-face with Bram Everstone. And I never would have known to fear him, and I never would have been so terrified of falling in love with his son.

It seemed like such an everlasting series of circumstances cycling through my mind, with no end and no beginning. And now that Bram Everstone was back in the States, what would that mean? Nathan's illogical belief that he'd thought of only my best interest over the year seemed rather too good to be true. And

hadn't Professor Silvious as much as admitted to me that the slanderous letter he'd received had been penned by Bram Everstone?

Who else would do such a thing? And why? Bram Everstone
had the reasons and the means to exact his revenge against my dead
mother by destroying the life and dreams of her only daughter.

And now, here I was, willing to take a chance at loving this
man's son and perhaps giving up my dream of having my own music
academy in Washington. Not that Nathan had asked me to give
up the dream, but what exactly were his plans for our future? Did
they sincerely involve going back to Washington, as he'd alluded to
the day we'd first met?

Suddenly the garnet and diamond ring hanging around my
neck, for safety's sake, created a barrier of protection and love
I'd never felt before, though I still could hardly comprehend that
Nathan had truly meant what he'd said the last time we'd spoken.

Marry him? Of course! Even if the name "Amaryllis Everstone"
sounded atrocious, I would accept it if that was what it took to be
with him. He was the one and only person who'd ever made it past
the barriers of my hard-hearted existence. And now that he had, I
couldn't imagine my life without him.

I hardly knew how to stop the bombardment of new feelings
that had overwhelmed me on a daily basis ever since the Everstone
Ball. I couldn't help but think of seeing him again; being so near
him, being able to look at him to my heart's content—to kiss him
until we couldn't breathe—all seemed so perfectly...dangerous.
But it was all I wanted.

After about half an hour, I heard quick, even footsteps coming
down the rickety wooden stairs along the bluffs behind me. My
first thought was more of a memory of Bram Everstone tromping
down those very stairs already knowing just *whose* I was before
making it all the way down to ask me the question point-blank.

I shifted to sneak a look around the tall boulder and saw that it
was, in fact, Nathan. I hated what a simple glimpse of him was able

to do to my insides. He was wearing worn trousers cut off below the knees and a tattered white shirt that matched the raggedness of the old dress I'd put on that morning.

Before I knew it, he was standing on the ledge above me, pulling off his shirt and tossing it onto the rocks to my right.

I closed my eyes.

I heard the splash and let my breath out slowly, trying to calm the racing of my heart. Witnessing him swimming in the ocean wearing only some raggedy cutoff trousers was definitely not what I needed at the moment. Or at any moment.

I sat curled up in a ball with my back pressed to the boulder, my hands covering my face. He would eventually see me. There was nowhere to hide.

"Amaryllis?" I heard him yell over the rolling waves. "What are you doing out here?"

"I was sitting." I peeked at him from between my fingers and noticed his wet hair standing straight up from his having pushed it out of his eyes. After wading in closer to the rocks, he pulled himself from the water, giving me entirely too much of him to feast my eyes upon.

I kept my eyes open behind the barrier of my fingers. It was rather hard not to. My lungs heaved with the deep breaths I kept forcing myself to take as Nathan quickly pulled his dry shirt over his wet skin.

A moment later, he stood next to me, reaching down to help me up from my seat. His shirt was soaked and clung to him, showing me each line of every sculpted muscle. I noticed how close he was standing to me, and I stepped away.

"You and your adorable love for big rocks." He smiled and moved closer to fill the gap between us. "I went to Truesdale a while ago; Claudine said you were out walking, but I couldn't find you. I never imagined you would have come here." He reached out and fingered a ratty piece of material hanging off my dress. "We make a matched pair today, don't we? I could get used to this—having a beautiful, young, enchantingly love-struck fiancée waiting for me upon the ledges of the rocks."

"As long as you don't expect me to swim in the ocean with you...."

He still hung on to the piece of tattered fabric, as if he knew I was ready to turn away with embarrassment. "You know, at Castle Rock, I thought you were finally going to admit that spending time with me was what you enjoyed so much. I hated that you had me contending with boulders. What do you think now? Will you finally admit you like me more than rocks?"

"I do." I thought the words were safe enough, until they were out. They sounded incredibly meaningful. The wind picked up, whisking my loose hair about. I grabbed and held the mass of it tightly in my grasp. "Oh, my wretched hair."

"Your hair is gorgeous, Amaryllis. Just like the rest of you. I love seeing your hair down like this, tossed all about. It's so thick and long." He took the long dark strands from me, wrapped them around his hand, and rested his wrist upon my shoulder. "Did you get my letter?" His fingers strayed to the back of my neck.

"Just this morning." I looked up to the sky, in order to avoid seeing the heated look I knew all too well would be in his dark green eyes.

He took my left hand in his. "Where's your ring?"

I silently pulled at the chain around my neck, producing the ring for him. I'd been in the habit of wearing it on my finger only at night, in order to avoid having to speak about it with my aunt and cousins.

"Hiding it from everyone, are you?"

"I didn't want to lose it in the ocean." I shouldn't have been surprised at how well he understood me. This was Nathan Everstone, after all—the man who could read my heart as if it were a book written specifically for him.

He unclasped the chain and released the ring. Then he held it out and placed it back on my finger. "I thee wed, Amaryllis Brigham. Forever."

My eyes shot up to meet his, and suddenly I didn't care what Bram thought of me, or just what Nathan's plans were for the future, as long as he wanted me beside him for the rest of his days.

"Just practicing for later."

"Later...today?"

"You know, later...during the wedding, whenever it will be. That reminds me, we still haven't had time to speak about the details. As you already know from the letter, I was planning to announce the engagement tonight, but if you'd rather elope, we could skip the party altogether. The Justice of the Peace in Bar Harbor is an old friend of mine, and he'd be more than happy to perform a small, discreet ceremony." He gave me a devilish grin, telling me he was quite willing to change his plans. He tugged me by the hand, leading me back to my hidden little seat facing the ocean.

"That does sound rather diverting...at least the part about skipping the party," I teased, almost shocked by the playfulness Nathan was able to evoke from me. "But what on earth would everyone say?"

"Probably that it was about time. Oh, except for Crawford. I'm sure he would be furious." Nathan sat and pulled me down to sit close beside him.

"I wish I'd known the two of you were playing mix-up from the very beginning."

"Mix-up?"

"I never would have guessed you would be the trustworthy one, and that he, the missionary, would turn out to be the liar."

"Now, Amaryllis." Nathan took my face in his hands. "While Crawford has his flaws—pursuing you when he knew how I felt about you being among the worst...." His fingers moved down my face to my neck, sending tingles all the way through me. "I, for one, can't blame him for that. You are the best, the most compelling, young lady I've ever met."

He slipped his hands into my hair, tilted my head back, and lowered his face to mine. He kissed my jaw, and then his lips slowly traveled up my cheek to my ear as he whispered, "I adore you."

Forgetting myself once again, I nuzzled my face against his neck, savoring the taste of the salty water still clinging to his skin. My dress would be soaked before too long, sitting so entirely close to him as I was, but I didn't care.

"And look how well it all turned out," he said breathlessly, his vocal chords reverberating beneath my lips. I took a deep breath. Where had this intoxicatingly captivating man come from, and however had he come to fall in love with me?

I placed my hand on his, interlacing our fingers. His were so much bigger and longer than mine. I couldn't help but feel sheltered, protected, and safe.

"There's something I need to tell you, Amaryllis." He held both of my hands tightly between us. "Before going to Washington, I wasn't someone you would have ever wanted to associate with, much less marry." Lifting our hands, he nudged my chin upward, forcing me to look at him. "I'm not proud of how I've behaved in the past."

"Nathan, you don't have to tell me. I know you're not that person—"

"Let me finish," he shushed with a gentle whisper. "I've not only sinned against God, but I've sinned against you, Amaryllis. I've done so many things in my life that I regret. I love you, but I know I hardly deserve you. True, I didn't know you back then. Well, I knew your name, but I didn't know you were...*her*. The one I should have been waiting for all along."

I forced him to release my hands so that I could get a better grasp on his arm, and I rested my head upon his wet shoulder.

"If I could, I'd go back and change everything." Nathan caressed my cheek, then my hair. "I know I have God's forgiveness, but I needed to confess to you also, though it might kill me not to have yours."

I looked up to see tears swimming in his eyes. "You do have it."

He clenched me to him, tighter than I'd ever been held in my life.

"Nathan, if just one circumstance had played out any differently, you might not be here now, making me love you more than I thought I could love any man." I nuzzled my face again into the crook between his neck and shoulder. "And I'm the one who doesn't deserve you."

"None of us deserves any kind of love, and yet, here, God is giving us each other's."

"You believe God wants you to love me?"

"I know He does. I've been praying for these last few years that He would make it clear, and He did. Never mind that He made sure you were the one woman in all of New England who wanted nothing to do with me."

"Oh, but I've changed my mind, Nathan. I want everything to do with you now."

TWENTY-SIX

*"She no longer felt, she no longer knew, she no longer thought;
at the most, she only dreamed."*
—Victor Hugo, *The Hunchback of Notre Dame*

After spending the late morning hours with Nathan at The Cleft Stone, I realized that it was probably best we not see each other in such seclusion, and also probably a good idea that we marry much sooner than later. It was rather difficult for me to understand the feelings he evoked in me, wanting to be so close to him. I felt as though, if it were at all possible, I would crawl inside of him and be truly contented for the rest of my existence.

When I walked alone through the back door of Truesdale, I heard voices from the front parlor. It was Claudine speaking with her attorney, Wyatt Harden.

"The Everstones have been family friends of mine for years, Wyatt. You know that. I don't believe you can tell me a single thing I don't already know about any one of them."

I stopped where I was and listened, wide-eyed.

Claudine continued, "I'm completely aware of the situation, and it's nothing like you say. And I certainly don't see how it's any of your concern. As my lawyer—"

"I care for your niece, Miss Abernathy, and I don't want to see her reputation soiled by a rake like Nathan Everstone. Do you sincerely believe he loves her?"

I must have made a noise, for they stopped talking. I quickly began walking through the hall as if I'd come in the door just moments before.

Wyatt poked his head out through the opening of the parlor. Once he saw me, he excused himself from Claudine and strolled down the hall, looking me up and down in a way that made me cringe.

"Good morning, Amaryllis. I saw you walking up from the coast. Were you out there alone?"

"I often take a good, long walk in the morning." I shrugged, as unladylike as the gesture was. It wasn't a lie. I often walked alone either through the gardens or along the edge of the woods.

"So, where's Nathan about now?" he asked, pinning me with his icy blue eyes.

"I haven't the faintest idea, Mr. Harden," I told him with an amazingly straight face. And really, I didn't. He'd gone back up the steps toward Rockwood, while I'd walked home along the rocky shore.

"Your dress looks as if you perhaps went for a swim." He narrowed his eyes and cocked his head. I could tell his mind was conjuring up something shocking.

"Yes, well, if you'll excuse me, Mr. Harden, I must change before the rest of the family arrives home for lunch." I slipped past him and started up the stairs.

"Of course. But do hurry back down. I have something I know you'll be interested to hear. Perhaps you'd consider taking a stroll through the garden with me?"

"What a superb idea," Claudine said as she entered the hall. "I'm certain that by the end of your visit, Mr. Harden, you will understand how things are."

How was it she was able to trust Wyatt so entirely?

"Certainly, Mr. Harden," I responded automatically, obeying Claudine's wishes. "If you'll just allow me to freshen up, I'll be right down."

The thought of consenting to such a thing made me nervous, but in a completely different way than I'd ever felt regarding Nathan. While something about Nathan had always begged to be trusted, I knew with certainty that there was not a trustworthy bone in Wyatt's entire body. However, as Wyatt Harden was Claudine's attorney, whom she had entertained for dinner at Hilldreth almost weekly all spring, I knew that consenting to almost anything he asked, even while on Mount Desert Island, was expected of me.

Wyatt met me at the foot of the stairs when I came back down. I hadn't seen him in weeks, and truthfully, I would have been perfectly happy never to see his face again for the rest of my life. He took my arm and led me through the back door and then all the way to the edge of the garden, where an ivy-covered stone wall made a nice border along the edge of the coastal rocks.

From there, I had a clear view of The Cleft Stone; and the thought of seeing and, very likely, kissing Nathan again made me suddenly rather warm and breathless.

Wyatt was silent as he walked beside me, but I feared what he would say when he opened his mouth. It was no secret, based on what I'd heard of his conversation with Claudine, what he thought of Nathan's interest in me.

"I've been watching you these last few months." He stopped walking, let go of my arm, and placed his forefinger to his mouth in thought. "No, let me be honest—I've been watching you for years now."

"Because of my grandmother's will?"

"Eleven years to the day, to be exact."

"And why?" He was making no sense whatsoever.

"Because I knew a perfect chance when I saw one." He walked up beside me and again took my arm in a possessive grip. "Who in all of Boston's elite society would settle for an unknown, untrained recluse of a young woman who was more country bumpkin than social debutante, no matter the inheritance—besides me?"

I tried to escape his firm hold, but it was useless.

"I'm sorry to disappoint you, Mr. Harden, but I already have a suitor whom I am very much inclined to marry." Wyatt must have seen the ring; I'd had it on ever since Nathan had last placed it on my finger. It wasn't going anywhere, and I was ready to tell the world. No matter what they thought of me.

"You must have been overjoyed when you found out Nicholette decided to take Will in Nathan's place. I, for one, never expected it. And I know Bram didn't."

"Were you at the ball?"

"Unfortunately, I wasn't invited. Although her husband and I have long been friends, Natalia Livingston doesn't necessarily approve of me."

"For good reason, I'm sure." I finally broke free from the clutch he had upon my arm.

"So, you've finally accepted Nathan's generous offer. I'm not surprised, after he went to all the trouble of coaxing you into the study of Rockwood, and all." His presumptuousness perturbed me. And how did he know so much if he'd not been to the ball? "It is hardly a secret to anyone anymore that he wants you, just as I told you he did months ago. But you don't really believe he will marry you, do you?"

I walked toward the house, resolved to finish this garden stroll as quickly as possible.

"What's the matter, Amaryllis?" Wyatt followed me, taunting me with every step. "You know, whatever he's said to you is a lie. He will never marry you."

I walked even faster for a few moments but then stopped altogether and turned to face him. "That you would think such things of him, Mr. Harden, proves to me that you know nothing about the man. If you would take a moment and look past the jealousy you harbor against him, you might notice that he is nothing like you say."

"He has you so entirely fooled. You remember what I told you at the DeLagrange Ball, don't you?"

"Nathan's already told me everything."

"Everything? I doubt that. Perhaps just enough to make you trust him." At the wicked sneer on his face, I again started toward the house. "But has he told you he wants you to marry him after all these months of chasing after you? Has he actually told you he's in love with you?"

"Yes," I stated boldly. I lifted my hand to his face, flaunting Nathan's mother's ring. "He proposed, and I said yes. He gave me his mother's ring."

"You do believe him."

"I believe a true gentleman at his word, Mr. Harden."

"Such high esteem," Wyatt snickered. "If it is true, then it's simply so sad…Nathan doesn't realize he's planning to knit his soul to the one person on earth responsible for the death of his beloved mother."

"What are you talking about?" I tried not to look as frustrated as I felt.

"On the evening of July the fourth, eighteen seventy-nine, a ship called the *Aurora* sank to the bottom of the Atlantic Ocean just off Nahant Island."

"What does that have to do with anyone's mother but mine?"

"Grace Everstone was also on the ship that night."

"You're lying." I wanted to doubt him, but the same fears that had compelled me to keep my walls up for so long were again emerging.

"And tell me, Amaryllis, why was your mother on that ship in the first place?"

"She was running away. You know the reason as well as I do." Surely, he knew every detail about the whole altercation…and more.

"Do you not remember seeing me at Truesdale earlier that morning? It was the first time I saw you." He strolled around me, seemingly quite content with having such information to abuse me with. "I knew you were Elinorah's daughter the moment you and Lawry passed me in the hall. Your thick, dark hair and that bent nose of yours reveal as much to anyone who ever knew Elinorah Landreth. You look just like her."

"You knew her?"

"I knew what your mother looked like from the massive portrait of her hanging in the study of Rockwood. Bram had it painted as soon as their engagement was announced. It was on display until the day she died."

What a sick man Bram Everstone was, flaunting his obsession with one woman in the face of the one he'd married. What had Nathan thought of my mother's portrait hanging there all those years?

"If I remember correctly, you and Lawry were both headed outside to this very garden that day. I remember quite specifically Lizabeth telling you to stay in the garden—she didn't want you leaving the grounds for any reason. However, I could tell by the impetuous look in your eyes that you had no intention of listening to her. Was that the first time you broke the rules of Truesdale, or simply the first time you got caught?"

"It was the only time."

"Hmm. That doesn't surprise me in the least."

"Why were you at Truesdale? Claudine was in England at the time."

"Now, Amaryllis, please stop with the interruptions. Do you want to hear this story or not?"

"Go on, then."

"I was there merely to deliver some important papers to Edward. Your aunt and uncle were quite distracted by them and had better things to think about than watching over two rebellious adolescents. Before I left Truesdale that day, however, I took a stroll, right through here, actually." He motioned with an outstretched arm to the garden. "I saw you and Lawry climbing the rocks on your way to The Cleft Stone."

I stopped trying to pretend that what Wyatt was saying didn't affect me. It did, most significantly. And it made me feel sick to my stomach.

"Are you the one who told on us?"

"I had better plans laid than to simply tattle on you. What fun would that have been? I went straight to Rockwood and told Bram that I'd seen Elinorah Landreth's daughter and that she was likely headed straight his way, with her mother, whom I was certain your aunt and uncle were striving to keep hidden away from him, sure to follow."

"Why would you do that?"

"One usually has to find a way to buy one's way into Bram's good graces."

"How did Nathan's mother come to be on the ship?"

"Let me see if I can remember everything correctly. Upon our return to Rockwood, Bram was quite livid. Actually, enraged was more like it. Grace was as white as a ghost when we walked in the door, and she heard him ranting about you and your mother. Grace hadn't seen her in nearly twenty years. I could tell that seeing her again was the one and only thing on her mind. You see, I am very observant when it comes to reading people. It is what makes me such a valuable attorney."

The facts were only starting to become clear to me, but I was already beginning to think of the implications of my being at fault for Grace Everstone's death.

"You killed her just as much as you killed your own mother, by that single act of defiance in leaving the grounds of Truesdale that day."

His words hit a chord in me, shaking my resilience. They were the very expression of the thoughts that had inhabited my soul since the moment I'd learned that my mother was dead. It was my fault. If I hadn't left Truesdale that day, she would still be alive. We would have eventually concluded our visit and reunited with my father. We would have gone back to Washington within the week.

But that wasn't what had happened.

Estella's dark, glaring gaze every time she'd been anywhere near me flashed across my mind. But then, there was Natalia, with her tragic green eyes, always smiling at me, so insistent that she was overjoyed at Nathan's feelings for me. Could they have known already?

It was too complicated to figure out, so I went on to the more pressing matter. "Bram Everstone thought I'd destroyed his chances of ever having her. And he was right."

Wyatt nodded. "He'd been searching for her since the day she ran off with Peter Brigham, whom she'd so recklessly eloped with while visiting his family in England. Bram was certain that he could have convinced her to leave your father. Why do you think she took the first ship out of Bar Harbor that day? She knew it was true but was set on honoring her hastily made vows." His blue eyes roved over me.

Surely, if Nathan had known anything, he would have told me, especially today at The Cleft Stone, as it was the anniversary of the shipwreck. The more I thought of it, the more complicated everything seemed. How on earth had I ever let myself get into the middle of such a mess? Oh, yes—by allowing myself to fall in love. Mistake number one. That it had been with Nathan Everstone was mistake number two.

My earlier thoughts concerning him now seemed so out of place. And the ring on my finger...what on earth was I to do?

Whether or not Nathan knew any of the details already, I was convinced he'd never be able to forgive me once he knew everything.

If it hadn't been for my disobedience in leaving Truesdale that day, Bram Everstone would never have seen my mother at The Celft Stone, and Nathan's mother would never have followed her onto the ship that ended up sinking off Nahant Island.

TWENTY-SEVEN

The Cove Party

"Her passions are made of nothing but the finest part of pure love."
—William Shakespeare, *Antony and Cleopatra*

I was in no mood to attend the Summercourts' Cove Party, no matter that it was to be held just down the coast. However, Lawry's mother and both of his sisters made it their mission to ensure I would have a good time that night. And so, directly after lunch, I was on my way with the entire Hampton family, walking the short distance down the coast by way of the horse trails to Summerhouse, the Summercourts' cottage.

I made certain to walk with Lawry, who had arrived while I'd been speaking with Wyatt in the garden. It had been two weeks since I'd last seen him, and I was curious as to what exactly he'd been doing in Bangor. But the strained silence between us as he strolled beside me prevented me from even speaking. Finally, I decided to say something, regardless of how he was acting. "Meredyth and Garrett just came from Boston last night with their parents."

"I know."

"Have you been in contact with them? I haven't heard from Meredyth since they went on back to Boston right after the ball at Rockwood. She didn't seem quite herself that night. She hardly spoke to me."

Lawry huffed under his breath but made no other response. And so, I reverted to silence once more.

When we arrived at the cove down the coast from Truesdale, I found there was little more to the party than a large, flat-stoned area meant for dancing upon, a small orchestra playing, a tent full of refreshments, and a large bonfire.

I didn't care what Lawry thought about my refusal to let go of his arm as we stood just outside the caves, which some referred to as "The Ovens." Meredyth came up to us and tried to pull me in the direction of the dancing, but I wasn't about to separate myself from Lawry and take the chance that Nathan might find me alone once Meredyth had secured a partner. I wasn't quite certain how I was going to survive seeing him again after hearing everything Wyatt had said.

"How do you like Mount Desert Island, Amaryllis?" Meredyth gave up trying to entice me away from Lawry and smiled her customary, sunny smile. Did she really have no idea how much she seemed to be bothering my cousin?

"I understand why the Hamptons choose to stay here year-round," I said. "I forgot how much like Whidbey Island it is up here." When I turned to Lawry, his eyes, focused upon Meredyth, had a steely glint to them.

The fog around us suddenly grew thick, and I heard footsteps on the gravel. I couldn't tell who it was until Will and Nicholette were standing before us. Just as I let out a sigh of relief, Nathan stepped out from behind them, his gaze catching mine.

He smiled at me, and I nearly wanted to melt, or to run into his arms. But instead, I forced my feet to stay cemented to the rocks, while my grip remained on Lawry's arm. Looking away from Nathan, I focused on everyone else.

Will tipped his head in Meredyth's direction. "You still think your waiting around will pay off?"

"Yes," Meredyth replied stiffly, as if she weren't at all happy to answer his question.

Lawry's muscled arm tensed under my fingers.

"Have we heard anything of Vance's plans to return to the States?" Nicholette asked rather guilelessly. The fog had so quickly and so densely wrapped about each of us, I could hardly see anyone's reactions, only Lawry's—and for some reason, he suddenly seemed blazing mad, his dark eyebrows lowered, his jaw clenched.

"Not any time soon," Nathan said in his smooth voice. "Maybe never, by the way Father talks." I could hardly tell he was there anymore, the fog was so thick.

"Surely, he'll come back for your wedding next summer," Meredyth said.

"He's not coming back." Will pointed a finger in her face, causing her to draw back. "Not for you, and not for anyone. It's better that you simply come to terms with the facts."

With an exasperated groan escaping her lips, Meredyth turned and stalked away toward Summerhouse. I'd never seen her so worked up about anything.

Lawry wrenched his arm free from my tight grasp to go after her. Will and Nicholette also decided to follow in their stead, which left me standing alone with Nathan and quite confused as to what exactly I'd just witnessed.

I turned and found Nathan standing surprisingly close beside me. I tried not to acknowledge the immense relief I felt by having him so near. It felt strange having let down my guard for someone. Although I knew what I needed to do, I was having the most difficult time rebuilding that wall between us.

"Is there a reason Meredyth would especially want to see Vance hurry home?"

"Vance and Meredyth have something of a history."

"And all this time, Lawry's been...." I hoped I sounded stern, or at least solemn. I really didn't know how I was ever going to convince Nathan I didn't care.

"Frustrated...concerning her? Yes, I suppose he has been. She was the reason we came back from Washington last spring. He thought he might have given her enough time to get over Vance." His gaze had followed our friends and still searched the fog in the direction in which they'd gone. But then he cocked a smile down at me and caught me staring. "That you'd come to stay with Claudine was an added advantage."

So Lawry was in love with Meredyth...and had been for a very long time. How unfortunate.

I turned to look in the direction of Summerhouse, which was lost in fog. "What is he going to do now? Give up?" I twisted the ring nervously about my finger.

"I don't know," Nathan answered, so ordinarily.

What would Nathan do—what would he say—if he knew what I intended to do with that ring by the end of the evening?

"His father wants him to stay in Bar Harbor for the next six or so months, something to do with the firm—probably wants to make him partner, I would imagine. I guess we'll have to wait and see. Personally, I don't think Lawry should give up. Not if he loves her."

My eyes roved over the beach in search of anyone else familiar to link myself to besides Nathan. But the fog was still so dense, I could hardly recognize anyone standing nearby. The voices of others all mingled together in a jovial sound. "No, not if he loves her," I repeated sadly.

Nathan took my hands in his, which I regretfully allowed. I didn't know how I'd ever give him up and go on as if it were nothing.

"Nathan." Natalia walked up, facing him squarely, as if she'd not noticed me there. "Have you seen Estella? The last I saw her, she was dancing with Jay— Oh, forgive me, Amaryllis. I didn't see you."

"Great. Just what she needed," Nathan said, obviously more concerned for Estella's whereabouts than my being privy to their conversation.

"I didn't think anything of it. I merely hoped that they'd resolve whatever issues were standing between them, but I haven't seen either one for a good while." Natalia grabbed our entwined hands and pulled us along.

The fog that had tried its best to overtake the party for a time was gradually being banished to the trees. And that was where we began our search.

It really took only a minute for the three of us to find her.

Estella was sitting alone on a fallen log at the edge of the dense pine forest, still partly hidden by the mist. But we didn't need our eyes to determine her location—her sobs could have been heard by anyone willing to listen past the music and the cheery sounds of the party.

Nathan and Natalia sat on either side of her while I stood nearby. I could just make out their forms as Estella put her arms around Nathan, pressing her cheek to his chest.

"He left," she sobbed into his shirt. "He left without me… again…and this time for good."

"Perhaps it's for the best, Elle. How many chances do you think he deserves—"

"No more, that's for certain." Estella's voice had a certain edge to it, making me almost believe she meant it.

I looked up to see dark clouds shifting across the sky above us. "I do believe it's about to rain." I stepped forward.

The drips began to fall in warm, heavy droplets, and I could hear the crowd of partygoers behind me begin to squeal and scamper up the trail to Summerhouse. Natalia and Estella both stood and quickly followed the masses, while I simply stood in the rain, unwilling to leave Nathan—who didn't seem to be going anywhere.

"We really should follow—"

"I have a better idea." Nathan put a hand firmly around my waist and pulled me in the opposite direction from where everyone else was headed. "The caves are just around this bend, if you'd like to have a closer look at them."

"Why not?" Hadn't I resisted him for months on end? Five more minutes in his presence wouldn't kill me. And it was something I had to endure in order to give him back his ring.

His hand caught mine, and before I knew it, we were standing before a large, jagged opening. The sky was filled with bright blues, pinks, and purples, the clouds stretching in strange formations across all we could see of the horizon. The cave itself was dark with looming shadows as we walked to the edge of the entrance. I ignored the muggy raindrops hitting the tops of my head and shoulders.

"It's absolutely dreadful-looking, isn't it?" My words echoed back, and I turned away. "We're not going inside, are we? It's so black."

"You're not afraid of the dark, are you? Not with me by your side." Without waiting for an answer, he lifted me into his arms and walked through the large threshold of the cavern. He bent his head just enough in order to kiss me soundly.

I let him, of course—I couldn't help it.

Just one last time.

I wrapped my arms around his neck, pressing in farther. He dropped my feet to the ground but continued to kiss me, his arms wrapped about my shoulders—until I stepped away, severing our heated embrace.

"Is something wrong?"

"No. I mean, yes." I took the ring from my finger. "Your mother's ring—"

"You mean *your* ring. It's yours now, Amaryllis."

I sucked in a breath, determined to simply have everything out. "Your mother died in the same shipwreck as mine."

His brows lowered into a momentary frown, but then he replied, "I know."

I could sense the tears inching up into my eyes. "Have you known all along?"

When he finally answered, he spoke so softly, I could barely hear him. "You told me your mother died in a shipwreck...and then I saw the date on her gravestone."

I thought of everything that had happened between us since that day at the cemetery. "And yet you—"

"And yet I what? Fell in love with you? I was already in love with you by then. And nothing is going to make me stop loving you, Amaryllis. Not Bram Everstone, and certainly not a shipwreck that happened eleven years ago."

My only response was to walk away. He followed on my heels, and when he reached me, he grabbed hold of my shoulders, turning me to face him. "Amaryllis, does it mean nothing that I still love you regardless of the fact? You said you loved me, too—that you wanted to marry me."

Hardening myself against the feelings his words produced, I barely whispered, "That was before...." But I knew he heard me.

His hands moved down from my shoulders to my elbows. "I know how you felt when your mother died. I was going through the exact same thing—"

"You have no idea of the guilt I've been subjected to since that day." I wanted to spit the words, but when they came out, the sound was more like a whimper.

I held the ring between us. He refused to take it.

"Your tough exterior doesn't fool me," he said without an ounce of emotion. But suddenly his arms enveloped my shoulders, and I could feel him shaking. "You can't keep pushing everyone away because of what happened to you in the past. The way your father and your grandmother treated you was unfortunate, but does it mean nothing that Claudine, Lawry, and even Meredyth all love you? That I love you?"

"None of it means anything. Not when I have to live with the kind of self-loathing I have these past eleven years. Knowing what I know now, I don't think I'll ever be able to accept your love—no matter what you say." I astounded myself with my exceptional ability to be so hard-hearted toward someone I loved so much.

He stared down at me with an unwavering yet hurt countenance. I almost thought about putting the garnet ring back on my finger—anything to change that wounded look on his face.

"You won't accept my love?" He let go of me and stepped back, almost dumbfounded.

"No." The word fought against every wish of my heart, and I knew that what I really wanted more than anything was him, that ring, and our love. But it was impossible.

"You forgave me my past, even said it is what has made the way for our future together. How can you exonerate me, exempt me from all blame, for the things I've done, yet hold on to your own—pardon me if I use the word lightly—misgivings so tightly?"

"It's not the same. And I've already decided," I said, again resolved to end everything as quickly as possible.

Just as I dropped the hand holding his ring to my side, he was next to me, jerking it from my fingers.

After putting the ring in the breast pocket of his suit jacket, he turned around and walked down the slope of the rocks toward the ocean. As I watched him stalk away, my heart was weighed down with grief, and I could hardly prevent the sob that escaped my chest. I was completely unprepared for the utter despair I felt in my heart.

Nathan stopped walking, combed his fingers through his dampened hair, and turned around to face me again. I tried to quickly school my facial expression from revealing the wretchedness I felt, but he'd already seen it and came storming back.

It was the determination on his face that startled me the most, and I turned to run in the opposite direction down the gravelly beach, the warm rain pelting my face. His steps quickened behind me, but by the time he caught up with me, I'd made it all the way to the deserted dancing rock.

Nathan's hand hooked the crook of my elbow, propelling me around to face him. I stiffened against his touch as he grasped my arms, but I couldn't keep from searching his green eyes—the anguish I saw in their depths prevented me from looking away.

Thunder cracked through the dreary, dusky sky.

"I will love you forever. Why won't you believe me?" His words wrenched my heart, and I struggled against his hold until I lost my balance. My footing slipped on the large, wet stone, and Nathan strived to catch me but ended up only stumbling and coming down with me. He broke my fall, and I landed flat on his chest with his arms around me once more.

He immediately rolled us to our sides, but then, without warning, he leaned in and covered my lips with his, the intenseness of the kiss bringing to mind everything I was set on giving up. I could tell he half expected me to fight him off, for when he realized my arms were again around his neck and I was willingly kissing him back with just as much fervor, his hands tightened hungrily around me.

I hardly cared that we were both soaking wet and practically covered in mud, or that I was going to have to think of some very good reason for being found in such a disheveled state. I couldn't very well tell everyone the truth—I'd never known I was capable of such reckless behavior. But never in my life had I ever felt the way Nathan made me feel—consumed and unafraid.

Nathan's left hand roved from my waist up my back and around my shoulder until he gently held my face. "Amaryllis," he mumbled against my lips. "Amaryllis...."

I pushed him away, shoving my fists against his chest. Fumbling to my feet, I focused my attention on the examination of my favorite blue dress. The mud stains all up the back looked extremely scandalous, especially when paired with the filthy streaks up the side of Nathan's suit.

"Amaryllis." Nathan quickly stood at my side. There didn't seem to be anything else he could say, only my name, pleading me to change my mind.

I turned from him and made my way toward the trail up to Summerhouse. I hoped he wouldn't realize just how much of the water on my face was from my tears and not the rain.

"I am going home now." Not that I knew where my home was, apart from with Nathan Everstone.

"Is it that difficult to trust my love for you, to believe I will always love you?" He came around me and blocked my way up the wet, stony trail.

"Let me by." I didn't trust myself to get past him, since that would involve touching him.

He stood before me, rigid and unmovable. "You're being completely unreasonable!"

"I am not being unreasonable. I am doing the most logical, the most sensible, thing possible. Just like always." I shoved my shoulder into his ribs, not caring any longer if I touched him or not. "How can I allow myself—" I just wanted to get through, to get back to Truesdale. Finally, I barged past him and fled.

"Amaryllis!" he called out, still right behind me.

Once I reached the yard of Summerhouse, soaked through and through, I turned around quickly, causing Nathan to nearly run into me. He tried to take me in his arms again, but my best imitation of a hateful glare stopped him cold.

"I never should have allowed myself to fall in love with you in the first place. I hardly know what I was thinking." The sound of the now-pouring rain nearly swallowed my words.

"Did you fall in love with me, Amaryllis?" Such words, combined with the angered look on his face, stopped my breath for a moment. Even though I'd purposefully taunted him into saying them, they cut deep.

"Yes, but I really should have known better." I knew I had to keep the argument going, no matter how I hated the cool, calculated way he was suddenly looking at me. I had to, in order to keep him from wanting anything to do with me.

"Yes, and I suppose I knew it was a mistake from the very beginning, as well, but leave it to my stubborn affinity for rising to a challenge, even when it's a seemingly impossible one." His voice sounded as even as ever, but there was a new edge to it, an edge I alone had created. I'd never seen his brow so furrowed or his facial expression so troubled. His countenance had been so clear and bright when he'd been with me earlier that day.

Unable to sustain the play of hard-hearted contempt toward him, I stifled a sob, then turned and headed up the slope of the grassy hill to Summerhouse, stopping one last time to add, "And please refrain from following me too closely. We really don't need anyone to see how perfectly the mud stains upon our clothes match. Anyone would be able to tell what we've been doing out here."

And then I ran as best I could to Summerhouse in order to make my excuses for leaving the party early. I longed to be alone in the confines of my bedchamber. I didn't know how I was going to respond to questions about my muddy dress or where I'd been for the last twenty minutes, but I would find some way. Just like I would find some way to live with the burning, hollow pain in my chest caused by my rejection of Nathan.

I looked to the sky, now suddenly rainless. The dark clouds had blown away to reveal a kaleidoscope of light purples and pinks, with a single, bright ray of sun shining through.

Ultimately deciding to forgo seeing everyone at Summerhouse and having to explain my tardiness, as well as the mud on my dress, I stepped quickly along the wooded horse trail to Truesdale. As I made my way through the misty woods, I could feel something in me breaking. With each step, the pain that I'd tried for so long to ignore threatened to overwhelm me with the knowledge that, deep down, I knew precisely what I was doing.

I was walking away.

Willingly.

From the party. From my friends. From their world.

And from Nathan Everstone.

I knew Nathan's last words were born of his frustration with me, and what else could I have expected? His response was exactly what I'd hoped it would be.

I also knew it was infinitely better that way.

At least, that was what I had thought before realizing that in giving back his mother's ring, I would effectively break my own heart. Was there no turning back from this path of destruction I kept forcing on myself? Would I ever truly be able to break free from the past? Could I, by the love of one strong-hearted man, somehow be released from this bondage that so much hatefulness and abandonment had produced in my lonely life? Was it possible?

After wandering aimlessly down the trail, lost in thought, I found myself stopped at the front doors of Truesdale. I was glad to be home, despite the fact that it really wasn't home at all. It was only *a* home, for now.

Determined to put an end to my musings regarding Nathan and whatever it was my future would hold without him, I thought again of Bram Everstone. That was when I realized that that particular man had been strangely absent from my mind for some weeks, except for when Wyatt had brought him up. I was rather surprised by how the sudden thought of his being somewhere between Boston, Newport, and Bar Harbor hardly had the same effect on me as all those nightmares of him had produced over the last eleven years.

I didn't know what to do, so as I ran up the stairs to my bed-chamber, I prayed that God would somehow show me. I couldn't stay at Truesdale or at Hilldreth. I couldn't do it; it would be too difficult. Traveling cross-country with nowhere to go would be preferable to ever seeing Nathan again and to the torment it would cause me to pretend I felt nothing for him.

TWENTY-EIGHT

The Letter

*"Heaven knows we need never be ashamed of our tears,
for they are rain upon the blinding dust of earth,
overlying our hard hearts."*
—Charles Dickens, *Great Expectations*

M y tears would not stop once I crumbled onto my bed in the safety of my bedchamber, even with all the practice I'd had at preventing them for so many years.

I wanted nothing more than to sleep, but I didn't know how I'd ever accomplish such a thing. I pulled my pillow out from under the coverlet and buried my face, willing myself to forget about the party and my friends who were all still at Summerhouse, having a good time in their fake, gilded world of luxury. Well, everyone but Nathan. I couldn't even imagine what he was doing or going through, and all because of me.

Noticing an envelope upon my bedside table, I quickly sat up and lit the lamp to investigate, hoping that whatever it was would be enough to distract me, at least a little, from the misery I felt in my heart.

I tore the envelope open.

June 3, 1890

Dear Miss Brigham,

I have pleasure in writing to offer you the post of Instructor of Piano at The Redding Academy of Music in Redding,

California, at a starting salary of $400 per annum beginning August 1, 1890. You may wonder at us for offering to hire you without, as it seems, an application or references—but I shall explain.

One of my colleagues, while in Boston last spring, had a chance encounter with your abilities at a Musicale Benefit held at The Boston Conservatory. She was so impressed with your abilities and your reputation from serving so willingly at The Trinity School for Girls, she specifically remembered your name and recognized it when an old acquaintance of mine recently wrote to us on your behalf.

If you choose to take the position, please send me a telegram at your earliest convenience. You will be provided with room and board for the full cycle of the year, regardless of there being no students in the summer session. You are welcome to move in to our facilities at any time before August 1, if you so choose. We are all very much looking forward to enjoying your company before the school year begins.

Virgil G. Bromley, Esq.
President of The Redding Academy of Music
194 Rosemont Lane
Redding, California

I was stunned. Someone wanted me, even without references.

It had to have been Lawry who had made it possible. Who else would have such a connection, or knew my hope of attaining such a position?

I immediately went about pulling everything I owned from the dresser drawers and wardrobe. I knew I couldn't take all of it, not if I had to ride Truelove up the bridge to Ellsworth in order to catch the earliest train. With the exorbitant weekly allowance Claudine had insisted upon granting me all spring, I would be more than able to afford my train ticket, as well as passage for Truelove. It was exactly what I'd been saving up for. Only now, I had my destination.

Redding, California.

I stuffed the letter into my corset for safekeeping.

Surely, this was God's answer to my prayers. Teaching at this school in California was obviously His will for my life. If only I hadn't been so caught up in Claudine's society and so preoccupied by Nathan Everstone, perhaps God would have brought the position to me that much sooner.

Still in my muddy blue dress, and with just the essentials packed to take with me, I tiptoed out of the practically empty house, making sure not to wake Claudine, who had stayed home from the festivities. I headed to the stable, still trying to convince myself that leaving Nathan behind was the best thing to do. Obviously, Lawry had thought so, for he'd contacted The Redding Music Academy on my behalf in the first place.

I knew, from riding with Ainsley almost every day during those first few weeks of the summer, that the path of the wide carriage roads went straight through the hills bypassing Bar Harbor. No one would know I was gone until late into the night, when Lawry and his family returned home from Summerhouse, or perhaps even the next morning.

After I'd saddled Truelove, I reached up and wrapped my arm around her stout neck. I loved my horse; I had ever since the day she'd arrived in Boston three years prior. But I couldn't remember that day without also remembering who, as I'd discovered at the Granary Burial Grounds, was ultimately responsible for her arrival in the first place.

Nathan Everstone.

Even before I'd met him, he'd been giving me more than I ever would have dared ask for. It still boggled my mind how intricately our lives had been entwined all those years. My heart ached at the thought, and a sob escaped my chest.

Truelove turned and lowered her head, nuzzling her soft, velvety nose against my cheek. It wasn't until I felt the wetness of my tears on her skin that I realized I was crying...yet again.

$\sim$

I hadn't taken more than five steps out onto the gravel drive, leading Truelove by the reins, when I realized we weren't alone. I heard Wyatt's voice before I saw him.

"Is it not a rather strange time for a ride, Amaryllis?" He walked straight for me, his hands casually buried in the pockets of his trousers.

"What do you want?" I asked, unease winding inside me at the cold look in his eyes.

"Why, what a generous question to ask." Wyatt gave me an imperious smile as he stepped closer. "You might as well know I intend to marry you by the end of the night."

My eyes grazed past him to the house. I considered running there and locking myself safely behind closed doors. But the house was a good twenty yards away, and he would surely be able to stop me.

"You see, Nathan Everstone seems to want you so very badly, I thought I'd better act before he had the chance to run off with you himself." He took a step closer. "But don't worry—by tomorrow morning, he won't be able to stand the thought of you."

My stomach tightened. "Why would Nathan not—"

"I mean to take all I can from him—the woman he loves, as well as his peace of mind." His pale blue eyes bristled with lust.

My blood chilled. "Why do you hate Nathan so much?"

"He was born an Everstone, one of the wealthiest families in the country, and he acts as if it were something awful. He's had whatever he's wanted since he was born, and I will be gratified knowing that once you're mine, he'll finally realize just what it's like to want what he can't have." The malicious look in Wyatt's eyes grew more and more deranged as he went on. I backed into my horse, which only caused the man to inch closer. But then he turned to look at Truesdale. "And I want your inheritance, of course. I've waited a great many years, after all. I was getting a bit impatient, and that's when I decided to take matters into my own hands last winter concerning your schooling."

"You're the one who wrote the letter?"

"Are you really surprised? It was clever of me to involve Bram, wasn't it?" He stared down at me with a sinister smirk, as if he were disappointed I hadn't given him the credit before. "Are you also then surprised that I'm the one who burned your father's precious horse farm in Maine? Really, Amaryllis, what have you been so focused on all spring? Oh, wait." Wyatt snapped his fingers and turned to me sharply. "I remember. Nathan Everstone."

I stood stunned, unable to move, frozen upon his admission of having murdered my father.

"Why would you kill my father?"

Wyatt shrugged, meticulously picking a piece of lint from his jacket. "I'd already waited around for too many years. I can't tell you how frustrating it was to wait three years more than I'd planned while you attended that stupid music school. I wanted you to have nowhere to turn but to Claudine." He turned his wicked eyes back to me. "Which worked out quite perfectly, since she trusts me so entirely."

While Wyatt had maintained a small space between us, it was quite plain that he wouldn't be keeping that distance for long. I needed a plan of escape, and a fast one. If he had, in essence, killed my father, nothing would stop him from doing the same to me once he compromised me, married me, and officially secured my inheritance. I searched the walls of the stable, looking for anything I could grab to use as a weapon.

He reached for my arm, but I bolted back in time to get away. "I'm sorry, Mr. Harden, but I'm afraid I have other plans this evening."

Wyatt seemed more than a little perturbed by my resistance and stared down at me steadily with his devious blue eyes. "There is no use fighting, Amaryllis."

He seized me about the waist and pulled me away from Truelove. In response, I tightened my grip on her reins and yanked her closer.

Wyatt smacked Truelove on the rump, and she shuffled from side to side, not willing to leave me. But when he hit her again, harder, she was spooked enough to run, the reins slipping from my grasp. She raced out of the stable, whinnying loudly as she went.

Wyatt lugged me outside and across the drive. I kicked my heels against his shins and screamed, knowing full well that Claudine would never hear me. Truelove was running back and forth across the lawn, clearly scared yet still unwilling to leave me.

"Amaryllis, I don't think you quite understand." Wyatt brought an arm up to my neck and squeezed, calmly breathing near my ear. "You don't have a choice in the matter."

He yanked me toward the far side of the stable, and I was sure he was about to take his revenge then and there, when he flung me over his shoulder. The pressure against my lungs, added to the tightness of my corset, took my breath away. As Wyatt tromped past the stables, I beat his back with my fists, still screaming as best I could. When he finally released me, he hurled me bottom-first onto the dirty floor of a small enclosed buggy.

"I'm sorry, did I hurt you?" He leaned casually against the wheel, blocking my escape.

"My corset—"

"I have just the remedy." He pulled me up roughly by the arms, turned me around, and ripped open the back of my dress, the buttons popping off and pinging against the metal frame.

"Claudine! Claudine! Oh, please—"

Grabbing hold of my waist, Wyatt climbed over me and picked me up to sit next to him, my blue dress falling off of my shoulders, completely ruined. He pulled at the material and continued to rip it all the way down my back to the hem. Then, after yanking off my sleeves, he shoved the mass of blue satin and lace to the floor, cursing under his breath. "I don't have time for this."

With both of his arms firmly around my back, he positioned us chest to chest, his rough day's growth of whiskers scratching against my cheek. He pinned my arms awkwardly behind me and worked at tying my hands together. But that did nothing to stop me from trying to wriggle out of his grasp. I had to get away.

"I knew you'd be a feisty one," he whispered in my ear as he finished his task.

Then he took up the reins and hurried his horse down the drive. That was when I realized he'd actually tied my wrists to the buggy, and that there was simply no way of escape.

Surprisingly, he didn't take me far. We were soon parked at the back entrance of Rockwood. Why Wyatt had chosen Natalia's home—so close and so obvious—as the site for his deplorable crime against me, I couldn't understand. That is, unless he wanted someone to know…unless he planned for Nathan to find us.

Once he'd untied me from the metal frame of the buggy, Wyatt swung me over his shoulder and carried me up the stairs to the covered porch. He kicked open the door with a loud thump that echoed through the empty hall. My mind raced, still trying to come up with a means of escape. But, as he'd proved again and again, I was simply no match for him.

Still holding me, he crossed the threshold, leaving the door open behind us, and carried me down the hall and then up the sweeping marble staircase. I fought against his ever-tightening hold, trying my best to scream for help. Surely, someone was home, with so many lights on! Surely, someone would hear!

Surprisingly, when we'd reached the top of the staircase, Wyatt placed my feet upon the richly carpeted hall floor. His eyes narrowed to slivers as he lowered his gaze, slowly and meticulously taking in every detail of my embroidered white chemise and corset. I'd never felt so shamed in my life, and he'd hardly touched me. I backed myself against the dark paneled wall.

He reached over and grabbed me under my arms, tugging me close, my face inches from his.

"Why would you bring me here?" I asked in tears. "Nathan will come looking for me once they find Truelove saddled and running about without me."

"Oh, I'm counting on that. Only, by the time he finds us, it'll be too late." His hot breath burned against my cheek. "I know for a fact Natalia gave her entire household the night off in order to attend the festival; and, fortunately, her husband trusts me just as much as your auntie Claudine does. You see, I'm the one watching over Rockwood for them while everyone's away. How shocked they're all going to be when they find you've come here searching for the perfect opportunity to seduce me."

"I'd never—"

Quickly grabbing me by the arm, Wyatt dragged me down the hall. As we approached one of the bedchamber doors, my knees locked, and the heels of my boots dug into the thick carpet, causing me to trip over my petticoats. As I fell to the floor, he growled, "Come on, Amaryllis, you're making this entirely too easy."

I was exhausted, and my shoulders hurt from my wrists having been tied in such an awkward position. I'd used my every ounce of strength fighting against him, and I was nearing the point where I had to admit he was going to get what he wanted.

He reached down, ungraciously lifting me by the front of my corset, as if I were nothing more than a rag doll. I was suddenly so numb, I hardly comprehended that his fingers were touching my skin. Oh God, was this all my life would end up coming to? Being ravished by and then forced to marry Wyatt Harden?

"What's this, a love letter?" Somehow Wyatt had the letter from The Redding School of Music in his hand. He held me against the wall with one hand in order to whip open the page. My knees buckled beneath me, and I crumpled onto the plush red carpet. "Looks like I took action just in time. Were you just leaving for California?"

"Yes," I whimpered, my face pressed uncomfortably to the floor, my hair fallen loose about my shoulders. He picked me up under my arms again and pressed me to the wall once more.

"You have Nathan Everstone wrapped around your little finger, and you were going to leave him?" He paused to take another look at the letter. "To teach piano for a measly four hundred dollars a year? By Jove, seeing that would've been almost as satisfying as this!" He pressed his chest roughly and painfully against mine. "Well, almost."

I heard footsteps hurrying up the marble stairs.

"Help me! Oh, someone help me!"

Wyatt crushed a thick hand over my mouth and hissed, "Remember, you're here because you want to—"

I kicked against him, screaming all the more.

"What do you think you're doing in my house?" demanded a gruff, angry voice—the same voice from my nightmares.

"Taking my pleasure of the infamous Amaryllis Brigham, of course," Wyatt replied snidely, as if ruining innocent young women in someone else's house was part of his normal routine.

"And since when is anything to do with Amaryllis Brigham your concern?"

TWENTY-NINE

Bram Everstone

> *"Happiness is like those palaces in fairytales whose gates are guarded by dragons:*
> *We must fight in order to conquer it."*
> —Alexandre Dumas

When Wyatt turned, I saw Bram Everstone standing upon the landing of the staircase.

My feet were plastered to the floor, and my heart pounded in my ears, as I watched him take the steps two at a time—surely coming for me. But then suddenly, with one swift movement, his fist connected with Wyatt's face, laying him out upon the floor before me with a thud.

I couldn't help but stare down at Wyatt's awkwardly sprawled body, watching for any sign that he would get up to fight back—but he didn't move a muscle.

When Bram's footsteps stopped before me, I finally lifted my eyes and saw a look I'd never expected his face to make. His eyes—dark brown, almost black—were emanating compassion…toward me.

That didn't stop me from being scared nearly to death of what he might say now that I faced him eye to eye once more. But as I stood there, shaking in my skin, I realized that my debilitating fear of him throughout the years suddenly seemed quite irrational.

"That should take care of him for a while. Let me untie your wrists."

I swallowed hard and willingly turned around to face the wall.

He gently untied whatever it was that had bound my wrists, then turned me back around to face him. He held tightly to one of my hands, as if he could tell I wanted to run.

Was this truly Bram Everstone, this calm-spoken gentleman with such kind brown eyes? What had happened to the bitter and angry man from the past? Where was the hate-filled tormentor from my nightmares?

His hair was still dark and thick, though now peppered with gray. I could hardly perceive that he was indeed the same frustrated man from years before. But then, I suddenly realized how justified he'd been in harboring such deep anger toward my mother. She'd married my father instead of him—for reasons still unknown—and then asked him to marry her friend as a special favor. Would I not be just as bitter if I were found in the same situation?

Memories of my last conversation with Nathan flashed through my mind. Would he, because of my heartless treatment of him, carry the same mixture of love and pain for the rest of his days?

I jerked my hand free and hurried down the stairs, intent on leaving Rockwood and Mount Desert Island as soon as I was able. The only thing that made sense was to find Truelove and be on my way west—that was what I'd always wanted, wasn't it?

"Amaryllis, wait."

I stopped upon the landing halfway down the stairs, unable to move at his command. I shook with the realization of how close I'd come to being a pawn in Wyatt's terrifying plan to get his hands on my inheritance—as well as his intent to exact some sort of revenge upon Nathan.

"Did he— Has he hurt you?" Bram followed me to the landing, seeming almost embarrassed as his eyes grazed past the state of my undress. "Please, tell me what happened."

I focused my gaze on the rich dark wood lining the wall of the great hall at the bottom of the stairs. "Wyatt wrote the letter. He killed my father—" A sob broke through. I knew it was probably not what Bram had been referring to, but it was the only thing I could focus upon. It was Wyatt, all along, who'd been trying to ruin my life...and not Bram Everstone at all.

He rested a hand upon the intricately carved railing beside me and turned to look me square in the eye. I gathered every ounce of courage I could, for if anyone knew the answers to all my questions regarding the last eleven years, it was this man.

"Why didn't Father want me?"

"It wasn't that Peter didn't want you, Amaryllis. He simply wanted you to have the life you deserved as the eventual heiress of the Landreth fortune. He knew your being raised on a horse farm was a far cry from what society would someday expect from you—"

"He knew all along?" I hugged my arms over my chest, once again realizing I was standing there in only my underclothes.

"Not really. It was only a well-informed guess that played out just as we'd expected. When your grandmother discovered you were attending Madame Pelletier's, only then did she seriously begin considering leaving everything to you."

"And you funded my way because...?"

"Your father couldn't afford to send you to boarding school, let alone to Mount Holyoke or The Boston Conservatory. And I felt guilty. I knew that if it hadn't been for my inane reaction to seeing you and your mother that day at The Cleft Stone, neither she nor Grace would've been on that ship. You and Nathan both lost your mothers that day, Amaryllis—because of me."

I was shocked that he felt such similar emotions about the shipwreck as I did. Yet it did nothing to take away my own guilt. "Why exactly was your wife aboard the ship that night?"

"When Grace heard about my confrontation with Elinorah, she went directly to Truesdale, but Elinorah had already left for town. When Grace returned to Rockwood, I insisted on taking her into town, hoping that if she accompanied your mother on the ship to Boston, she'd be able to convince her to turn around and head back. I knew Claudine was in England, and that your grandmother had still not forgiven her for marrying Peter. Grace and I both knew Elinorah was simply setting herself up for even more heartache in going to see her mother. If only she'd waited for your father to return to Truesdale instead, we wouldn't have lost them when we did."

"But it was because of my disobedience that day, in leaving Truesdale when I'd been strictly forbidden to do so, that they died. You never would have seen her if she'd not come looking for me."

"Yes, but it was also because of my reaction to seeing her. You see, Amaryllis, for all those years, I'd thought I still loved her, and finally seeing her again made something snap within me." Bram had both hands gripping the stair railing as he stared at the massive crystal chandelier suspended from the ceiling in front of us. "But when I heard about the shipwreck, I found that it wasn't your mother I grieved losing at all, but Grace."

"You did love her, then?"

"I did. I did love her, I just didn't know how much until it was too late." He motioned toward the prostrate form at the top of the stairs, as if we'd already covered enough on the subject of him. "Speaking of love...Wyatt, here, has sent me more than one telegram this spring concerning you, obviously thinking he was on to something transpiring between you and Nathan that I would disapprove of."

I stared down at my feet, hoping not to get too deeply into the subject of Nathan. It hardly mattered anymore. Then I started back down the stairs.

"Is it true that you're in love with Nathan?" Bram, of course, followed on my heels, down the stairs and then through the great hall, our steps upon the marble floors echoing throughout the great corridor.

"Not at all. How could I?" I lied, sprinting toward the glass doors behind the twisted staircase.

He caught up to me, smiling in response to what he clearly perceived as lies. "How could you, indeed? But I believe, for once, it's Wyatt who's telling the truth—"

"What does it matter?" I tried the latch, desperate to escape the knowing look in his fathomless black eyes.

"It matters very much if you're in love with him...if you're going to marry him." He held his arms out at his sides, barricading my way. But even then, I felt as if he were doing it out of concern for me.

"Oh, but you're mistaken! I'm not going to marry him." I darted in the opposite direction down the hall, then began to pull open a heavy pocket door to one of the back parlors.

"Why ever not?" He reached out from behind me and stopped the door from opening any further. Then he stared down at me, his dark eyebrows lowered. Was he seriously upset that I, Amaryllis Brigham, didn't want his son?

"He doesn't— I mean, I don't—I don't belong here. I don't deserve him. And I'm responsible, at least in part, for the death of his mother."

"Amaryllis, the shipwreck wasn't your fault. Believe me, I've struggled with similar guilt myself, and I've been forced to conclude that everything happens for a reason. I can see now how it's all come together for good. I'm convinced that you and Nathan were meant to be together, that God meant for you to love each other at this particular time in your lives, for His purpose."

It was the same thing Nathan had told me earlier at The Cleft Stone, but, coming from Bram Everstone, the words penetrated my very being. And I actually almost believed them.

He opened the door to the parlor, allowing me to enter before him. I walked into the room, almost in a trance, completely overwhelmed by the realizations running through my mind and heart. I sat upon a beige velvet sofa, finally grasping how dreadfully mistaken I'd been about so many things.

Bram followed me into the room and began pacing back and forth from the fireplace to the wall of windows. "Throughout the years, I've done my share of pushing Nathan in directions he simply wasn't interested in pursuing. You see, I could tell he wasn't happy, could tell that no matter how well—at least outwardly—he seemed to adjust to the lifestyle he was born into, it simply wasn't in his blood. He and Natalia are both very much like their father, you see, which I've been told you know all about. That's why I allowed Nathan to go off on his own to Washington two years ago. I knew that when he came back, if he did, he would know just what he was looking for. And, oddly enough, it's turned out to be you."

I hadn't realized my mouth was gaping until it snapped shut of its own accord.

"And from everything he's told me of you from the moment I returned from Europe, I heartily congratulate you for achieving what has been thought by many over the years to be quite impossible." Bram took a step back and leaned against the table behind him, watching me intently, much like Nathan had always done before I ever understood why. "And I'm more than happy about the idea of having you as a daughter-in-law." Bram gave me a knowing grin. "What have you thought all these years? That I hated you?"

"Yes." Relief poured through me as I finally spoke the truth.

All the reasons I'd broken my engagement to Nathan, and my determination to travel to Redding to teach at the music academy, now seemed so insignificant. There was only one question left to be answered. Only one question mattered anymore.

Would Nathan ever forgive me for my thoughtless words—for hurting him so?

Suddenly, there was a commotion from the hall, which sounded much like someone clambering down steps. I immediately stood up as Bram crossed the room and leaned hard upon a particular book in the bookcase next to the fireplace. Then he pulled at a small piece of wood trim, which resulted in the entire shelf moving quietly away from the wall.

"Come quickly. There's no telling what he'll—"

I was already at Bram's side, already entering the hidden passage, resolved to hide from Wyatt any way I could.

Bram didn't follow but quickly took a large book from a nearby shelf and shoved it at me, whispering, "Lock the door behind you. Take this up and then back down from the attic, and get back to Truesdale. I'll take care of Wyatt." And then he closed the secret passageway gently in my face.

Right away, I heard Wyatt's loud, angry voice through the wood door. "Did you have a productive little reunion? Where the devil is she?"

"She's already gone," Bram answered, and then I heard the explosion of a gunshot.

And nothing more.

I strained my ears in an effort to determine who had fired. If it had been Bram, and Wyatt was dead, he would open the secret door to retrieve me, would he not?

But he didn't.

Bram was likely dead, and Wyatt still after me.

I stood stunned for a moment, a little terrified, since I wasn't sure just where the tunnel led, and I was left in the darkness to find out. But as my eyes adjusted to the dimness, I realized there was some sort of light coming from above.

I turned around with my free hand outstretched before me. Immediately I came to a stair rail that spiraled up the central wooden beam of the tightly wound staircase. As I climbed the steep spiral staircase, I made my way closer and closer to the light, which was coming from a very small tower room with tall, narrow windows.

The large book Bram had hurriedly handed to me was still in my arms, and I held it up to the streaks of dim light beaming in through the tiny window. Inside I found a pistol tucked into a compartment of hollowed-out pages.

I carefully put the book down and lifted out the pistol. It had been a long time since I'd fired any sort of gun, but I knew that if I had to face Wyatt once more, I would shoot him before ever letting him get away with his dreadful plans for me.

Resolutely, I turned from the window with the pistol held firmly in hand. The light revealed a small wood-plank door, and if my orientation served correctly, I'd reached the uppermost attic rooms. I tried the handle and found it was unlocked. I opened the door slowly, which only made the awful squeak of the hinges that much more pronounced, echoing through what I soon realized was a huge, empty room. There were three more windows in a row to my left, likely the ones I remembered seeing high atop the terra-cotta roof between the two turrets facing the front of the mansion.

Fortunately, my search throughout the room was fruitful; I found another passageway, identical to the first, and dashed down the stairs as fast as I could. When I made it to the end of the tunnel, I opened the narrow door just a crack. I immediately heard another door slam shut. I retreated back into the darkness of the tunnel, unable to breathe. Someone was unmistakably in the house, but who? I heard the same door open again.

"Estella! Do calm yourself. There's no need to be slamming doors!"

It was Natalia. She and Estella must have left the Cove Party early. And what would they think, seeing me in such a state? And in their house at such a time!

"No, I will not! I'm sick to death of acting like everything is wonderful! Living with a broken heart is not wonderful! And now Nathan, too? Talia, you have no idea how it feels!"

Hearing such a fiery response from Estella was surprising, and I felt the pang of what she meant by those telling words. Nathan had confided in her, had told her everything. I was shocked to learn that Estella also hated the masquerade of the elite society she'd been born into. The kind of society where all the people were supposed to act happy because they had all the money they could ask for and everything they could ever want, only at the expense of never attaining what they wanted most—the one thing that money couldn't buy.

And the one thing I'd thrown back in Nathan's face.

I listened as Natalia and Estella's voices became more muffled as they continued their conversation further down the great hall. I opened the door a crack and realized I was in the coatroom near the front door.

"Oh, Father!" I heard Natalia cry from down the hall. "What are you doing here? Are you all right?"

Estella shouted, "Father, have you been shot?"

"Believe me, it looks worse than it really is." Bram's voice echoed through the great hall to reach my ears. "It's just a graze. Wyatt Harden took a shot at me before getting away...he made it to his buggy before I could catch him. He's likely on his way to the mainland by now, if he knows what's best—"

"What has he done now?" Natalia asked.

"He had Amaryllis Brigham—"

"Amaryllis was here with Wyatt?" Estella exclaimed.

"He had her here by force, believe me."

"He wanted Nathan to find him, didn't he?" Natalia practically gasped the entire string of words. "Oh, what a scoundrel!"

I had hurried halfway down the main hall when I looked down and again noticed how little I was wearing. Remembering that there were a few lightweight capes and shawls in the coat closet, I went back for one. I grabbed a dark green velvet cape off one of the many hooks, wrapped it about myself, stuck the pistol in a pocket, and again headed down the hall to find Bram Everstone and his daughters.

Only, as I walked down the great hall, I no longer heard their voices—or anything else, for that matter. The house was utterly silent. I ran from room to room in search of them, but they were gone. At suddenly finding myself alone in the massive house, the terror of everything that Wyatt had tried to do that day caught up with me. What if he was still here? And where had Bram and his daughters disappeared to in such a hurry?

Hearing carriage wheels traveling down the drive outside, I looked out the nearest window just in time to see Natalia's carriage disappear behind the trees on its way out to the road. The three of them were, in all likelihood, heading to Truesdale in search of me.

My fears of Wyatt coming back to find me alone again overwhelmed me as I tried to think. But then I thought of Bram's logical supposition that Wyatt had run off. Surely, he was on his way... somewhere. Anywhere was fine with me, as long as it was far away.

I ran to the back of the house in the direction of the stables. Being that the estate was so entirely void of servants, it made the house and stables seem eerily deserted. I searched, but there wasn't a single horse to be found.

Of course, good-natured Natalia Livingston wouldn't just give her servants the night off; she had also permitted their use of every one of her horses. Not that I blamed the servants for taking the night off, since it had been offered. I only wondered that Natalia and her husband felt secure enough to have only Wyatt Harden watching such an estate for hours on end.

Having no other option, I walked steadily down the slope toward the sea until I came to the edge of the woods. With determination, I started along the horse trail, not caring about anything but getting safely back to Truesdale. Only after I was safe would I figure out what to do about my missing horse, the job in California...and Nathan Everstone.

THIRTY

The Ruins

*"There is one friend in the life of each one of us
who seems not a separate person,
however dear and beloved, but an expansion, an interpretation,
of one's self, the very meaning of one's soul."*
—Edith Wharton

I kept walking, one foot in front of the other. As dark as it was in the woods, I kept moving, no matter what. Thoughts of Wyatt crept back into my mind, and my hand brushed against the hard metal of the pistol. I would use it if need be. But having the pistol in my pocket did nothing to stop me from thinking back to how intent he'd been on ruining my life on so many levels throughout the years.

The scene at The Cleft Stone between my mother and Bram.

The slanderous letter written to The Boston Conservatory.

The burning of the horse farm.

My father's death.

And now...Nathan.

Would he ever want to speak to me again? And would I ever be able to go a minute without missing him for the rest of my life?

Suddenly, something Bram had said earlier crashed through to the surface: *"Everything happens for a reason."*

Oh, what did Bram Everstone know about it? How could anyone ever believe that today's events were part of God's will for me? Why would a loving God torment me with feelings for someone I'd known better than to surrender to in the first place? Just like Nathan had insinuated—he'd known better, as well.

Perhaps it was best that I simply found Truelove—hopefully, the saddlebags of money I'd attached were intact—and ride to Ellsworth, like I'd planned...even with only a cape covering my utter indecency.

Oh, God, can You really hear me? All the way down here, lost on this island in Maine, so far from everyone and everything? Can You truly read my heart? Have You indeed heard my unspoken prayers all these years? If so, if Bram was right, and all this is just as You designed, please, please find a way for Nathan to forgive me. And please help my heart handle whatever tomorrow may bring.

The bright pinkish-purple light streaming down the trail through the fog appeared as if it was from heaven. I hoped it would eventually lead to the coast, for then I would at least know something of where I was. Even with all the trails Ainsley and I had ridden during the weeks I'd been staying at Truesdale, this one was unfamiliar. For some reason, we'd always avoided going anywhere near the ruins of the old Everstone Castle, which were somewhere between Rockwood and Truesdale.

Ainsley had indicated that her mother's irrational yet stern belief that they were haunted had something to do with my mother and the shipwreck. How Gothic of Aunt Lizabeth to think the ghosts of Elinorah Landreth and Grace Everstone roamed the ruins of Everstone Castle seeking restitution.

Being that I was lost in the same dark woods where those ruins were located, the thought wasn't quite comforting.

After walking along the trail for what seemed like hours, I heard a horse snort farther down the hill through the trees. I immediately left the trail and headed further up the hill, which was covered densely with pine trees, terrified it was Wyatt and that he would soon detect my location. I didn't care in which direction I was going by then; I just wanted to disappear. The fog was still thick, thankfully, even along the high trail of the ridge I followed.

It was hard keeping quiet while climbing the steep, tree-covered hill; my hands constantly reached out for the next tree or root to grab on to, so as to not fall backward down the slope. When I made it to an alcove of huge rocks sticking out beneath the high ridge, I stopped to listen. I didn't hear anyone traipsing through the woods. But I did hear something.

The ocean.

I ran closer to where the wonderful sound came from. For if I'd found the coast, hopefully I'd be able to tell just how far I was from Truesdale. I walked on through the fog and finally heard the blessed thundering of waves crashing upon the rocks.

Walking slowly on, still trying desperately to not make a sound, I eventually came to a small grove of pine trees. I walked around them, the sound of the waves growing louder, until I was standing upon the cliffs overlooking The Cleft Stone.

The same stairs Nathan had tromped down earlier that day were to my right.

I would be safe at Truesdale soon!

I turned, and not twenty feet beside me, through a scattering of mature, misplaced oak trees, stood a great limestone structure situated upon the cliffs, half hidden in the fog like a castle in the clouds.

The ruins of Everstone Castle.

From what I could see, it was two stories tall, with at least a dozen evenly placed openings; the once-massive, costly windowpanes were long gone. Turning my back to the wooden steps heading down to the rocks, and to Truesdale, I left the edge of the cliffs and walked toward the dilapidated mansion. Wyatt, and the memory of all that had occurred earlier, dissipated into the fog surrounding me. Something about the ruins inexplicably pulled me forward, until I realized I stood in the very background of my haunting nightmares.

I quickly realized that it was the scene of not just my nightmares but also the dreams I'd consistently had about Nathan since meeting him—the dreams that had, in essence, almost replaced my nightly reminders of my mother's death and Bram Everstone's anger.

I entered the ruins through an arched doorway. Directly inside, along the wall, were stone steps that led up to what was once the main house. I ascended them, with the fog dispersing from around me, until I stood in a great room overgrown with about half a dozen century-old oak trees. The sun reflected off something across the room.

I walked slowly in the direction of the glare and quickly realized it was a mosaic of colorful, oddly shaped tiles put together and cemented onto the limestone wall near the corner of the room. As I drew closer, I realized the tiles composed a name—a name that stopped me dead in my tracks. I couldn't turn away, no matter that it hurt to breathe as I read the words again and again.

Grace O'Basney-McGreaghan Everstone
Cherished Wife and Mother
June 20, 1840–July 4, 1879

It wasn't your fault. The words echoed in my heart as if from God Himself—and this time they took hold. A final wave of freedom permeated my soul. It was everything I'd never allowed myself to believe yet always wished I could.

I fell to my knees in the wet grass at the edge of the mosaic, staring at the name with tears running down my face, my mind void of everything but a wretched prayer having to do with one certainly now quite unattainable man.

Footsteps pounded upon hard stone, and I turned. Someone stood in the arched doorway at the other end of the room. And just as in my dreams of him, I recognized the outline of Nathan's physique, cut to perfection by the purple sky behind him.

Were my eyes playing tricks on me?

"Amaryllis."

At the desperation in his voice, I stood and raced into his arms. "Wyatt tried to take me— He took me to Rockwood and tried to—" I couldn't even say the words. "But your father...he was there, and he saved me."

Nathan reached up and held my face in his hands. He looked tired and a bit ragged but glad to see me.

"I know. Father told me." Taking a closer look at my attire, he fingered the green velvet of the hood draped about my shoulders. Anyone could tell I was far from properly dressed underneath. With his brows drawn together and his eyes closed, he didn't say anything for a while. "He told me what Wyatt tried to do to you." He almost growled the statement.

"Where's Wyatt now?" I asked.

"Still missing. I doubt he's around, but nevertheless, we should get out of these woods and back. Father's at Truesdale now, along with Natalia and Estella. They've been consoling your aunts and your cousins, while Lawry, his father, and I have been searching and searching for you. Ever since Father came looking for you, worried, I've been nearly sick thinking—" Nathan tightened his arms around me, bringing his head down nearly to my shoulder. He took the length of my hair in his hand and brought it to his face. "Amaryllis...."

That was when I realized he was crying. And what a perfect gift I'd been given.

Nathan lifted his head. "There is one thing I don't understand. We found Truelove wandering about, fully saddled and ready for what seemed like quite a journey."

"Yes. When Wyatt found me in the stable, I was just leaving."
Nathan held me firmly by the shoulders. "Leaving?"

"I received an offer from a school in California. I was being foolish, and I could see only my guilt. I was just going to run away...from everything."

"It wasn't your fault, Amaryllis." Nathan's green eyes brimmed with tears. Did he think I was still intent on holding my ground from earlier that night?

"I know that now. And believe me, Nathan, I'm so sorry I broke our—"

With one finger, Nathan lifted my face closer to his and nuzzled his nose against mine for a moment. His lips slowly brushed my cheeks. "All evening, God kept leading me back here to the ruins, to the grave. Every time I came back, and you weren't here, I just kept praying, trusting that His will was best, no matter the outcome."

"Do you still want to marry—"

He cut short my breathless whisper by pressing his lips to mine, apparently unwilling to discuss the subject any further, at least for now. "I should've taken you off and eloped with you the night of the ball." And just like that, he was back to his confident, charming self. "You would have let me, too. Am I right?"

I nodded my head slightly into the crook of his neck. There was no use denying it.

"And tonight, would you?" Drawing back, he reached into his breast pocket and produced my engagement ring. And again, I let him take my left hand and slip it back on my finger.

"I'd like nothing so much, Mr. Everstone." I smiled.

"Well then, what do you say we take a detour on our way back to Truesdale? The Justice of the Peace in town is a friend of mine, if you recall—"

Before I could answer, the sharp click of a pistol broke through the fog.

THIRTY-ONE

Nathan Everstone

"Love…cannot be found by looking for it or
by passionately wishing for it.
It is a sort of divine accident."
—Sir Hugh Walpole

"How sweet." Wyatt's voice echoed from the edge of the pine forest.

Nathan grabbed me around the waist and dropped to the ground as a bullet hit the stone wall where we'd just been standing. We were a tangle of legs and arms as we took cover behind the limestone wall. My cape was all askew, but I didn't have time to think of my modesty—only that Wyatt had a gun and seemed to want to kill one or both of us.

I reached into my pocket, produced my pistol, and handed it to Nathan. "Here, use this."

He raised an eyebrow and gave a crooked smile as he took the pistol from my hand. "My ever-ready Miss Brigham. Whatever would I do without you?" With skillful movements that told me he knew how to handle a gun, Nathan checked the cylinder and deftly clicked it back in place. "I love you." He leaned in and kissed me.

"The lovebirds reunited…too bad it's only momentarily." Wyatt fired another shot, which ricocheted off the stones outlining the open archway where Nathan and I had been standing just moments before. "You want her that badly?"

Nathan didn't answer. Kneeling beside me, he leaned against the wall with his left shoulder, his torso facing the empty archway. He held the pistol with both hands tucked near his chest ready to swiftly take a shot through the arched opening in the wall.

"Well, so do I," Wyatt went on.

Tremors raced up my spine. I didn't doubt him for a moment.

Nathan crouched closer and whispered, "You need to hide." He took a moment to look about the ruinous, tree-filled room, then motioned with his eyes to our right. "Can you climb that short wall into the next room?"

Another bullet whizzed by.

I slunk along the high walls until I reached the crumbled one Nathan had indicated. It was about five-and-a-half feet tall, for I was just able to see over it when I stood on some nearby rubble. Inside the smaller tree-filled room were stone steps leading to the level above what used to be the carriage house. Reaching that higher level was our best bet of ultimately gaining control of the situation.

"You dead yet, Everstone?" Wyatt called out.

Nathan still knelt near the archway, and I wondered if he meant to come with me—I couldn't bear the thought of hiding from Wyatt without him. He turned to me and pointed to the partially collapsed wall.

"You're coming?" I whispered.

He closed his eyes for a moment, shook his head, and mouthed the words, *"Climb over the wall."* I'd never seen him look more serious.

Wyatt fired another shot, which soared past Nathan through the archway, the bullet hitting the stone wall on the other side of the room.

With his attention on Wyatt, Nathan finally whispered, "I'll be right there, I promise. Just go."

Using the fallen stones at the base of the crumbled wall, I made my way over, then landed with a thump on the ground. I didn't dare move; I just sat there—my back to the wall, my cape a mess about me, my knees to my chest, and my hands clamped to my face—and prayed.

Oh God, save him!

I heard another shot hit the wall, and then another bullet struck something with a metallic ping. And then nothing but the rustle of leaves overhead.

"Nathan?"

Too many seconds later, Nathan answered in his normal voice, "I'm fine, Amaryllis. I've got him."

"Got him...already?" I stood to look over the wall. Nathan's eyes and pistol were both focused on Wyatt, who was now somehow unarmed. Nathan walked over to where Wyatt's pistol had landed.

"Where on earth did you learn to shoot like that?" I asked. "Did you not want to kill him?"

"I had a lot of free time in Washington, and firearms quickly became a favorite hobby of mine. And no, I didn't want to kill him. He'll get his punishment regardless."

Wyatt stood with his hands raised, a frown contorting his bruised face. Obviously, he hadn't counted on being cornered so easily.

I walked through the maze of stone rooms to rejoin Nathan. Wyatt narrowed his blue eyes, piercing me with a hateful look. Remembering just what his intentions had been regarding me, I made certain to position my cape properly.

"You know how to use this?" Nathan asked, indicating Wyatt's gun. "There still might be one bullet left."

"Yes, I've shot one before—at Bruckerdale."

Nathan handed me the pistol. I checked the cylinder for that one last bullet, found it, and aimed the pistol steadily at Wyatt, daring him to accost me again.

Nathan circled nearer to our prisoner. "What do you say we take a little trip into town? Amaryllis and I were just on our way to go see my friend Henry. I'm sure he'll be more than happy to hear all about what you've been up to tonight."

"And I'm sure everyone else will, as well," Wyatt replied. "You know they will forever think of her as damaged goods now, no matter what you say to deny—"

Nathan took a swing at Wyatt, his fist hitting him squarely between the eyes. Wyatt's hands went to his face as blood gushed from his nose.

Nathan shook his fist, stretching out his fingers. "I do believe her reputation will be just fine."

$$\smile\!\!\!\!\frown$$

The sun had set by the time we pulled up in Wyatt's buggy outside the large white house in town with a sign out front that simply read, "Justice of the Peace and Notary Public."

Nathan exited the buggy, helped me down, and then helped Wyatt dismount Thunder. His face was bruised and bloody, his hands tied behind his back with horse reins. Nathan gripped both his arms in a stronghold for extra measure as I knocked on the door while drawing Estella's green velvet cape more tightly around myself.

A very tall, nice-looking man around Nathan's age answered the door. He smiled as soon as he recognized Nathan. "Well, isn't this the night for visits from old friends? Crawford's here, too, having stopped by on his way out of town."

Henry didn't stop smiling as he invited the three of us into his home with an outstretched arm. "Come in, come in. It's good to see you again, Nathan. What can I do for you?"

Jayson Crawford-Castleman stepped into the foyer, and his eyes widened. "Are you all right? What happened?" His gaze traveled over Wyatt to Nathan and finally to me.

"I need you to perform a marriage ceremony." Nathan was all seriousness. I didn't miss the seething look that passed between him and Jay.

"For these two—" Henry began to ask.

"Good grief, no. I'm marrying Amaryllis myself." He reached out with his left arm and put it about my shoulders, pulling me close yet making sure I didn't come anywhere near Wyatt. "Henry, let me introduce you to my fiancée, Amaryllis Brigham. Amaryllis, this is an old friend of mine"—he paused just long enough to look at Jayson—"a good friend of ours from Dartmouth, Henry Goodenough. And this, Henry"—Nathan motioned to Wyatt— "as you know, is Wyatt Harden, who is guilty of kidnapping Amaryllis this evening with the intent of defiling her and thereby forcing her to marry him against her will come morning, all in an effort to gain control of her inheritance."

"He did all that, among other things," I affirmed. "He admitted to me that he forged a slanderous letter, and he killed my father—"

"You have no proof of any of that," Wyatt said with clenched jaw. He was still restrained by Nathan but looked as if he wanted nothing more in the world than to charge at me.

"As if you won't hang simply for what you've done tonight," Nathan growled from behind Wyatt.

"He kidnapped you with the intent...but he didn't...?" Jay seemed to have a difficult time meeting my eyes.

"Wyatt took me to Rockwood thinking everyone was at the festival, yet hoping they would come home to find him—" I swallowed hard. "Only, Nathan's father was there, and he helped me escape. But that didn't stop Wyatt." I shot daggers at him with my eyes. "He came after me on my way home to Truesdale and caught up just as Nathan found me."

"Jay, would you be kind and escort Miss Brigham to the parlor?" Henry indicated the first room off the hall. "Nathan, if you'll bring Wyatt and come with me, I'll contact the sheriff."

After Henry, Nathan, and Wyatt disappeared down the hall, Jay led me into the parlor, where we sat upon the quaint sofa situated in front of a large bay window.

"Amaryllis, are you truly all right? I had no idea Wyatt was so...." Jay took my hand in his, and I could tell by the defeated look in his eyes that he knew exactly what the ring on my left hand meant without my having to tell him.

He'd never even had a chance.

"I really am fine now," I said.

"I didn't realize you were missing—"

Nathan came into the room from the foyer without Wyatt. "Well, you couldn't have known. You left the party early also, didn't you? Right after the conversation you had with my sister." Nathan scowled as he leaned against the doorjamb.

"Henry said you were on your way out of town...?" I said to Jay. Suddenly I felt sorry for him. He had failed in his task of finding a "mission-minded" wife to take with him to Aberdeen. Did that mean he wouldn't be able to claim the mission? Would it go to someone else? What would he do then?

Before he could answer, Henry returned, also without Wyatt. "I have a cozy cell out back that will hold him until the sheriff gets here."

"I was just about to tell Nathan and Amaryllis of my plans to head home to Concord," Jay said to Henry as he took a seat in a nearby chair. "You see, I'm giving up the idea of taking on the mission in Aberdeen...at least for the immediate future."

Nathan sat next to me on the sofa and put his arm possessively around my shoulders, as if Jay were still a threat. Sitting in between them as I was, I could sense the tension in their lack of words for each other.

"Nathan, do you indeed want to marry this young lady in such a hurry?" Henry asked, getting straight to business. "You're not doing this simply to be the hero, are you? With your father's account, the girl's reputation will be spared. You don't need to go through with this if you don't want to."

"Marrying Amaryllis is the only thing I know I do want, Henry. We were engaged before this whole turn of events, and, quite frankly, we should have eloped weeks ago."

Henry turned to me. "Is this true, Miss Brigham?"

I nodded. "Indeed. We've been secretly engaged since June nineteenth." I lifted my left hand to show him my engagement ring.

"I didn't really think he was serious," Jay whispered so only I could hear.

Henry slowly nodded, his chin propped up by his thumb and forefinger. "I just like to know that all the stories line up." He glanced my way again. "And you truly want to marry this rascal Nathan Everstone?" He smiled, as if he already knew the answer.

"More than anything."

Henry stood, walked over to the staircase in the foyer, and hollered, "Lindy, dear, come on down. I'll need your services as witness. If you can believe it, Nathan Everstone's down here requesting to be married!"

Even from our seat in the parlor, we heard a commotion on the upper floor, followed by hurried footsteps coming down the wood stairs. Jay, Nathan, and I were standing when Henry followed his wife into the room.

The tiny blonde crossed the parlor and came straight for me, extending her hand. "You must be the lucky young lady. My name is Lindy Goodenough. What's yours?"

I put my hand in hers, and she shook it vigorously. "Amaryllis Brigham," I answered automatically, not having expected such straightforwardness.

"Soon to be Everstone, though, eh?" She most definitely had a Canadian accent, and the way she rounded out all her words made me smile. "He's a fine catch, your fiancé is. Been friends with my Henry, here, for years. And Henry's always had the best things to say about Nathan Everstone." She let go of my hand and looked to Nathan for the first time. "Finally found one you liked enough, did ya?"

Nathan gave her a crooked grin, then simply said, "I did."

"So Crawford and I shall be the witnesses, then?" Lindy asked as she situated Jay, Nathan, and me in front of the tall fireplace. She immediately turned to her husband. "Henry, what were you thinking, not taking her cape? Amaryllis, let me take that for you. Surely, you don't want to marry Nathan Everstone wearing this dirty old—"

"Actually, I would like to wear it," I insisted. "It's much better than what I'm wearing underneath." I felt my face flush as Nathan grinned down knowingly at me.

"Let's begin, then; it's getting late," Henry said. "I'm sure you have places to be after this." He strode across the room toward us and put on his spectacles. Without another word of instruction, he opened to the front of his Bible and said, "Nathan Everstone, do you take Amaryllis Brigham to be your wife?"

Nathan took my hands in his and held them tight, holding my gaze with his.

"Do you promise to love, honor, cherish, and protect her, forsaking all others, and hold only unto her?"

"I thee wed, Amaryllis Brigham, forever." His words were purposefully reminiscent of what he'd said at The Cleft Stone only earlier that day when he'd "practiced" putting on my ring. Nathan's eyes told me he meant every word, and really, I couldn't think of a time his eyes hadn't been telling me what they were just then.

He'd loved me all along. I'd simply been too stubborn and scared to believe it.

"Amaryllis Brigham, do you take Nathan Everstone to be your husband? Do you promise to love, honor, cherish, and protect him, forsaking all others, and hold only unto him?"

"I thee wed, Nathan Everstone, forever." I made his words my own, and tried my best to tell him as much with my eyes as he was telling me with his.

"Nathan and Amaryllis Everstone, insomuch as the two of you have agreed to live together in matrimony and have promised your love for each other by these vows, I now declare you to be husband and wife." Henry took our clasped hands in blessing and said, "Congratulations, Nathan. You may now kiss your bride."

Nathan didn't waste any time in letting go of my hands to wrap his arms around me and lift me off the floor. He kissed me for a long time before putting my feet gently down upon the rug. We quickly realized that Henry, Lindy, and Jay had left the room, and we were alone again.

Only married now.

"Mrs. Everstone, I believe your family is still wondering just where you are," Nathan said into the crook of my neck.

"True," I replied, not moving from his arms. "And I suppose we should tell them what we have just done. I hope they won't be too terribly disappointed. They probably would have liked to attend the wedding." I could only imagine what their responses would be to the news. "Well, everyone except Daphne, that is. She was quite set on making a conquest out of you this summer."

"As if anyone could ever succeed in making me fall in love with her. Doesn't everyone know that I only prefer young ladies who can't stand me?"

⌒

After our unconventional wedding, Nathan and I took Wyatt's buggy, with Thunder trailing behind, to Truesdale to tell everyone our news.

When we arrived at the front door, Ainsley answered in the midst of a fit of hysterics, something I really hadn't ever expected from her, as she was the most sensible of all the women in her family. "Amaryllis! Oh, Amaryllis is home! Where did you find her, Nathan? Is she all right? Did you kill Wyatt for trying to steal her?"

As soon as she'd said my name, everyone else in the house came rushing into the large foyer, encircling both Nathan and me. I quickly realized, because of Bram's account of what had happened at Rockwood, that most of them already knew about Wyatt's kidnapping. Nathan filled them in on what had happened at the ruins and how he'd captured Wyatt and handed him over to the authorities.

Nathan didn't come right out and share the news of our wedding, but I was beginning to realize that this was simply part of his character.

"Amaryllis." Bram was beside me, taking my hands in his, so much like a father. His right shirtsleeve was torn and rolled up making room for a bandage just above his elbow where Wyatt's shot most likely had grazed him. "I'm so sorry Wyatt was able to get away from me at Rockwood—"

"It wasn't your fault." As I said the words, I realized just how powerful they were. "And it turned out for the best, regardless. Just like you said—the way God wanted it to be."

I was thinking of the marriage certificate in Nathan's jacket pocket, which he still hadn't produced. He stood next to me, observing the two of us with his searching green eyes—those green eyes that still gave me uncontrollable flutters in my stomach.

Lawry came over and wedged himself between Nathan and me, putting an arm around both our shoulders. He winked at me playfully before saying, "You'll have to marry Nathan now, Amaryllis, just to appease the gossipmongers all over New England."

Nathan reached into his pocket and produced our marriage certificate. "Already took care of that, Hampton." He handed it over. "Now it's your turn."

EPILOGUE

"God's gifts put man's best dreams to shame."
—Elizabeth Barrett Browning, *Sonnets from the Portuguese*, XXVI

September 3, 1890 · Washington State

After nearly two months of honeymooning across America in one of the Everstones' private railcars, Nathan and I were finally nearing Whidbey Island from the south, having traveled through California and Oregon. We'd brought Thunder and Truelove with us, with the goal of settling near Seattle.

We were taking the ferry from Port Townsend to Coupeville, my shoulder crammed against Nathan's side as he held me tightly. The joy and familiarity I felt at simply seeing my Whidbey Island again seemed to calm whatever it was in me that was usually affected by the motion of boats. But still, I relished having Nathan's arms around me. I knew he was concerned for me.

I was eager to see Bruckerdale again and hoped that the new owner would be obliging enough to let me wander through the big old foursquare house and stables. I wondered if it was still a horse farm or if the new owners were doing something else with the hilly, forested bit of land. I knew Nathan had quit the house only earlier that year, having lived there under lease from my father while taking his lengthy sabbatical from his rigid and demanding life in Boston. But so much could happen within a year.

Or even in five months.

Nathan squeezed my arm. "Would you rather found your music academy in Seattle or on Whidbey Island?"

I turned to face him, confused. "If it were an option, you know I'd choose Whidbey Island. Only I'm not sure if I'd be able to stand being so close to Bruckerdale and not actually calling it mine."

"We'll have to see what we can do about that." Nathan smiled down at me with that same gorgeous, crooked grin I'd first seen in the photograph of him at Deception Pass.

"You really wouldn't mind settling on Whidbey Island for good?" I stared into his eyes, hopeful.

"We'll have to see," he repeated. He wouldn't say anything more. For the first time since he'd kissed me, I wondered what he was up to.

Once we were in Coupeville, we rented a carriage, loaded it with our belongings, and traveled south about thirteen miles to Greenbank. The next step would be to catch another ferry, this one from Whidbey Island to Seattle. Suddenly, I didn't think I could be satisfied to stay only a day on Whidbey Island. I wanted to stay forever.

It was still before noon by the time we made it to the drive off Smuggler's Cove Road that led to Bruckerdale. The wrought-iron archway with the name "Brigham Shires of Bruckerdale" was still in place, even after all these years. I cuddled close to Nathan, unwilling to look at him, for fear of bursting into tears.

We drove up the hill, and finally I saw it again—everything I'd wished to see for so long. The brick Victorian farmhouse appeared to have a new coat of fresh white paint on the trim about the windows. From every window at the front of the house, I could see billowy lace curtains, just like my mother had always used.

Were they possibly—? Could they be hers?

Nathan parked the carriage right in front of the porch steps, as if we owned the place. After exiting the carriage, he turned to help me down. I could not keep my eyes from gazing up at the house.

My house—the one place my heart had longed to dwell for well over a decade.

I didn't realize what Nathan was doing until he'd lifted me in his arms and carried me up the steps. The front door was just as I remembered, extra wide with a beautifully designed lead-glass window. He shifted me in his arms and awkwardly reached for the door handle.

"Nathan, what are you doing? The people who live here are going to think we're breaking into their—"

"It's your house, Amaryllis." And with one turn of the knob, Nathan proceeded to carry me in.

His forest-green gaze held mine for what seemed like minutes, and a million silent questions flooded my mind before I managed, "*You're* the one who bought the land from my father?" I pounded my balled fist against his shoulder. "Why didn't you tell me?"

"And ruin this surprise?" He kicked the door closed behind us.

"You should have told me back in March when you met me!"

"I was going to, but when I learned of your irrational fears concerning my father, and then I realized I was falling in love with you...well, it all got rather complicated."

I crushed my face to his neck. "Oh, Nathan, you're right. You certainly didn't need any other reasons for me to think the worst of you. How did you do it?"

"Easy. Your parents left the farm in the care of some trusted friends of theirs who ended up taking the job quite seriously. Even when your family never returned, they continued to live here, simply waiting for you to someday show up." Nathan put me on my feet, and I had a good look about the place. My mother's curtains, her furniture, her old box grand piano...everything was just as we'd left it.

"However, your father was concerned it was becoming too much for them in their old age—and it was. That was about the same time Lawry and I decided to head west, and your father and I formulated a plan to—"

"And that's how all my mother's things are still here...everything in its place?" I instinctively drifted to the piano. My fingers slid over the old ivory keys, and I started right in to the middle of Chopin's *Raindrop*, my favorite.

Nathan stood leaning against the casing of the pocket doors, simply watching and listening. His green eyes laughed when he recognized the piece. I played for only a few seconds, just as I had months before, at the mission society.

Then I walked about the room, taking everything in. I still couldn't believe my beloved Bruckerdale was all mine once again. Everything looked just as I remembered, even the portrait of me in the red-wallpapered front hall, painted when I was around the age of fourteen—right before we'd left for the East Coast. I stepped forward to take a closer look at my likeness. It had been such a long time since I'd been that carefree little girl. It was amazing to me that I was even there at Bruckerdale, able to look once more upon the long-forgotten portrait.

Nathan came up beside me, took my hand, and threaded his fingers through mine. "Lawry told me the moment I walked through this hall for the first time that this was a portrait of you—the cousin he'd met that summer, whom he never seemed to cease speaking of. Amaryllis Brigham. That stunning, staring face haunted me every day for the two years I lived here. And it did ever since I saw you in person at the train station in March." He looked from the portrait to me and then back again. "Who knows where each of us would be right now if I hadn't seen this portrait and become so intrigued by you, even before ever meeting you?"

I laughed. "Well, thank the Lord for silly girls who demand to have their portrait painted."

"Yes, otherwise I don't know if I'd have been able to put up with all the rejection you put me through this spring." Lifting our entwined hands to his chest, Nathan wrapped his other arm around my waist and turned me to face him.

"God knows you needed it," I replied. "It was clear from that first evening's dinner party that you believed all you had to do was speak to me, and I would want to die of love for you."

"Now really, Mrs. Everstone." Nathan again lifted me into his arms and headed toward the wide wooden staircase. "Is that any way to speak to your doting husband, who has, with God's help, just made all of your dreams of Whidbey Island come true?"

"Oh, let me assure you, Mr. Everstone—as much as I hate to admit it, you ended up being quite right about me, too. I'm still a bit mortified by how easily I fell in love with you."

Coming Soon

The Bound Heart

The Everstone Chronicles ~ Book Two
Preview

THE EVERSTONE CHRONICLES

The
Bound
Heart

DAWN
CRANDALL

PROLOGUE

The Cave

"All human happiness and misery take the form of action."
—Aristotle

June 19, 1885 • Mount Desert Island • Bar Harbor, Maine

Come on, Meredyth..." Vance Everstone urged with a smile.

"Only if you go first." I called down to him as I sat upon a large boulder, positioned higher than his lanky six-foot frame.

Vance suddenly seemed so grown up as he gazed at me with that gorgeous grin. In that moment, I had the first inkling of what it might be like to have Vance Everstone fall in love with me. I had loved him, had waited for him to love me—for years—while I'd been at boarding school, and then as I'd suffered through my first season while he'd finished his last year at Harvard.

I wasn't truly afraid of going into the cave or of anything possibly inside those familiar caverns that were accessible only during low tide along the coastline of my family's summer cottage on Mount Desert Island. However, Vance didn't know anything about my fears or the lack thereof. All he knew, as evidenced in his eyes, was that I had changed in the last year.

And I *had* changed. I would soon turn nineteen, and I'd finally grown up enough for Vance Everstone to notice me. I was finally more than just my brothers' little sister.

We'd known each other since the day I was born. Every summer, our families would sail from Boston to Bar Harbor to enjoy the cooler weather. And for as long as I could remember, the boys had ruled the summers: the three Everstone brothers, my three older brothers, and Lawry Hampton, whose family lived in the house in between.

This left me with only Estella Everstone, who had just turned fifteen, and Ainsley Hampton, who was only twelve. It was apparent, at least to Vance, why I would want to seek out his company that day. He was the most intriguing person in the whole bunch, and he knew it well.

Vance's only response to my declaration was a hooded look, added to the assertive gaze he'd already been giving me. I knew he could see my wet and sandy bare feet, as well as my ankles. The very same ankles he'd seen above those bare feet my entire life.

Instead of tucking my feet beneath my petticoats, I lifted them an inch higher. I extended my right foot, moving it this way and that, and laughed. "What dirty feet I have!"

He took a step closer to the high rock I sat upon and grabbed my foot, gently brushing off the sand. Then he did the same for my left.

The touch of his hands on my skin made me uncomfortable, but instead of shying away from the feeling, I wanted more. It became almost addictive.

When he finished brushing off the caked-on sand, he placed his hands firmly upon my ankles and positioned my feet against his chest, particles of sand getting all over his white shirt. He stood there, holding my ankles, staring at me with a new look in his eyes. One I'd never seen before.

I didn't know what it meant, but I wanted to find out.

He suddenly let go of my ankles and stepped back. I wasn't prepared for this, and I slid down the gently sloped rock, landing upon my feet directly before him.

His deep brown eyes took me in, and he repeated his question: "I dare you to go into the cave, all the way to the back—where it's deepest and darkest."

It was the same request, the same exact phrase we'd always taunted each other with, ever since we were children, playing together on those very rocks. However, with no one else present, it sounded like a completely different kind of question.

With a brand-new, soaring self-confidence, I stood my ground. "I'm not going in there alone."

It took him a few seconds of deliberating to decide whether to remain standing only inches from me or to do as I'd requested.

"Meredyth." He almost choked on my name. He surprised me by taking my hand and leading me into the familiar crevice of the tall, mountainous rocks. It really wasn't that dark in the caves during the morning hours, and so we could see where we were going quite well as we followed the rough, uneven floor of the cave until it narrowed. And that was where we stopped.

"When did you get so beautiful?" In the time it had taken for him to lead me to this place, my confidence had doubled, if not tripled. I loved the way I felt with his eyes on me.

Knowing that I'd produced that look created a new power within that I hadn't known I possessed until that moment. I stepped closer, testing it.

"I must say, this old dress makes you appear rather...uncivilized." Vance fingered the tattered ruffles of my torn-up, ratty dress and then my collarbone just above them. Emboldened, I took his other hand and placed it at my waist. Since I wore a corset under my dress, I really didn't think I would be that affected by this touch—but that was before his hands slid up the material of the bodice.

Watching Vance's face as he apparently enjoyed himself pushed my new feelings along and made me wonder, if he liked touching my feet and my waist, what else would he enjoy?

I soon found out. His fingers grazed my arms, traveling upward, past my collarbone again, then tunneled through my hair at the back of my neck, setting my long tresses free.

"Vance." His name upon my lips darkened the desire on his face. I had yet to touch him after years of wanting to, and I was deliriously happy to find I could now make him want me.

My hands were behind me, pressed against the rough wall, out of the way. For all my bold thoughts, I didn't know if he would welcome my doing the same things to him...or if I dared. This was all too new, and while he was enjoying my newfound beauty, which I had presented to him willingly, I wasn't sure if I had the courage to enjoy him in the same ways.

It was simply enough to enjoy him with my eyes.

"Meredyth, where are your hands?" he breathed.

I pulled them out from behind me, palms up, between us, splaying my fingers for him to see.

"What are you doing with them?"

"Nothing."

"I noticed," he said with a smile. He took hold of them and caressed my palms with his lips, then moved on to my wrists, which made my blood boil through my veins.

Without another thought, I put my arms around his neck, drew his face to mine, and kissed his lips. It was a tentative, almost innocent, first kiss, but when I realized how ardently he kissed me back, my boldness grew once again. I pressed myself to him, clutching his neck. I let him delve deeper and deeper into that kiss until it was all I knew.

Finally, Vance Everstone wanted me. Surely, he loved me.

I sank into the kiss, relishing the power of the emotions I'd evoked from him, kissing him back with equal desire. He pressed me against the hard, jagged wall. The force of the rocks in my back, and his groping hands as he grabbed at my skirts, brought me to my senses.

"Vance." I pushed at him with my fists.

His ragged breath passed my ear as he kissed my neck, not slowing in his exploration of my skin.

The balance of control had suddenly shifted, and my confidence turned to distress.

I tried to break free from his kiss, from his ever-searching grasps of my skirt. "Vance!"

He didn't listen; he only continued to kiss me more urgently.

And I didn't know how to stop him.

Shame replaced my earlier courage as the course of my actions became all too clear. I'd led him to that cave—to me—never knowing where my actions were headed.

Until it was too late.

About the Author

A graduate of Taylor University with a degree in Christian Education, and a former bookseller at Barnes & Noble, Dawn Crandall didn't begin writing until 2010 when her husband found out about her long-buried dream of writing a book. Without a doubt about someday becoming published, he let her quit her job in 2010 in order to focus on writing *The Hesitant Heiress*. It didn't take her long to realize that writing books was what she was made to do. Dawn is represented by Joyce Hart of Hartline Literary.

Apart from writing books, Dawn is also a first-time mom to a precious little boy (born March 2014) and also serves with her husband in a premarriage mentor program at their local church in Fort Wayne, Indiana.

Dawn is a member of the American Christian Fiction Writers, secretary for the Indiana ACFW Chapter (Hoosier Ink), and associate member of the Great Lakes ACFW Chapter.

The Everstone Chronicles is Dawn's first series with Whitaker House. All three books composing the series were semifinalists in ACFW's prestigious Genesis Writing Contest, the third book going on to become a finalist in 2013.